PRAIRIE

PRAIRIE

WALTER J. MUILENBURG

Introduction by Nathan Tye

Hastings College Press | Hastings, Nebraska

Production Staff

Stephanie Bloyer

Destiny Curtis

Nicky Georges

Ruthanna Johnson

Vaughn Harper-Marcel

Lauren Stull

Renee Williams

ISBN-13: 978-1-942885-97-9

Note on the text: This edition has been reset from the first (1925) edition. Original spelling and grammatical conventions have been maintained, except in the case of publishing errors in the first edition. The original punctuation has been maintained but updated using modern conventions (e.g., eliminating spaces around dashes).

INTRODUCTION
Nathan Tye

Walter J. Muilenburg's *Prairie* came and went like a prairie fire. A critically acclaimed short story author, Muilenburg appeared poised for success when his only novel appeared in 1925. The first book published by newly established Viking Press, *Prairie* arrived at a high point for rural Midwestern fiction, but its harsh landscape, bare plot, and stark characters drew mixed reviews. When no subsequent publications emerged, Muilenburg's work and early praise faded from regional literary memory. *Prairie* is a hard book to come by, with scarce copies appearing and disappearing quickly from the rare book market. It also remains a hard book. "It has not and will never become anyone's favorite book, offering very little to warm the human heart," argued James Schaap in his 2016 reappraisal of the novel.[1]

Nevertheless, *Prairie* is worth renewed attention and wider appreciation. The novel's descriptions of the prairie rival those of Willa Cather or O. E. Rølvaag. Unlike its romanticized contemporaries, Muilenburg's unflinching depiction of homesteading underscores the harshness of the prairie, its fires, storms, and isolation. Across the durable cycle of farm life, a slower cycle, of alienation and disdain, stirs. A father rejects a son, who in turn rejects his son. Early in the novel Elias Vaughn leaves his Calvinist father after he refuses Elias's pleas for a social life with his peers. Drawn by dreams of the West and need for human connection, despite the promise of inheriting the family farm, Elias marries Lizzie Dalton. Marrying her breaks the bond between father and son. The newlyweds head West and begin a new life on the prairie.[2]

The land, isolation, death, and a prairie fire degrade the bond between Elias and Lizzie, however. The former throws himself further into work, transforming into his father, whereas Lizzie rarely ventures outside. Children slightly alter these dynamics—a sickly son, Joey, arrives and a baby daughter dies four days after birth—but Lizzie's devotion to Joey renders him ill-suited for farm labor and the demands of his father. Paralleling Elias's own paternal rejection, Joey leaves the home and finds work in town. On her deathbed, Lizzie believes Elias is Joey returned. Elias's kind impersonation eases Lizzie's passing but hardens Elias. When Joey returns, Elias turns him out into the winter night. There Elias's last human connection is consumed by the landscape, which ultimately envelopes him too:

> There was no sound; a vast silence lay upon the winter prairie, which stretched away from him until it was lost in the night. Slowly the man turned back to the house. For a moment he stood outlined sharply in the lamplight that streamed through the doorway. Then the door closed. (279)

The promise of the West is empty in the novel. The prairie strips away your soul for a land that can be altered and refashioned but will ultimately never be *yours*. "After all, this prairie country takes everything and doesn't give much in return," warned one of Elias's neighbors (177). A prairie fire, a bad season, and a broken family all serve as reminders of the fleeting and fickle reality of the settler experience. Elias's new life in a new place costs him everything, the triumph of isolation over family.

Walter John Muilenburg was born near Orange City, Iowa, on August 10, 1893, to John W. Muilenburg and Gertrude (Van Rooyen) Muilenburg. The large Muilenburg family (Walter was one of ten siblings) farmed northeast of Orange City. Part of the area's large Dutch population, John Muilenburg's father had migrated from Pella, Iowa, in 1872 along with other early residents.[3] Education was important to the family. Walter graduated from Orange City high school and the University of Iowa. At least four other siblings attended college, as well, with two earning doctorates.[4]

In Iowa City Muilenburg joined the nascent campus literary group, Athelney, organized by the English chair and dean of fine arts, Clarke Fisher Ansley. One of their aims was to explore Midwestern culture. To further this, Muilenburg's friend and fellow Athelney member, John T. Frederick, established *The Midland* literary magazine in 1915.[5] Muilenburg graduated in 1915, and the following year leased the *Grant Chief*, a village paper in Montgomery County, from his brother.[6] Muilenburg then taught high school in Iowa and Michigan.[7]

Ansley left the university after a nervous breakdown and settled onto a farm outside Glennie, Michigan, in 1917. Two years later, Frederick and his father moved to adjoining property.[8] Muilenburg followed not long after. At his cabin in Glennie, he wrote and enjoyed his hobbies, "hunting, fishing, smoking."[9] Teaching high school at the time, he spent his summers outdoors, visiting neighbors, and writing. Glennie became *The Midland*'s "permanent spiritual home."[10]

There Muilenburg built a home overlooking a lake and surrounded by old growth forest. A nearby stream provided good fishing. "Everything is quiet, except for an occasional call of a whippoorwill or owl," he shared in a surviving letter to his brother James. He was well stocked with necessities: books, canned food, tobacco, music, and dynamite (to remove stumps). Muilenburg had everything he needed. He wrote to James, "To most people this hermit life would be eerie; to me it is ideal."[11] He considered this an improved version of Henry David Thoreau's *Walden*, a draw to the area his neighbors also appreciated[12]:

> Thoreau put this idea in my head, and the matter has worked out with wonderful satisfaction, I work from morning to night. In the evening, after a hard day's work, I don't feel sleepy, and read until eleven o'clock. The writing itch has come back, and I have been able to write between one and two thousand words easily in an evening. My appetite is boundless.[13]

Muilenburg "became something of a recluse," recalled his brother, but his letters record regular socializing with neighbors and visits from his family.[14]

In 1923 he joined Iowa's English faculty.[15] He supported the department's nascent creative writing efforts by teaching narrative writing.[16] Between the novel's announcement and publication Muilenburg joined the faculty at Michigan State College (now University), where he remained for twelve years.[17] Muilenburg died from a heart attack in Phoenix, Arizona, on November 30, 1958. He is buried in Orange City near his parents, to whom he dedicated *Prairie*.[18]

Although Muilenburg's output was small, a novel and eight short stories, he received critical praise and was anthologized for decades. His champions considered him a promising voice within regionalist literature, but after *Prairie* he did not publish any fiction.

THE SHORT STORIES, *THE MIDLAND*, AND MUILENBURG'S LITERARY APPRENTICESHIP

Muilenburg's literary career was tied closely to John T. Frederick and his Iowa City–based journal *The Midland*. Six of Muilenburg's eight short stories appeared there between 1915 and 1922. Frederick was Muilenburg's college classmate, a Glennie neighbor, and later faculty colleague in Iowa. Dissatisfied with the Eastern dominance of the American literary scene, Frederick established *The Midland* to foster Midwestern writers and readers. "The magazine is merely a modest attempt to encourage the making of literature in the Middle West," Frederick declared in the first issue.[19] It promoted the best of Midwestern literature until its closure in 1933.

Frank Luther Mott recalled decades later that those "who wrote short stories for the *Midland* would show that most of them were then and now unknown to fame."[20] While certainly true, Muilenburg was one of the few who achieved fame through the journal. His most critically praised stories, "The Prairie" and "Heart of Youth" appeared during the journal's first year.[21] These stories emerged from Muilenburg's life. He confessed, "[T]he greater part of both have been taken from my own experience, and the circumstances are reproduced rather than fancied."[22] Muilenburg also published elsewhere. "At the End of the Road" appeared in *The Forum*, and "Thanksgiving Lost and Found" was published in *Today's Housewife*.[23] Further stories appeared off and on in *The Midland*, "Brothers of the Road" in 1916, "The Last Spring" in 1918, "Peace" in 1921, and "The Ways of His Fathers" in 1922.[24]

The Midland's critical success owed no small part to Muilenburg. "Heart of Youth" was anthologized in Edward J. O'Brien's inaugural *Best Short Stories* volume in 1915. O'Brien selected ten stories from *The Midland* for his honor roll, but republished only Muilenburg in the book. He argued that these stories offered "the most vital interpretation in fiction of our national life that many years have been able to show."[25] The following year O'Brien once again pointed to *The Midland* as an important literary venue and included Muilenburg's "At the End of the Road" among the year's best stories.[26]

O'Brien's support was sincere and unwavering. As a colleague recalled, "Whatever excited him usually boiled into vibrant enthusiasm."[27] He often ranked *Midland* among the top publishers of distinctive short stories.[28] Of the 337 short stories the *Midland* published from 1915 to 1933, O'Brien included 324 in his annual best stories list, or ninety-six percent of the journal's total fiction output. In addition, O'Brien awarded three stars to 105 *Midland* short stories, a feat few publishers matched.[29]

In a rare public letter in *The Editor*, Muilenburg confessed his writing advice was limited, "owing to the fact that I am young, callow, and have few published stories to my credit." Moreover, his experience was not representative of most aspiring writers. His early stories were included in *Best Short Stories*, astonishing recognition for a novice.[30] "To be starred in [O'Brien's] annual was success, and to be three-starred or reprinted there was fame," recalled Frank Luther Mott.[31] Yet, that fame was hindered by Muilenburg's themes and style.

Muilenburg knew his shortcomings: disinterest in plot and preference for pessimistic narratives. "In spite of the fact that I have read definitions of plot until I am blue in the face and my brain reels, I have not the least idea what it all means," he confessed to *The Editor*. Instead, he tended to produce "sketches" rather than fully-fleshed-out stories. He did so, partially in response to public demand for "cheerful" and romantic stories, "wherein everything is loveliness to the nth degree." Rather, he considered his best short stories those "where darkness and pessimism are featured." This demonstrated a remarkable self-awareness of his own psyche and his approach to art:

> I have come to the opinion that I will continue to work this out as it will and if it has been decreed that my work must be of gloomy themes, I shall at least try to brighten it with the best art I am capable of.[32]

Elsewhere he considered his deemphasis on plot and attention to characterization key to writing. "For me the best story is the one that gives the reader the greatest after-mood, and this can be done with very little action," he argued. Instead of plot, setting and characters were primary to Muilenburg. "To give the feeling of an environment, to show character absolutely in a life-like manner, and to give nature and man an equal place: these I consider necessary to almost every story," he wrote.[33] Thus, rather than correct himself and adopt a more commercial and optimistic approach, Muilenburg sharpened these characteristics in *Prairie*.

Although Muilenburg did not point to Willa Cather's 1922 essay "The Novel Démeublé," his approach echoed her concerns about art, commercialization, and the aims of writing. Cather argued that art relied on higher attention and sympathies, a creative practice that sought "the inexplicable presence of the thing not named, of the overtone divined by the ear but not heard by it, the verbal mood, the emotional aura of the fact or the thing or the deed." This distinguished art from commercial writing. Rather than adopt a romantic posture for commercial gain Muilenburg accepted his "gloomy themes" and strove to imbue them with art. His short stories succeeded in this, envisioning an artistically grounded form of realism drawn from the writer himself. Or, as Cather asked, "But is not realism, more than it is anything else, an attitude of mind on the part of the writer toward his material, a vague indication of the sympathy and candour with which he accepts, rather chooses, his theme?" [34] The novel challenged Muilenburg to develop his "gloomy themes" into a larger work. It also provided a space to reject the romantic and heroic frames dominant within commercial Western literature. Grounded in recollections of his youth and the experiences of his elders, *Prairie* recorded the hollowing out of a homesteader and the disintegration of his family, hardly a romantic vision of the West.

THE PRAIRIE

Muilenburg's correspondence with the Canadian writer Raymond Knister records the novel's development. Knister found Muilenburg's stories after requesting copies of *The Midland*. Impressed with the journal and the community that supported it, he briefly moved to Iowa City and joined the staff.[35] Muilenburg and Knister shared an office, where both dreamed big and worked late, which the latter recalled after *Prairie* appeared. "I know you'd do it and that those evenings we spent in the office rattling typewriters, smoking, would not come to naught."[36] Muilenburg was, by his own observation, "creatively slow."[37] He reworked the scenes and themes of his 1915 *Midland* stories "The Prairie" and "Heart of Youth" into a longer narrative.[38] These stories appeared while he was a student, but they were grounded in his childhood outside Orange City. *Prairie*, then, was something he was working on, consciously or not, for much of his life up to then.

Extant correspondence documents a novel manuscript underway in 1922, which Knister read and returned to Muilenburg with comments and recommendations. This manuscript could be an early iteration of *Prairie*, but the male protagonist was a musician. While this does not preclude him also being a farmer, as the characters are described as living "in the country," the manuscript departs from Muilenburg's farm stories. This suggests he was stretching beyond his established themes and material. What can be gleaned about the plot echoes *Prairie*, though. A wife leaves a husband and child in the country—Knister's letter does not disclose her motivation—and travels elsewhere, presumably to a city. Muilenburg may have transformed this into Lizzie and Joey's trip east in *Prairie*. According to Knister, he struggled to narrate these parallel, but geographically distinct, stories. Knister recommended alternating chapters for each spouse, as Edith Wharton had in *Glimpses of the Moon*. Otherwise, he suggested separate parts or books within the novel for the wife and husband. In the published version of *Prairie* Muilenburg sidestepped this by focusing solely on Elias.[39]

By the fall of 1924 Muilenburg had a nearly complete *Prairie* manuscript, lacking just the final chapter and substantial revisions. He wanted it to be "a fairly finished piece of work" before prospective publishers saw it.[40] Four publishers rejected *Prairie* before B. W. Huebsch, the American publisher of James Joyce and D. H. Lawrence, accepted it.[41] The company also published influential regional literature, like Sherwood Anderson's *Winesburg, Ohio*.[42] Between signing his contract and the book's release, Huebsch merged with the newly established publisher Viking Press. *Prairie*, in fact, was Viking's first book, which the publisher touted in advertisements: "New book, new novelist, new publisher."[43] Muilenburg was excited to see it in print and hoped for positive reviews. His contract gave Viking the option for his next two novels.[44]

"Prairie does credit to the Viking Press, which makes its *début* in the publishing world with the volume," commended an early review. "The print and binding are good, and the general format is conservative and pleasing."[45] Others welcomed the new publisher and its promising young voice: "The Viking Press is to be congratulated on this auspicious beginning of its publishing career, and Mr. Muilenburg is to be hailed as a welcome addition to the ranks of the younger American novelists," proclaimed *Commonweal*.[46]

Inaugurating a new publisher into a crowded market was no easy task. Muilenburg, to his credit, had a clear vision of the novel's trajectory. "I do not look for the book to be much of a seller, but I am hopeful of a fairly cordial reception at the hands of the better critics," he wrote to Knister.[47] Viking, however, marketed *Prairie* within the commercial frame Muilenburg rejected. In fact, an early advertisement claimed Muilenburg "finds romance in the prairie."[48] Later advertisements said Muilenburg extracted "the pure gold of romance … from the quartz of our pioneer history" and fashioned it into art. By fall 1925 reviews were available and highlighted by Viking. For example, Ellen Glasgow's comment, "As fine and true as any work that has come from the Middle West – a book of unusual significance," was used in later advertisements.[49]

Prairie received welcome reviews but was overshadowed by releases from established writers at bigger publishers. That fall

Doubleday, Page & Company released Glasgow's *Barren Ground*, while Alfred Knopf published Cal Van Vechten's *Firecrackers* and Willa Cather's *The Professor's House*. Meanwhile, Sherwood Anderson's *Dark Laughter* was published by Boni & Liveright, and Harcourt, Brace released Sinclair Lewis's *Arrowsmith*. Writers interested in Midwestern writers or rural settings had many options. Nevertheless, Viking was happy with the novel's reception, and Muilenburg earned a small profit even though it was not a best-seller.[50]

AT THE HANDS OF THE BETTER CRITICS

Muilenburg left Iowa for Michigan State College (MSC) by the time *Prairie* appeared. He found fewer literary folks about campus, but the pay was better, and a quick walk brought him into timber and solitude.[51] Their alumni magazine lauded Muilenburg's novel. Paraphrasing a letter from Frederick to MSC English professor W. W. Johnston, the magazine shared "that he has never known of a first book by a mid-western writer which has had such widespread critical recognition." Moreover, Johnston himself believed "it has more of intensity" than Knut Hamsun's similarly themed 1917 novel *Growth of the Soil*.[52]

More positive reviews were forthcoming. *The Bookman* welcomed the arrival of Muilenburg, Ruth Suckow, Glenway Wescott, Sherwood Anderson, and John T. Frederick. All were Midwestern novelists "who have known the soil and nature in all her capricious and frequently cruel manifestations" and transformed them into literature. Rather than romantic pastoral tales, Muilenburg and his peers revealed a hostile reality. "Sometimes the fierce struggle against nature is a brutal picture and sometimes a tragic one, but always there is in it a fierce kind of splendor," tensions found at the novel's heart. Ultimately, *The Bookman* reviewer wrote, books like Muilenburg's *Prairie*, Suckow's *Country People*, and Anderson's *Poor White* "have in them something of the fire of immortality because they are related closely to truth."[53] Elsewhere in the same issue, Louis Bromfield identified *Prairie* as one of the best novels he read the previous month, and a short review deemed it a "fine and sturdy story told with realism and yet with beauty."[54]

In *The New York Times Book Review* Lloyd Morris argued the novel "has the effect of an epic; it is more than a novel of promise; it is a substantial achievement in art."[55] Its epic quality was recognized by other critics, as well. In *Commonweal*, John Kenny welcomed Muilenburg's turn to the novel. The "material is simple, though its implications are large," he found. Muilenburg infused drama into the smallest details of prairie life, from river crossings to town visits. *Prairie* served as a testament to the "heroic pioneer," accorded Kenny, a figure who "is pictured with a realism that is none the less honest because it does not blight the romance of the adventure."[56] While certainly a warm review, however, its positioning of *Prairie* as another romantic Western adventure misreads Muilenburg's attempt to subvert the genre.

For an aspiring writer, one voice mattered above all: H. L. Mencken. Known for his sharp wit, poison pen, and advocacy for up-and-coming voices, Mencken supported regional voices and unknown writers. This included *The Midland*, as noted above. John T. Frederick encouraged Ruth Suckow, for example, to send her stories to Mencken, who published her in *The Smart Set* and in the first issue of *The American Mercury*.[57] This suggests Mencken was familiar with Muilenburg's stories, but he was unimpressed with *Prairie*: "Nor am I moved by Mr. Muilenburg's peasants in

'Prairie.' They never seem real to me for an instant. I can't get rid of a feeling that they are set up in front of me, not by one who has lived among them and sweated with them, but by a spectator from the Ford of some agricultural experiment station."[58] Muilenburg confessed his disappointment in Mencken's review in a letter to his brother, but considered the critical response largely positive. "Mencken was not favorably taken with the book," he wrote. "The last *Bookman* had some pleasant things to say about it. Taken by and large, the book has been successful, and I am more than satisfied, even though the sale promises to be small."[59] He told Raymond Knister Mencken's comments were "a wicked slam" and that he was displeased with Laurence Stallings's "unenthusiastic" review in the *New York World*.[60]

Supportive letters found their way to Glennie, including one from Glenway Wescott.[61] Although his initial letter does not survive, Muilenburg's reply does. He told Wescott he welcomed reader's letters, which differed from the "too stale" opinions of newspaper critics. Nevertheless, he found those critics "accorded me better treatment than I deserve."[62] Closer to home the book was welcomed. Appropriately, Frank Luther Mott published the novel's longest review in *The Midland*. Mott welcomed the novel's sincerity and harmony. Rather than forwarding trendy experimentation or a blatant attempt to reach the "jazz-hungry public," Muilenburg wrote an honest book. The book's "singular harmony" unified its tone, structure, and form into a bleak, but revealing portrait of Great Plains homesteading. Although he disagreed with Muilenburg's depersonalization of Elias Vaughan, he found the depictions of the landscape and Elias's struggle within and against environmental forces the heart of the work. Multiple reviewers pointed to the Biblical, mythic, or epic quality of this struggle, which Mott viewed as mystical encounters. He deemed Elias "the farmer-mystic," whose contact with the land and environment defined his being.[63] Mott concluded his review by disclaiming the existence of a *Midland* literary school. Certainly Muilenburg, not to mention Suckow and Frederick, published in and/or edited the *Midland* at one point or another, but there was "no Midland school," claimed Mott, just Midwestern writers each interested in their particular locales and people, and all of them could write about things beyond "farm and village life" if they wanted.[64] Had Muilenburg published fiction after *Prairie* then sufficient distance between he and the journal may have formed. Instead, Muilenburg is bound up with *The Midland*. Overall, American reviewers commended his depictions of homesteading's harshness and the brutal struggle to survive. Yet, most found his muted characterization and bare plot limiting. Nevertheless, critics saw a promising future ahead.

John Lane published a British edition in 1926 to familiar criticism.[65] English critics welcomed its captivating depictions of settlers' struggle against nature's brutality. "This is an unusually promising first novel," confessed *The Guardian* reviewer. They commended the novel's stark setting, from which he produced a compelling novel. "Out of these materials, drab enough in themselves, Mr. Muilenburg has made a story which holds our interest closely. It is very quiet, very faithful to life, and the one character who rises above mediocrity is Elias himself."[66] Further praise followed. *Prairie* was a "sombre story, but great and powerful in its truth," commended *T.P.'s & Cassell's Weekly*. They pointed to Lizzie's death scene as "almost Biblical" in its telling.[67] Another review proclaimed Muilenburg "a force to reckon with."[68] Muilenburg appreciated the positive English response.[69]

Other European critics found much to praise. A Welsh critic enjoyed that this "book of short sentences" puts readers directly into the fire, frost, and loneliness of prairie life. "There is no plot, in the usual sense, but the book grips with its reality and simplicity."[70] The *Irish Independent* welcomed Muilenburg's departure from short stories with "a study of singular intensity of loneliness." Nevertheless, the story suffered from its narrow and intense focus.[71] French critic and translator Régis Michaud praised *Prairie* in *Revue Anglo-Américaine*. Michaud was regarded as the leading interpreter of American literature in France.[72] Michaud found Muilenburg's realism precise and penetrating. *Prairie* was a "veritable document épique," on par with the best of Sherwood Anderson, Sinclair Lewis, and Willa Cather. It was a magnificent start to Muilenburg's literary career, he proclaimed.[73]

In the coming years Muilenburg's work was still anthologized and appreciated, but without any new publications, Muilenburg faded from the forefront of Iowa's literary canon. John T. Frederick kept the flame of Muilenburg's fiction alive through frequent anthologizations, such as the first *Midland* anthology, published by Knopf in 1923.[74] To support this volume he had "The Prairie" reprinted in *The Iowa Alumnus*.[75] He also included it in *Present-Day Stories*, published in 1941 by Charles Scribner's Sons.[76] Frederick's next anthology, *Out of the Midwest*, published in 1944 by Whittlesey House, McGraw-Hill, included the story alongside those of Willa Cather, Ernest Hemingway, and Carl Sandburg.[77]

In 1930, Iowa's state librarian, Johnson Brigham, published an overview of the state's literary history with biographical and critical overviews of key authors. Brigham argued that Muilenburg's work was "marked by an active sense of significance of men's relation to the earth and by a profound grasp of emotional values."[78] Frederick listed

Muilenburg as part of the Midwestern literary vanguard, alongside
Glenway Wescott, O. A. Rølvaag, and Ruth Suckow in an essay on
Suckow. These writers and their predecessors, "constitute what is
unquestionably the most considerable contribution to American
literature which the century has to show thus far."[79] However, as vital
as Muilenburg may have been to Midwestern literature in the 1910s
and 1920s, few continued to champion his work.

Other promising *Midland* authors found wider success in the
1920s and 1930s: Ruth Suckow, August Derleth, James T. Farrell,
and John G. Neihardt, for example. Not to be outdone, Frederick
published two novels as well.[80] In 1938, Wallace Stegner published
a literary history of Iowa in *The Saturday Review of Literature*.
Since the turn of the century Iowa had developed a vibrant literary
culture, fostering young writers and imprints to support them.
"Iowa has become as fit a subject for books, and as reputable a state
for a writer to live in, as any other," Stegner concluded. Central
to this was John T. Frederick and *The Midland*. Unlike previous
accounts of the journal and its success, Muilenburg was not
mentioned.[81]

Attention from academic critics was slow and remains limited.
Roy Meyer engaged with *Prairie* in *The Middle Western Farm
Novel in the Twentieth Century*. He was unimpressed, marking it
as a "crude but not negligible" predecessor to *Giants in the Earth*.
He argued it was little more than "an expanded short story, not
sufficiently expanded for the scope of the theme."[82] It would take
a generation before another literary scholar considered *Prairie*.
Mary Engel's 1978 dissertation on prairie novels is Muilenburg's
most sustained scholarly treatment. Her generous reading of
Muilenburg and his work argued for the novel's place alongside
other contemporary writers. She found *Prairie* "a novel of

potentially epic proportions" that arrived at the wrong moment, published between two better received novels with similar themes, Knut Hamsun's *Growth of the Soil* and O. E. Rølvaag's *Giants in the Earth*. Moreover, critical attention to literary modernism undercut the reach of Muilenburg's forbidding realism. Nevertheless, Engel found that the novel's revelation of the "spiritual desolation" at the heart of prairie settlement warranted further study and attention.[83]

This scant scholarly attention suggests *Prairie* was not entirely forgotten. Popular Library republished an inexpensive paperback edition in the early 1970s.[84] Ever the book's champion, John T. Frederick celebrated its return. In a note to Davenport columnist Jim Arpy he declared it "perhaps the finest achievement of an Iowa writer in [the 1920s]." Frederick implored readers to pick it up: "[*Prairie*] deserves a permanent place in American literature, and a place in the library of every serious Iowa reader." Arpy had never heard of the book and asked, "How many Iowa readers, serious or otherwise, know about Muilenburg?" Despite his obscurity, Arpy hoped it would lead Iowans to "a chunk of our useable past."[85]

Others rediscovered the novel in recent years, an effort the present volume furthers. James Schaap's reassessment in 2016 suggests the novel still finds curious readers. Framing it within the Muilenburg family's Reformed faith, Schaap argues *Prairie* "is an argument for despair." He concludes it is a story of a man whose fight with the land left no time for his family. Schaap's reading echoes the novel's initial critics. He found that Muilenburg's "[c]haracters appear less human than they are functions."[86] This unknowingly echoes Mencken's observation that the novel was written "from the Ford of some agricultural experiment station."[87]

PUBLIC NEGLECT

Muilenburg's biography in *A Book of Iowa Authors* foretold future literary success: "American literature will be enriched by his special contribution to it, and many readers are looking forward with eagerness to the second novel on which he is working."[88] Yet, shortly after *Prairie* appeared he confessed that writing was hard arriving. In a letter to his brother that fall he reported his voracious reading. Reading was easy, writing was hard. Muilenburg concluded his letter, "No I've lost the thread of this. One thing I remember was on my mind, and that was: Write!"[89] Three months later he told Glenway Wescott that his drive to write was exhausted:

> What with teaching at college here and a paradoxical hatred of what I want most to do – writing – I get very little done. I envy the fellows who are consciously inspired. I used to be that[,] a sense of beatitude came over me when I was writing. It doesn't any more, largely because the thing is self conscious, I suppose the yearning youngster has a flame that the older writer has lost through inhibitions – he's studied methods and mechanics too much, or else has burned out in classroom study of fiction. Do you find it so in your own case?[90]

Two years after its release in the United States, Muilenburg confessed that *Prairie* was "beginning to bore me as something to talk about." He also admitted that he was falling away from most of friends and acquaintances from Iowa City.[91] Given Muilenburg's struggle to write, one wonders whether he said all he had to with the novel. The novel was not kind, romantic, or welcoming.

Its raw, brutal, and unyielding depiction of prairie life was not appreciated by many. Schaap goes so far as to ask, "Was Walter Happy? I don't know, and I wish I did."[92] Muilenburg crafted a story to last, not one to appease readers or critics. It did not ignore the difficulties of homesteading; rather it drew this process into itself, revealing a struggle that once overcome was nevertheless defeating. "Isn't it possible," he observed, "that only the stories that have some situations where the characters must be shown in primitive fashion are enduring?"[93] His story was bare, but not simple. It got to the heart of settlers' relationship to the land and their self-defeating conquest.

As difficult as he found writing, though, Muilenburg did not stop. He won first prize for a story "Alone" from the Michigan Authors' Association in 1930.[94] This remains unpublished. In all likelihood much of his work remained in manuscript. He shared in 1917, "that editorial opinion does not gibe with my own" and as a result few were willing to publish his work. Instead, "[s]old as waste paper, my rejected manuscripts now on hand should bring in a goodly sum."[95] Presumably Muilenburg's manuscripts do not survive, a result of critical inattention and the passage of time.[96]

After leaving Michigan State College in 1937 he moved to Glennie to farm alfalfa, raise sheep, and band birds. He wrote occasional articles for *The Country Gentleman, The Flower Grower,* and the Department of Agriculture. He lived off the land, hunted, fished, and gathered berries and nuts, recalled his brother.[97] To return to Schaap's question, yes, Muilenburg was happy. His letters with Raymond Knister and Glenway Wescott show he was pleased by the novel's reception and sales. He found joy on the land in Glennie, living simply, but hardly solitary. He was surrounded by life-long friends and family with whom he socialized as he pleased.

He enjoyed teaching at Michigan State College, loved Glennie, and kept writing, although with a lower public profile.

His later commercial writing shows continued discernment with the themes of his literary endeavors. For example, in *The Flower Grower* he reflected on the cultivation of plants ill-suited for Michigan: "But some of us have a further reason for gardening— we like to gamble, and so we try to grow things that simply don't belong in our climate and our soil, on the off-chance that we may get them to settle down and feel at home." He recounted his failure to cultivate American holly around his Glennie farm and middling success with azaleas and rhododendrons.[98] While this article may seem banal, it suggests Muilenburg continued to turn over the themes of his fiction: locality, land, and finding a place in the world.

Later he suffered from an unrecorded illness and was taken care of during his final years by his sisters, Josephine and Anna. He also moved to Arizona.[99] He did not forget *Prairie*, though, renewing the novel's copyright in 1952.[100] After moving to Arizona he sold his Glennie property to the Fredericks, who allowed him to use the cabin until his death. Sadly, his brother believed he never returned.[101] A heart attack killed Muilenburg in Phoenix on November 30, 1958. He is buried in Orange City.[102]

All but forgotten in his lifetime, his absence was noted in some quarters. Arnold Mulder, a Michigan newspaper editor, critic, and novelist offered a pointed eulogy for his literary career in 1939:

> An East Lansing novelist, Walter J. Muilenburg, sometime
> in the middle twenties wrote a novel called 'Prairie' that
> is a beautiful prose poem of real distinction. Until now it
> remains alone on the shelf and I don't suppose there will be
> another. A career assassinated by public neglect.[103]

ENDNOTES

1. James C. Schaap, "Walter J. Muilenburg's *Prairie*: Review Essay," *Pro Rege*, Vol. 44, No. 4 (June 2016), 13.

2. Muilenburg's geography is intentionally vague, resulting in critics claiming it occurs in the Dakotas or Nebraska. The former is more likely, and it is possible Muilenburg drew on community memory of Dutch homesteaders who left Sioux County in the 1880s for South Dakota. See Henry S. Lucas, *Netherlanders in America: Dutch Immigration to the United States and Canada, 1789–1950* (Ann Arbor: University of Michigan Press, 1955), 376–86. Schaap, 16; Frank Luther Mott, "Sincerity in the Novel," *The Midland*, Vol. 11, No. 17 (October 1925), 304.

3. "Walter J. Muilenburg," *Sioux Center News*, December 11, 1958; Schaap, 13. For more on the Dutch in northwest Iowa see: Lucas, 334–51; Jacob Van Hinte, *Netherlanders in America: A Study of Emigration and Settlement in the 19th and 20th Centuries in the United States of America* (Grand Rapids: Baker Book House, 1985), 463–521.

4. "Walter J. Muilenburg," *Sioux Center News*, December 11, 1958; Douglas Firth Anderson, "'Our People Excel in the Love of Education': Northwestern Classical Academy, Iowa, 1882–1928," *Northwestern Review*, Vol. 5, No. 1 (2020), 21–22; Schaap, 14–15.

5. *The Hawkeye*, 1915, 333; *The Hawkeye*, 1916, 323; Milton M. Reigelman, *The Midland: A Venture in Literary Regionalism* (Iowa City: University of Iowa Press, 1975), 3–4.

6. "From Our Neighbors," *Adams County Free Press*, August 12, 1916.

7. "Muilenburg's Novel Appears in August," *The Daily Iowan*, June 17, 1925; "Ex M.S.U. Man Dies," *Lansing State Journal*, December 1, 1958; Johnson Brigham, ed, *A Book of Iowa Authors*

by Iowa Authors (Des Moines: Iowa State Teachers Association, 1930), 228–29.

8. Delight Ansley, *First Chronicles* (Stockton: Carolingian Press, 1971), 13; Reigelman, 12–13.

9. John T. Frederick, ed., *Stories from The Midland* (New York: Alfred A. Knopf, 1924), 317.

10. Warren Van Dine quoted in Reigelman, 13.

11. Walter Muilenburg to James Muilenburg, August 14, 1924, Letters to James [Muilenburg], 1924-1955, MsL M9538 m, University of Iowa Special Collections, Iowa City, Iowa.

12. Ansley, 35.

13. Walter Muilenburg to James Muilenburg, August 14, 1924, Letters to James [Muilenburg], 1924-1955, MsL M9538 m, University of Iowa Special Collections, Iowa City, Iowa.

14. James Muilenburg to Milton Reigelman, June 23, 1971, MsL M9534 r, University of Iowa Special Collections, Iowa City, Iowa; Walter J. Muilenburg to Raymond Knister, October 4, 1924, Box 2: Incoming Correspondence, Raymond Knister Fonds, RC0121, McMaster University Archives and Research Collections, Hamilton, Ontario, Canada; Walter Muilenburg to Raymond Knister, October 24, 1925, Box 2: Incoming Correspondence, Raymond Knister Fonds, RC0121, McMaster University Archives and Research Collections, Hamilton, Ontario, Canada.

15. *The State University of Iowa Catalogue, 1924–1925* (Iowa City: Published by the University, 1924), 21.

16. Stephen Wilbers, *The Iowa Writers' Workshop: Origins, Emergence, and Growth* (Iowa City: University of Iowa Press, 1980), 42n9.

17. "Muilenburg's Novel Appears in August," *The Daily Iowan*, June 17, 1925; "Ex M.S.U. Man Dies," *Lansing State Journal*, December 1, 1958; Brigham, *A Book of Iowa Authors*, 228–29.

18. "Ex M.S.U. Man Dies," *Lansing State Journal*, December 1, 1958; "Walter J. Muilenburg," *Sioux Center News*, December 11, 1958.

19. "The First Person Plural," *The Midland*, Vol. 1, No. 1 (January 1915), 1.

20. Frank Luther Mott, *A History of American Magazines*. Volume 5 (Cambridge University Press, 1968), 183.

21. Walter J, Muilenburg, "The Prairie," *The Midland*, Vol. 1, No. 8 (August 1915), 260–70; Walter J, Muilenburg, "Heart of Youth," *The Midland*, Vol. 1, No. 11 (November 1915), 362–77.

22. Quoted in Blanche Colton Williams, *How to Study 'The Best Short Stories'* (Boston: Small, Maynard & Company, 1919), 145.

23. Walter J. Muilenburg, "At the End of the Road," *The Forum* (May 1916), 583–90; Walter J. Muilenburg, "Thanksgiving Lost and Found," *Today's Housewife*, Vol. 23, No. 7 (November 1917), 3, 20.

24. Walter J. Muilenburg, "Brothers of the Road," *The Midland*, Vol. 2 No. 9 (September 1916), 266–78; Walter J. Muilenburg, "The Last Spring," *The Midland*, Vol. 4, No. 5–6 (May-June 1918), 129–36; Walter J. Muilenburg, "Peace," *The Midland*, Vol. 7, No. 4 (April 1921), 159–70; Walter J. Muilenburg, "The Ways of His Fathers," *The Midland*, Vol. 8, No. 3 (March 1922), 81–95.

25. Edward J. O'Brien, "Introduction" to *The Best Short Stories of 1915 and the Yearbook of the American Short Story* (Boston: Small, Maynard & Company, 1916), 9.

26. Edward J. O'Brien, "Introduction" to *The Best Short Stories of 1916 and the Yearbook of the American Short Story* (Boston: Small, Maynard & Company, 1917), 5.

27. Robert Whitehand, "Edward J. O'Brien," *Prairie Schooner*, Vol. 14, No. 1 (Spring 1940), 4.

28. Reigelman, 21.

29. Jacquelyn S. Spangler, "Edward J. O'Brien: *Best Short Stories* and the Production of an American Genre," PhD diss. The Ohio State University, 1997, 35.

30. "Contemporary Writers and Their Work: A Series of Autobiographical Letters," *The Editor*, Vol. 47, No. 9 (December 26, 1917), 270.

31. Frank Luther Mott, *Time Enough: Essays in Autobiography* (Chapel Hill: University of North Carolina Press, 1962), 128.

32. "Contemporary Writers and Their Work," 270.

33. Quoted in Williams, *How to Study 'The Best Short Stories,'* 145.

34. Willa Cather, "The Novel Démeublé," in *Willa Cather on Writing* (New York: Alfred A. Knopf, 1949), 33–43.

35. Raymond Knister, "Canadian Literati," *The Journal of Canadian Fiction*, Vol. 4, No. 2 (1975), 163–64.

36. Raymond Knister to Walter J. Muilenburg, September 14, 1925, Box 3: Outgoing Correspondence, Raymond Knister Fonds, RC0121, McMaster University Archives and Research Collections, Hamilton, Ontario, Canada.

37. Walter J. Muilenburg to Raymond Knister, February 14, 1927, Box 2: Incoming Correspondence, Raymond Knister Fonds, RC0121, McMaster University Archives and Research Collections, Hamilton, Ontario, Canada.

38. For a detailed comparison between "The Prairie" and *Prairie* see Mary F. Engel, "Bankrupt Dreams: The Isolated and the Insulated in Selected Works of Canadian and American Prairie Literature," PhD diss. Kent State University, 1978, 102–107.

39. Raymond Knister to Walter J. Muilenburg, October 7, 1922, Box 3: Outgoing Correspondence, Raymond Knister Fonds, RC0121, McMaster University Archives and Research Collections, Hamilton, Ontario, Canada.

40. Walter J. Muilenburg to Raymond Knister, October 4, 1924, Box 2: Incoming Correspondence, Raymond Knister Fonds, RC0121, McMaster University Archives and Research Collections, Hamilton, Ontario, Canada.

41. Walter J. Muilenburg to Raymond Knister, May 10, 1925, Box 2: Incoming Correspondence, Raymond Knister Fonds, RC0121, McMaster University Archives and Research Collections, Hamilton, Ontario, Canada.

42. Ann Catherine McCullough, "A History of B. W. Huebsch, Publisher," PhD diss. University of Wisconsin-Madison (1979), 217–336, 418.

43. Martha Sue Bean, "A History and Profile of the Viking Press," Master's thesis, School of Library Science, University of North Carolina-Chapel Hill (1969), 2–5; "Prairie by Walter J. Muilenburg," *The Publisher's Weekly*, Vol. 108, No. 3 (July 18, 1925), 157.

44. Walter J. Muilenburg to Raymond Knister, May 10, 1925, Box 2: Incoming Correspondence, Raymond Knister Fonds, RC0121, McMaster University Archives and Research Collections, Hamilton, Ontario, Canada.

45. Mott, "Sincerity in the Novel," 305.

46. John M. Kenny, Jr., "Prairie by Walter J. Muilenburg," *The Commonweal*, Vol. 2, No. 18 (September 9, 1925), 430.

47. Walter J. Muilenburg to Raymond Knister, May 10, 1925, Box 2: Incoming Correspondence, Raymond Knister Fonds,

RC0121, McMaster University Archives and Research Collections, Hamilton, Ontario, Canada.

48. "By Way of Introduction," *The Publisher's Weekly*, Vol. 108, No. 2 (July 11, 1925), 94–95.

49. "The Viking Gallery," *The American Mercury*, Vol. 6, No. 22 (October 1925), ix.

50. Walter Muilenburg to Raymond Knister, October 24, 1925, Box 2: Incoming Correspondence, Raymond Knister Fonds, RC0121, McMaster University Archives and Research Collections, Hamilton, Ontario, Canada.

51. Walter Muilenburg to Raymond Knister, October 24, 1925, Box 2: Incoming Correspondence, Raymond Knister Fonds, RC0121, McMaster University Archives and Research Collections, Hamilton, Ontario, Canada.

52. "English Instructor Publishes Novel," *The M.S.C. Record*, Vol. 31, No. 6 (October 25, 1925), 99.

53. "The Truth About Nature," *The Bookman*, Vol. 62, No. 3 (November 1925), 242–43.

54. Louis Bromfield, "The New Yorker," *The Bookman*, Vol. 62, No. 3 (November 1925), 322; "The Bookman's Guide to Fiction," *The Bookman*, Vol. 62, No. 3 (November 1925), 328.

55. Lloyd Morris, "Skimming the Cream from Six Months' Fiction," *New York Times Book Review*, December 6, 1925, 2.

56. Kenny, Jr., "Prairie by Walter J. Muilenburg," 430.

57. Reigelman, 20–21; Ruth Suckow, "Four Generations," *American Mercury*, Vol. 1, No. 1 (January 1924), 15–21.

58. H. L. Mencken, "The Library," *American Mercury*, Vol. 6, No. 23 (November 1925), 381.

59. Walter Muilenburg to James Muilenburg, November 17, 1925, Letters to James [Muilenburg], 1924-1955, MsL M9538 m, University of Iowa Special Collections, Iowa City, Iowa.

60. Walter Muilenburg to Raymond Knister, October 24, 1925, Box 2: Incoming Correspondence, Raymond Knister Fonds, RC0121, McMaster University Archives and Research Collections, Hamilton, Ontario, Canada. Viking was pleased enough with Stallings's review to quote in in their advertisements. "Prairie," *Chicago Daily Tribune*, September 19, 1925.

61. Walter Muilenburg to James Muilenburg, November 17, 1925, Letters to James [Muilenburg], 1924-1955, MsL M9538 m, University of Iowa Special Collections, Iowa City, Iowa.

62. Walter J. Muilenburg to Glenway Wescott, January 10, 1926, Folder 1215, Box 82, Glenway Wescott Papers, Beinecke Rare Book and Manuscript Library, Yale, New Haven Connecticut.

63. Mott, "Sincerity in the Novel," 302–306.

64. Mott, "Sincerity in the Novel," 305–306.

65. Walter J. Muilenburg, *Prairie* (London: John Lane, 1926).

66. F. R., "An American Farm," *The Guardian*, July 16, 1926.

67. "Like Father, Like Son," *T.P.'s & Cassell's Weekly* (July 17, 1927), 404.

68. Brother Savage, "Books and Bookmen: Literary Gossip from London," *Liverpool Daily Post*, August 7, 1926.

69. Walter J. Muilenburg to Raymond Knister, February 14, 1927, Box 2: Incoming Correspondence, Raymond Knister Fonds, RC0121, McMaster University Archives and Research Collections, Hamilton, Ontario, Canada.

70. A. H., "Short Sentences," *South Wales Argus*, December 20, 1926.

71. F. J. K., "Mixed Reading," *Irish Independent*, July 26, 1926.

72. F. B. Giovanelli, "The Useful Life of Régis Michaud," *Books Abroad*, Vol. 13, No. 3 (Summer 1939), 299–301; Alphonse V. Roche, "Régis Michaud on American Literature," *Books Abroad*, Vol. 13, No. 3 (Summer 1939), 301–303.

73. Régis Michaud, "Walter J. Muilenburg: Prairie. – The Viking Press, New-York." *Revue Anglo-Américaine*, Vol. 3, No. 2 (December 1925), 175.

74. "Group of Midland Best Stories Will Appear in Volume," *The Daily Iowan*, November 21, 1923; Frederick, *Stories from the Midland*, 182–203.

75. Walter J. Muilenburg, "The Prairie," *The Iowa Alumnus*, Vol. 21, No. 26 (April 7, 1924).

76. Walter J. Muilenburg, "The Prairie," *Present-Day Stories*. Edited by John T. Frederick (New York: Charles Scribner's Sons, 1941), 297–305.

77. Walter J. Muilenburg, "The Prairie," *Out of the Midwest: A Collection of Present-Day Writing*. Edited by John T. Frederick (New York: Whittlesey House/McGraw-Hill Book Company, Inc., 1944), 232–39.

78. Brigham, *A Book of Iowa Authors*, 228.

79. John T. Frederick, "Ruth Suckow and the Middle Western Literary Movement," *The English Journal*, Vol. 20, No. 1 (January 1931), 3–4.

80. Frederick's Glennie-set second novel, *Green Bush*, was published by Knopf the same month as *Prairie*. "Publish 'Prairie' and 'Green Bush': Novels by Frederick, Muilenburg Printed by Knopf, Heubsch," *The Daily Iowan*, September 18, 1925.

81. Wallace Stegner, "The Trail of the Hawkeye," *The Saturday Review of Literature*, Vol. 18, No. 14 (July 30, 1938), 3–4, 16–17.

82. Roy W. Meyer, *The Middle Western Farm Novel in the Twentieth Century* (Lincoln: University of Nebraska Press, 1965), 68.

83. Engel, 85–131.

84. Walter J. Muilenburg, *Prairie* (New York: Popular Library, 1970).

85. Jim Arpy, "Times-Democrat Tempo," *Sunday Times Democrat*, January 10, 1971.

86. Schaap, 16, 18.

87. Mencken, 381.

88. Brigham, *A Book of Iowa Authors*, 228.

89. Walter Muilenburg to James Muilenburg, November 17, 1925, Letters to James [Muilenburg], 1924-1955, MsL M9538 m, University of Iowa Special Collections, Iowa City, Iowa.

90. Walter J. Muilenburg to Glenway Wescott, January 10, 1926, Folder 1215, Box 82, Glenway Wescott Papers, Beinecke Rare Book and Manuscript Library, Yale, New Haven, Connecticut.

91. Walter J. Muilenburg to Raymond Knister, February 14, 1927, Box 2: Incoming Correspondence, Raymond Knister Fonds, RC0121, McMaster University Archives and Research Collections, Hamilton, Ontario, Canada.

92. Schaap, 18.

93. Quoted in Williams, *How to Study 'The Best Short Stories,'* 145.

94. "Awards Are Announced in Literature Contests," *The Flint Journal*, May 6, 1930.

95. "Contemporary Writers and Their Work," 270.

96. According to James Muilenburg, his deceased sister Josephine kept Walter's correspondence after his death. Whether

these materials survive is unknown. James Muilenburg to Milton Reigelman, June 23, 1971, MsL M9534 r, University of Iowa Special Collections, Iowa City, Iowa.

97. Muilenburg, "The Prairie," *Out of the Midwest*, 232; James Muilenburg to Milton Reigelman, June 23, 1971, MsL M9534 r, University of Iowa Special Collections, Iowa City, Iowa.

98. Walter J. Muilenburg, "Gardening as a Speculation," *The Flower Grower*, Vol. 32, No. 11 (November 1945), 540.

99. James Muilenburg to Milton Reigelman, June 23, 1971, MsL M9534 r, University of Iowa Special Collections, Iowa City, Iowa.

100. Front Matter, Walter J. Muilenburg, *Prairie* (New York: Popular Library, 1970).

101. Walter Muilenburg to James Muilenburg, February 23, 1955, Letters to James [Muilenburg], 1924-1955, MsL M9538 m, University of Iowa Special Collections, Iowa City, Iowa.

102. "Ex M.S.U. Man Dies," *Lansing State Journal*, December 1, 1958; "Walter J. Muilenburg," *Sioux Center News*, December 11, 1958; James Muilenburg to Milton Reigelman, June 23, 1971, MsL M9534 r, University of Iowa Special Collections, Iowa City, Iowa.

103. Arnold Mulder, "Novelists Who Drop Out," *The Grand Rapids Press*, March 31, 1939.

I

"Elias!"

A half groan, half sigh, filled with the misery of one drawn unwillingly from the depths of sleep, answered the heavy voice.

"Elias," the voice had a touch of finality, "it's high time to get up."

There was a commotion in the dark room, accompanied by the sound of deep breaths and partially stifled yawns. Then steps sounded on the pitchblack stairs, a door opened, and a young fellow stepped into the lamplight of a farmhouse kitchen. He stood still for a moment, ruffling his hair, dazed by the yellow light from the lamp on the table.

"I called you three times," the father grumbled, as he placed two cups on the table.

The son did not answer, but while his father poured coffee, went to the sink in the corner of the room, pumped a tin basin full of water, and splashed it over his face and arms. Then he groped blindly for the roller towel, scrubbed vigorously, and finally emerged from this exercise with cheeks dusky red and eyes fully open at last.

They drank the coffee black. When they had drained the cups, they drew on their short sheepskin coats that hung on nails beside the door, pulled their caps down over their ears, and went out. On the porch the boy lighted a lantern, lifted two milk pails from hooks on the wall, and followed his father into the cold darkness outside. The light of the lantern wove dim, flickering patterns on the ground, now revealing a row of posts strung with barbed wire, now a stack of corn stalks, and finally, the outline of a barn. He entered this, placed the pails on a salt barrel, and then left the barn by another door. In a few minutes he reappeared, preceded by four milk cows, which stumbled awkwardly into the barn and took their places with an air of humble dejection. One by one the ropes fastened to the low crib were snapped to the leather straps about the necks of the beasts.

It was warm in the barn and the young fellow, with his head pressed firmly against the flank of the cow, felt a return of drowsiness. The milk strummed rhythmically against the side of the pail. He was aware, without heeding it, of the warm, cloying smell of the milk. He drew the half filled pail away, took up the stool, and pushed the second cow over into a better position for milking. From outside came his father's voice, calling the hogs, "Hoo-ey, hoo-ey." Then followed a bedlam of grunting and screaming as the hogs fought over their morning meal of corn. The barn door opened whiningly, and a rush of sharp air flowed along the ground. The cattle stirred.

"Here, stand still!" the boy's voice commanded sharply.

"About ready, 'lias?"

"One more."

"Well, I'll be taking this bucket of milk up to the house and getting breakfast ready while you finish." The door opened again, and then shut with a slam.

Milking finished, the boy unsnapped the ropes and drove the reluctant brutes outside again. After that he carried the milk to the house. Even now, after the lapse of more than half an hour, there was no sign of dawn, and the stars were still bright in the darkness overhead.

The milk was strained into two pans that stood ready on a small table under the window, the pails were rinsed with hot water from the kettle on the stove and hung up again on the porch, and then he washed, scrubbing himself with soap and water with little less than a fury of motion. From the tin receptacle under the narrow mirror above the sink he drew a broken piece of comb, passed it rapidly through his hair. After that, he drew up a chair, seated himself at the table, where his father was awaiting him.

There was a moment of silence, and then the older man spoke in a heavy, unnatural voice as he petitioned a Divine blessing upon the morning meal. Coffee was poured, and they drew large slices of fried pork from the platter to their plates, poured the hot fat over this, and added thick brown molasses. While the first sharp edge of their hunger was being satisfied, they did not speak a word, each silently reaching for whatever he wished.

The father cleaned his plate with a bit of bread, finished the coffee in his cup, and sat back, relaxed.

"Do you think you'll finish the corn this week, 'lias?"

"I guess so; there's only about seven acres left to pick," the boy looked up briefly from his plate to reply.

"Goin' into November pretty well, and snow'll be coming any day now. Think I'll start fencing in the north side of the field so that when you've cleaned it up, we can turn the stock out right away."

The son did not reply but once more gave all of his attention to his food.

Seen in the yellow lamplight, there was little resemblance between father and son. The older man sat back in his chair, with a ruminative expression on his firm, almost heavy face. There was a compact grayness in him hard to express otherwise. The tanned, smooth cheeks were overlaid with this grayness, probably accented by the eyes, which also were gray. Above the broad, high forehead, the thin, light brown hair was roughly parted. The face suggested what the body was: well-set, not tall, but muscular. The boy, whose face was as smooth as that of his father, but thinner and with a high red color, was lean and tall, and heavy brown hair hung down to the gray eyes. The man gave an impression of solidity, of calm; the boy was more resilient, and his movements were quick, slightly nervous.

"It's gettin' light," observed the father, glancing out of the small window on the opposite side of the small room, against which the blackness of night had turned to the first pallor of dawn. "Guess I'll go hitch up your team while you fix up the lunch."

"All right."

The boy sat back in his chair after the father had gone, a lack-lustre look in his eyes. Then, stretching his arms above his head, he yawned and grimaced sleepily. He spread slices of bread thickly with butter, wrapped them in a newspaper, and placed the bundle in the pocket of his coat. After that, he poured what coffee was left from breakfast into a half gallon syrup pail. As he put on his coat, the tall clock on the shelf struck seven. "Didn't know it was so late!" he said to himself, aloud, and hurried outside.

The team was waiting for him. He touched the horses lightly with the reins and the wagon rumbled down the driveway to the road. The air was sharp, and the boy pulled the collar of his high coat about his ears. He knotted the reins, placed them about his shoulders, stuffed his hands into his pockets, and looked about him.

The gray in the east had taken on color; the subdued rosy light gave form and outline to the nearer cornfields, meadows, and plowed land, but at a little distance these faded into misty obscurity. To the west the light lost itself in the shadows of retreating night.

The team was drawn down to a walk and turned into a corn-field. The driver jumped down, threw his coat over the front end of the wagon-box, strapped the husking pin to his right hand, over the cotton glove, and set to work. His body kept to the same bent position as he grasped each ear of corn, struck sharply into the husk with the pin, pulled the rest of the leaves aside with the other hand, snapped the ear swiftly, and in what seemed to be all a single motion, threw it, without a glance upward, against the backboards of the wagon.

The corn husks were covered with a rime of frost that gathered on his gloves, melted, and then became icy again. In five minutes his hands were so stiff that his fingers would scarcely close. He straightened, swung his arms about his body until the blood beat its way to the finger tips, making them itch and burn, and again went back to his work, stripping two rows as he went, the horses keeping up his pace with only an occasional command.

The first hour, as always, was worst. Stooped over as he was, yet he sensed the growth of day. The cornstalks took on a sharper outline, became yellower. The east was still touched with red, but the blue of a cloudless sky had come into the void overhead. There was a sudden scurry at his feet and a cottontail, in a frenzy of haste, zigzagged away into the maze of cornstalks. The sharpness of the air had become a mellow and welcome coolness and the frost had disappeared, leaving the ground covered with a thin layer of sticky mud that gathered under his shoes until it fell away from its own weight.

When the rows came to an end, the pile of yellow corn in the middle of the wagon was well in sight above the sideboards. Elias climbed on the wagon, drew the lunch from his coat pocket and the coffee from the corner of the box where it was half buried.

Leveling the corn until he had a comfortable seat, he leaned against the backboard and attacked the bread with a sharp appetite, washing the food down with the coffee, which was now as cold as ice. Satisfied and a bit lazy, he stretched out as comfortably as he could on the uneven surface of corn in the wagon, and stared out and away with dreamy eyes. This short mid-morning rest was something he always anticipated during the first hours of work. The blood flowed warmly through his body. It seemed that, at such a time, he had no thoughts but felt only a hazy delight in life. He could see, about half a mile to the northwest, the farmhouse from which he had issued in the twilight of early morning, a small, dull-white house, trimmed with green that was blurred at this distance. Where it faced the road, a line of tall, leafless cottonwoods reared against the sky. To the east of the house were the other buildings. The largest of these, the barn, had gathered about its skirts a number of small, nondescript sheds. Even so far away, the boy could see the doves strutting on the sharp ridge of the barn. There was no sign of activity about the yard, and he wondered whether his father had already started with the fencing. Then, more eagerly, his eyes traveled away from the familiar and tedious features of the farmyard, and strayed out to the open western horizon directly before him. Far away, the groves were black against the thin light of the horizon. The nearer groves, each marking a farmyard, seemed more open, and glimpses of white and red, house and barns, came through the trees. On all sides lay what he loved: a sweep of almost open country, where a huge yellow triangle of cornfield standing in soft contrast to the gray blocks of plowed land on all sides gave a certain character to the view. Where the land dipped to the creek, a mile to the west, a broad belt of brown marked the hayland. Over all stretched a sky of as deep a blue as only autumn may bring, touched here and there with a small puff of white cloud that was born in the hinterland lying beyond the horizon, floated aimlessly over the blue, its edges dissolving slowly until, before it could traverse the span from northwest to southeast, it had been swallowed up in mystery.

He came to himself with a start and leaped lightly to the ground. "Hey, Bill! Nance!" he commanded, and the team moved forward a few steps in docile obedience. Again the "thud, thud" of corn striking the backboards came at precise intervals. He had rested longer than usual and he decided to work faster. His father would be waiting for him at a quarter after eleven, and he would have to hurry to get his load in time.

Under the lethargy of mind that came with physical concentration, time passed rapidly. The boy had almost reached the edge of the field when he heard the sound of a horse's hoofs. He looked up and saw a horse and rider pulling up alongside the road.

"Emory Reems," he thought to himself. "Wonder what he wants with me." He continued with the husking and in a short time snapped the last ear of corn from the stalk, threw it into the wagon, and straightened up.

"Hello!" The stranger, a tall, gangly youth with a red, good-natured face, accompanied his greeting with a broad smile.

"Hello, Em." The boy looked up curiously. "How does it happen that you ain't picking corn today?"

"Oh, me—I don't have to work. Guess I'll move to town one o' these days and take it easy. Farm life ain't what it's cracked up to be." He grinned broadly at this obvious pleasantry. Then his face became eager. "Say, 'lias, we're havin' a party up to our house tomorrow night, and we want you to come, and you got to bring a girl."

The boy leaned against the wagon wheel and seemed to hesitate before replying.

"You know a girl you can ask, don't you? Sure—Lizzie Dalton! You've been goin' with her, they say."

"Well," the boy admitted, with a slightly abashed expression, "not so much. Just a few times—now and then."

"She'll come if you ask her," Emory spoke reassuringly. "There'll be dancing, you know, an' she's a pretty good dancer."

"I'd like to come," the boy replied after a pause, "but I don't know what pa will say."

"Why, must you ask him?"

"Sure; I guess so. He'll want to know what I'm going to do with the horse and buggy. An' then, he doesn't like dancing such a lot, either."

"You c'n bet that my old man wouldn't handle me that way. Not more'n once, at least. Why, you're workin' for him, and you got a good time comin' once in a while. Sure, your old man will let you come. Tell you what you do! Go see Liz this afternoon some time and then you can tell your dad that it's all fixed up and can't be changed."

The boy's face was troubled, and a sullenness came into his eyes. Then he looked up. "All right, Em," he said, "I'll see Lizzie this afternoon. And thanks for asking me."

"Sure. That's all right." He kicked the horse lightly with his heel and started off. "See you again," he shouted over his shoulder. "So long."

"So long."

Elias climbed into the wagon, untwisted the reins, and the horses, knowing that they were homeward bound, eagerly straightened out the tugs. The wagon creaked heavily through the soft ground, bumped sharply as it struck the low grade of the road, and then, under the steady pull of the team, went up the slope toward the house.

As the horses stopped beside the corn-crib, the father came from the barn.

"You're late," he remarked. "I've had dinner ready for a quarter of an hour."

"Yes, I guess so."

"I saw somebody talkin' with you out there along the road. Looked to me like it was one of the Reems' young mares he was riding."

"Yes, it was Emory Reems. He just stopped for a little while."

"Funny for him to be chasing around like that when their corn isn't out yet. What did he have to say?"

"Oh, nothing much. He was joking a lot, like he always does." Then, casually, "Might as well let the load wait and shovel it off after dinner."

The man nodded. They walked up the bare, dusty yard to the house.

They ate the meal with hearty appetites, meanwhile preserving their usual silence. After the demands of hunger had been satisfied, the man sat back in his chair and glanced sharply at his son, whose face was turned toward his plate.

"Can't see why Reems doesn't hold in his boys a little more," the man said, as though continuing a conversation that had stopped for a moment. "I like the old man first-rate, but he's letting Emory and Joe run wild, I hear."

"Oh, there's nothing in all that. They just like to have a good time once in a while."

"Yes, that's where it always starts—with a good time. I wish you wouldn't have anything to do with them."

The sullenness returned to the boy's eyes, and he remained silent.

"You'd better take it easy and rest while I shovel off your load," suggested the man, scraping back his chair.

"Oh, I'm not tired," the son replied. "Better let me do it; I'd just as soon as not."

"It's a long time till evening, and you can stand the rest." The man opened the door and went outside.

The boy tilted his chair back against the wall and stared out of the window. What should he do? If he asked Lizzie this afternoon, and then told his father about it in the evening, there might be trouble, and if he didn't go, after asking a girl, the story would go through the neighborhood and he would be a laughing-stock. On the other hand, he was almost sure that his father would refuse. There had to be some way out.

Almost unseeing, his eyes took in the sweep of country that revealed itself through the window. Far away, hazy in the yellow light of an Indian summer afternoon, a line of leafless trees stood on the section line a mile to the west, black against the horizon. Even now, this came satisfyingly through the distraction of his mind, and he felt again a sudden leap of delight within him. There was something that he wanted, something not to be expressed, only an urgency that found relief when he thought of things far away, beyond the last low ridge in the distance. It was a place to which he longed to escape—a new country. Then, suddenly, he became aware of the quiet room, the slow ticking of the clock on the shelf, and his thoughts blurred into sleepiness. He was aroused by the entrance of his father.

"I've got the team at the gate. Time to start out, I guess."

"All right."

At the door, the son hesitated and turned toward the man who was busy clearing the table. The latter looked up inquiringly.

"Looking for something?" he asked.

"No, I was just thinking, maybe—" He stopped. "Well," he continued, "I'd better be gettin' along."

Once he was back in the cornfield, he began to berate himself. "Why didn't I ask him when I had a good chance?" he asked himself angrily. "It's got to come out some time." Then, while he worked steadily, automatically, his mind was a turmoil of plans. He rehearsed sentences that he would use to his father. He was getting too old to be afraid to ask a little thing like that! All of the other fellows got out once in a while and had a good time!

Under this preoccupation, time passed quickly. Unconsciously, he shouted at the horses when they failed to parallel his progress. Finally, when they refused to move in obedience to his commands, he looked up in vexation, to find that he had reached the end of the rows. In a few moments he had stripped the few remaining cornstalks. Then he walked to the other side of the wagon and looked toward the farmyard. He saw no sign of activity there. Very likely his father was back at the job of fencing, on the other side of the slope, invisible from this point.

In quick decision, he drove the team around into the next rows and then, with another hasty glance at the farmyard, he started out to the east, where a small grove stood, about half a mile away. He walked swiftly.

When he came to the edge of the grove, his pace slackened. Slowly he made his way through the trees and approached the kitchen door. As he knocked, he noticed that the screen door had not been taken down, although the flies had been gone for a month.

His summons was answered by a lean girl of medium height. She evidently had been occupied with some work, for she rubbed moist palms against her dress.

"Why, hello, 'lias. Won't you come in?" Her quiet voice had a slight touch of surprise.

"No, I've got to be goin' in a minute or so; I left the team standing in the field. You see," he continued, his face showing deep red through the tan, "they're having a party over to Reemses tomorrow night, and I was wondering if maybe you cared to go with me?" He shifted his weight to the other foot and smiled at her, awkwardly.

"Why, that's awful nice. Sure, I'll be glad to go, 'lias."

A surprised expression came to his face. "Don't you have to see your folks about it?" he asked.

Her voice became more animated. "Ask my folks! I guess not! And anyway, it won't make any difference to them."

"I wish pa was like that," he said wistfully.

"Doesn't he want you to go?"

"Well, I don't think so. I haven't said anything about it to him yet."

"Maybe he'll get mad about it, and then he'll think it's all my doin's. I always been afraid of your dad—he's so strict and religious. He never says much to me, but I just kind o' feel that he doesn't like me."

"Oh, no," the boy hastened to reply. "That's just his way."

They were silent. The boy's eyes were downcast. The pale blue eyes of the girl were fixed upon him meditatively.

"We'd better leave it this way, then," she said at last. "If you can come, be here by eight tomorrow night. If you can't, why, don't come, that's all."

"It will seem queer to your folks if I don't show up after I asked you," he objected. "They'll think—"

"They won't know anything about it. I'll just go upstairs when the dishes are finished, and put on my other clothes. If you don't come, I'll just go to bed. Nobody'll know the difference. We can tell the Reemses that something turned up so we couldn't come."

A great relief came into his face. "That's fine!" he exclaimed. "But I'll be here all right, I guess." An aggrieved note came into his voice. "Pa isn't goin' to tell me always what I may do. I'm goin' on to nineteen."

She nodded encouragingly.

"I must be gettin' along," he said. "The horses are standing loose in the field. Well, good-bye, Lizzie. See you tomorrow night, maybe."

"Good-bye." Then, as he was starting off, she called him back. "Here's a couple o' apples," she announced. With a touch of coquetry, she came close to him and stuffed two large apples into the capacious pocket of his sheepskin coat. Their glances met, and a warm bright look came into their eyes.

"Lizzie," he said softly, "if I can't see you tomorrow night, guess maybe I can take you home Sunday night?"

"We'll see," she replied, in a low voice, a slight smile touching her thin, almost sharp face.

When he returned, he found the horses where he had left them. He squinted at the sun, frowned, and set to work.

It was almost too dark to see the husks on the stalks when he finally finished. Before commanding the team to start, he leaned against the backboards, relaxing his back, tired after the unusual exertion of the past two hours. From far away came the insistent bawling of a calf, answered at regular intervals by the lowing of a cow. At that distance, the sound was mellow. There was something comfortable about it, something homelike. He took up the reins, touched the horses lightly, and they began the slow progress toward the grove. The air was sharp, but when the road dipped into the hollow, it became wet and cold. Out in the west, only a narrow line of red marked the last deep glow of sunset. Overhead, the stars were coming out in the shadowy blue. The whole world was quiet except for the creaking of the wagon and the heavy plodding of the horses which, with bent, nodding heads, were making steadily up-hill.

The boy noticed a light in the barn and decided that his father had come in late from his fencing and was probably doing the milking. He unfastened the end gates and started to shovel the corn into the crib. The ring of the shovel sounded sharply in the frosty darkness. In a short time the wagon had been unloaded. He unhitched the patient horses and placed them in the barn, where they attacked the oats in the boxes with a crunching relish while the harnesses were slipped from them. This done, the doors were closed for the night, and the boy walked to the house, where the window-panes of the kitchen were yellow with lamplight.

II

Ordinarily, during corn-husking season, Elias went to bed immediately after supper, but this evening he remained in his chair while his father removed the dishes from the table and took up the red-and-white checkered tablecloth that was used only for the evening meal, folded it, and placed it carefully in a drawer of a large cupboard standing in the corner.

"Better be goin' to bed, 'lias," he observed. "You'll be sleepy enough tomorrow morning when I call you."

"Oh, I don't feel much like sleeping yet," replied the boy. "Guess I'll help you with the dishes." He did not look up as he spoke.

"You don't have to help with the housework." The man glanced sharply at his son. "When you're doing field work, I'll take care o' things in here."

"Guess I'll go outside then, for awhile." He pulled on his coat and cap and stepped out into the darkness. After the warmth of the house, the sharpness in the air made him shiver, and he walked rapidly to the barn. Here it was warmer. He was so familiar with the place that, in spite of the darkness, he walked the length of the alleyway and threw himself down on a pile of hay.

Once more his thoughts took up the course they had pursued most of the day. Would his father let him go to the party? He'd have to, that was all. The other fellows in the neighborhood would go, and they'd have the time of their lives. Of course, this would be the first time that he'd appear in public with a girl, and the reports of the games they played at these parties made him quake inwardly, but his fear was compounded with delight. If he could have Sadie, the road horse, and the new buggy, he would show any

of them that he knew how to get along. He pictured the ride home
with Lizzie; he felt the intimacy that would fall on them as they
rode through the star-lit darkness. The buggy was new, and not a
horse in the neighborhood could beat Sadie if he let out the reins
and let her have her head. Then, the uneasy gnawing at the back
of his mind reasserted itself, and again he attacked the problem of
getting his father's consent. He was going, and that was all there
was to it! Why did his father have to be so much stricter than other
men? It was all right to be religious, but the other men went to
church on Sundays and still managed to enjoy themselves in ways
that his father wouldn't allow. And then, contemplation fell on
him, when his thoughts blurred away and he was conscious, with
the soothing sense that comes from the perception of usual things,
of the comfortable silence of the barn. There were sounds, but
they simply added to the feeling of quietness. Ahead of him, the
horses were rummaging through the manger for the choicer wisps
of hay, now and then blowing the dust from their nostrils. In the
pen to the right of him, touches of white in the darkness showed
where the calves were lying together in the fresh straw. Now and
then, one blatted softly, contentedly, as though knowing that the
mother was not far away, in the straw-pile just outside the barn. An
invisible hen, roosting high up in the darkness, objected sleepily
as some companion on the roost infringed upon her space. There
were scurrying sounds in the litter that was scattered over the floor
of the barn. Then, for just a second, there was unaccountable
silence, broken almost at once.

He was aroused by the sound of a slamming door. His father
had evidently finished the dishes. Well, now was the time to get
this thing settled. He hurried to the house. As he entered, the man
was stretching his arms and yawning. "I'm tired," he declared.

The son took off his coat and then faced his father.

"Pa," he began rapidly, "may I have the horse and buggy tomorrow night?"

The man turned abruptly. "Where do you want to go?"

"Why, you know Emory Reems was over to see me this morning and he asked me to come to a party at their house tomorrow night, and I was wondering if it would be all right with you."

The man was silent, his face turned meditatively to one side.

"I don't get out such an awful lot," the son continued, almost in a pleading tone, "and all of the other fellows in the neighborhood are going."

"I guess you better not, 'lias," replied his father.

"Why?" A sudden glint came into the gray eyes of the boy. "Why not?"

"Why not?" The face of the man became hard. "First of all, because I said you couldn't go. I knew that Emory Reems was up to something like this when he stopped out there in the cornfield, and I won't have you running around with the Reems' outfit. They're wild. Then there'll be dancing and other things, and I don't believe in them. That's why I don't want you to go."

The boy had moved over to the table, under the hanging lamp. He drummed his fingers on the boards. The red had faded from his cheeks into something almost like pallor, out of which the gray eyes, wide and half sick in expression, stared before him.

"I'm goin' on to nineteen," he said suddenly. "You ain't goin' to keep me from having a good time always, are you?"

"Not after you're twenty-one," the man replied, evidently with an effort to keep calm. "Then if you don't like my ways o' thinking, you may go away."

"But as long as I stay here I've got to do what you think?" the son sneered.

"Yes."

Neither spoke for some time. The man looked at the boy; the latter stared at the floor. At last he spoke again.

"I asked a girl to go with me," he said quietly, "and now they'll all be laughing at me."

"Who's the girl?" the man asked sharply.

"Lizzie Dalton." The boy spoke reluctantly.

"So you're going to take one of the Daltons to a party at the Reemses! You haven't much self-respect, it seems. One is the most shiftless family anywhere around, and the other is the wildest."

"Guess we must be about the only good folks left out here," the boy replied. His lips were crawling with his effort to keep them from quivering.

"I hope so," the man replied imperturbably.

There seemed to be nothing more to say. Nevertheless, instead of going to his room, the boy sat down on a chair, facing away from his father. After a moment the man, too, took a chair.

The wild gust of temper that had made him feel sick ebbed away in a short time and left the boy tired. After all, he had foreseen this and even planned for it. Lizzie wouldn't mind so much if he didn't come, and nobody'd ever know about it. He'd see her Sunday night and then he could explain all. Obstinately, he kept his face averted, wishing to make his father feel that he was still angry. Instead, his eyes were fixed on the glass pendants that hung down from the white shade of the hanging lamp. From their edges shone all of the colors of the rainbow, crystal orange and red and violet. He even moved his head a bit to make the pattern change.

"It's this way, 'lias," the heavy voice of the man was placating. "I've worked this farm for thirty years and I want to leave it to someone who is a God-fearing man and a good farmer. That's why I don't want you to go around with the Daltons and the Reems. If I *do* say so, we amount to more than those people put all together. They haven't any get-up in them. And if you're going to be like them, why—" He stopped. Then he continued, "Think it over. I'll let you be your own boss about this." The hard, strained look of temper had gone from his face, too, and he watched the boy almost eagerly. The latter did not reply. After a few minutes, he got up from the chair, stretched his arms, yawned elaborately, and made for the stairs.

"Good night," he said in a gruff tone.

"Good night, 'lias."

In the clean, cold air of his room the unpleasantness of his mood drained away. After he had undressed he stood still for a moment in the darkness, reveling in the sharp pinch of cold on his body, delighting in the warm surge of physical happiness within him. He stepped to the small window, opened it, and placed a splinter of wood under it to keep it from sliding down. He looked out. Through the fine twigs of a willow that stood out in the yard, gathering to themselves a haze of moonlight, he saw the new moon in the east, a sharply cut figure of light in the blue-black material of a clear night sky. For a moment he was unconscious of all that made up life for him, and a sense of the utter mystery and wonder of the great world filled him with ecstasy. And again, as in the morning, he felt a queer loneliness for far-away places he had never known. A slow sweep of cold air drew in through the window, and he jumped into the bed.

For a time he tried to stay awake and keep this mood, this sense of being without thought, but as soon as the blood had taken the chill from his body, he could feel himself sinking away, softly, into sleep.

On Sunday the wind, which had held from the northwest for the last few days, veered slowly through the north into the northeast. The sharpness drew out of the air. At noon, the wind died away altogether, and a queer weight of silence fell upon the earth. The usual sounds of the farmyard which, it seemed to Elias, were always less apparent on Sundays than on other days, as though all living things felt the Sabbatical influence, now died away, or became muted and indistinct. A white haze settled into the distances, shrouding the familiar vistas of far-away fields and groves with strangeness and mystery.

"Looks like it might snow tonight," remarked the father, as they ate their late dinner after having attended morning church services at town. "Maybe you'd better not go to Christian Endeavor this evening."

"Oh, it won't snow, I guess," the boy replied hastily, "and anyway, that wouldn't make any difference."

While his father dozed in his chair, the boy went outside and walked to a maple tree that stood alone on the highest point of ground in the pasture. Here he stretched out on the mat of dead grass and stared up into the sky with ruminative eyes. The silence, it seemed to him, was something alive, a wide-eyed being that was born of the haze and the thin yellow sunlight; it was something that had known the enchantment of far countries and strange lands, and now had come to him. His thoughts were dim, so unreal that they slowly added pattern after pattern to the delicate fabric of the phantasy. The quietness was breathed into his body until it seemed that he lay in suspended animation, with only the rhythmic beating of his blood and the faint steady ringing in his ears to betray the power of life that was held in thrall.

He lay there until the sun was midway between the zenith and the horizon. A deeper murk had thrown its obscurity over the country. A slow movement of damp air passed over him.

A bit stiffly, he got up and walked back to the farmyard. The horses and cattle, for some unaccountable reason, had come up to the barn, and he hastened to take advantage of this good fortune by opening the doors and fastening the horses in their stalls. Then he drove the milk cows into their side of the barn. Although it was rather early, he decided to start with the chores.

They had supper early. After it was finished, the man stepped outside for a short time. When he returned, he remarked again, "Maybe you'd better not be going to town. A six-mile drive— twelve miles altogether—won't be a joke if it starts in to snow."

"There won't be a storm," the son replied confidently. He went to his room and dressed. In ten minutes he was downstairs again, arrayed in a black, tightly fitting suit. For fifteen minutes he stood before the small mirror above the sink, trying to attain satisfactory results with the tie, which finally seemed to meet with his approval when the wide, ribbony ends were long enough to tuck between his vest and shirt. He drew up the soft collar of his shirt about his neck, pulling the tips back so that his throat was revealed. It took more time to comb his hair which, in spite of repeated applications of water, could be brought only to partial submission.

It was dark when he drove from the yard to the road. The horse, dimly seen ahead of him, was in the mood for exercise and the boy had to keep tight reins on her. As they passed swiftly through the darkness, his thoughts were on the evening that lay ahead of him. Surely Lizzie would be in town tonight. She always was, on Sundays. But then, she might not go to Christian Endeavor; her folks didn't care much if she went or not. Oh, she'd be there all right. It would be too cold to walk around outside. Would she be angry now that he hadn't taken her to the party? Well, he'd ask her to ride home with him, and then he could fix it up in some way.

Twice dim shapes loomed up ahead of him and he loosened his hold on the reins. Each time the horse sprang forward and pulled ahead of the other horse and buggy. There were shouts of greeting, and derisive, cheerful laughter. When the blurred lights of the town appeared about half a mile away to the southwest, he stopped the horse and descended from the buggy to tighten the check-rein to the last notch. The horse, her head held high, pranced impatiently.

He kept Sadie to a slow trot until he came out on the one long street of the town. Again he loosened his hold on the reins and the horse, her head thrown back, shot swiftly down the street. Whenever they passed the street corners, where electric lights cast feeble illumination, the boy glanced carelessly on all sides to discover if there were any to see him.

The horse was pulled up at the row of hitching posts on the south side of the square, and securely tied. Then, eagerly, the boy walked rapidly through the darkness until the outlines of a small round building, an ancient bandstand, appeared before him. He climbed up the shaky, circling stairs on the outside of the building, and came upon a group of indistinct figures, seated on the floor. Here and there, pipes glowed in the darkness.

"H'lo," he said in greeting, looking about for a place to sit down.

"H'lo, 'lias," came the scattered response. "Come out here," he heard the voice of Emory Reems. He made his way carefully among the extended legs and finally settled down beside his friend, his back braced against the side of the structure.

"Driving Sadie tonight, I see, 'lias," spoke up one of the figures. "I saw you come tearing down Main Street like you was in a race. That horse sure can lay herself out! Wish my old man would give me something better'n the old plug I got to drive."

"Sadie can go right along if she wants to," Elias responded in a pleased voice.

The conversation became general again. Emory turned to him and said, in a low tone, "Your dad wouldn't let you come to our party, would he?"

"No," the boy's voice, pitched so low that the others could not hear, was sullen. "He doesn't want me to have a good time like the rest o' you fellows have."

"Guess he thinks we're kind o' tough," his companion ventured. Then he added, in a slightly louder tone, "We had a mighty good time: walkin' games, forfeits, wink on th' sly, an' all that, y' know, and there was all you could eat. Then we finished up with dancing. Nobody started to think o' goin' home till it was past midnight. You sure missed it! And Liz Dalton did, too. Bet she'll show you the cold shoulder tonight."

"Oh, I don't know," Elias spoke in a casual way. "I guess she won't care so much."

They were silent, giving their attention to the others, whose conversation had become animated.

"I was tellin' the old man this morning," one was saying, "that I was thinkin' o' goin' out West. I ain't goin' to be tied down here all my life. I want to get out for myself—have my own farm."

Expressions of agreement came from all sides. Elias sat back, silent, his mind suddenly filled with a dazzling plan. Why shouldn't he go out West? Oblivious to his companions sprawled about him in the darkness, he pictured a shack on the distant prairies. He could buy a quarter section of land cheap, and he'd have a farm. He'd be his own boss. Then he thought of Lizzie Dalton and his mind, confused with the many angles of this dream that had been so suddenly thrust upon him, surged with excitement.

"Hey, fellows, it's time to be goin' to Endeavor," someone shouted.

There was a great scraping of feet, and they descended noisily down the short flight of stairs to the ground. Elias and his companion walked together, in silence.

The room where the young people held their evening service was very evidently an afterthought and clung to the larger bulk of the church proper, the windows of which were dark. The long line of boys shuffled in self-consciously and filled the last two benches. Ahead of them was row after row of young folks, evidently boys and girls from the farms. In front, behind a small table, sat a red-faced, uneasy young man who continually exhibited his handkerchief and seemed to find relief in staring at a certain discolored spot on the plaster ceiling.

The place was filled with half-heard whispers. Elias was crowded between Emory and another boy and listened silently to the broken flow of conversation. Behind him, the same one who had voiced his determination of going West, earlier in the evening, was bitterly bewailing his lot at home, where he couldn't have his own way and where he was constantly at the mercy of his tyrannical old man. The air was very warm and stagnant, and Elias noted hopelessly that all of the windows were shut. They would remain closed all evening, he knew.

The leader of the meeting rose and showed himself to be an able-bodied young fellow. His voice, however, was curiously out of relation with his bulk, and broke out, at odd moments, into tenor effects which set all of the boys at the rear of the room into subdued laughter that exploded nasally now and then. The young farmer who was presiding glanced toward them. Bitterness and pain, and a certain horror, were expressed on his open countenance.

"We'll open the meeting by singin' Hymn Number 267," he announced, and precipitately sat down. A lean girl, with narrow, stooped shoulders, walked from her seat to the organ beside the platform, where the leader sat. She played the entire selection. Then she drew down one shoulder violently and attacked the organ again. The leader struggled to his feet, made vague, upward motions with his hands, and the entire audience rose, somewhat unevenly. They all sang, even the boys in the last three rows. Elias was silent until he noticed that his companions were singing at the top of their lungs, and then he, too, essayed to sing. It was something he liked. He tried, tentatively, the bass, and thrilled with the deep power that rumbled within him.

The song was one that they sang at almost every meeting,

Throw out the life-line across the dark wave ...

They sang all of the verses and then sat down. The leader remained standing, and Elias, with mixed apprehension and sympathy, watched him. The round, red face was tilted toward the ceiling, the eyelids were pressed together so tightly that lines ran out from the corners of his eyes, and he lifted up his voice, unsteady at best, in prayer. Slowly the short, breathless sentences became easier.

A note of confidence crept into his voice. His language was that of the Psalmist David mixed with his own phrasing. "Oh, Lord," he cried, "may Thy mercy be upon us! Don't let us sin so awful much any more." He prayed for incredible dispensations in terms that he could not understand. But fervor was in his face, and clean honesty of heart.

The meeting went on. The leader recited some verses from the Scriptures, read ponderously from a paper, and then, after announcing another song in a voice filled with relief, sat down.

During all this time, in spite of his close attention to the speaker, Elias was conscious of the repressed talking about him. After the song, the confusion continued, and several of the older members, almost all of whom were young women, turned to glance meaningly toward the rear of the room whence the sound of talking came.

"Hey, shut up!" commanded one of the boys in a voice distinctly audible.

"Shut up yourself!" replied another, in a heavy, artificial tone. "You make enough noise to shake down the place."

This was so obviously a rarely good witticism that there was a general outburst of mirth that, because it was stifled at first, soon became uncontrollable and culminated in a heavy roar of laughter from Emory. It seemed to Elias, who was suffering an agony of embarrassment, that all the faces of those in front were turned toward him, and he felt his face grow hot. He hated the boys about him whenever these outbreaks occurred, and they came at almost every meeting. A spinsterly figure rose and prayed that those who had come to the meeting just to make fun might repent and be saved. Elias was utterly wretched. He hoped feverishly that God would note that, although he was among these irreverent mischief-makers, he really was not one of them in spirit. With relief he saw a sober-faced man rise from his seat toward the front and take his station, standing, behind them. Quietness was restored for the rest of the evening.

One after the other, members arose, either to announce a hymn, engage in supplication, or to exhort the others. Elias had ceased to listen for some time. His eyes scanned the backs ahead of him. Funny that Lizzie hadn't come! Then, row by row, he tried again, but with no better results. Suddenly someone well ahead of him moved aside, and he caught, for a moment, a glimpse of her profile. He sat back, contented.

The leader finally rose and dismissed them briefly. Elias stood aside while the others surged past him to the door. He could see Lizzie more plainly now. She was putting on her coat. He saw her coming. Quickly he took up his position just beside the door, and as she came up he said, in a low voice, "May I take you home tonight, Lizzie?"

She affected surprise and indecision. "I was goin' home with pa," she said dubiously. "He's over visiting with the Herrons, an' I was to go down there."

"Oh, come on!" he persisted. "We can go there and tell him that you're goin' with me."

"Well, all right," she said. Then, as an afterthought, she added, "I guess we won't have to go there anyway. I told pa that if I didn't show up by nine, he could go on ahead without waiting."

They formed an intimate part of the long procession that straggled down the street. At a corner a group of boys had collected.

"Hey, 'lias—got a girl tonight?" shouted one as the boy and girl passed.

Elias did not reply, but hastened his pace. He heard a laugh at his expense. "'lias is kind o' bashful," he heard the same voice again.

"That was Jerry Grimes," remarked Lizzie placidly. "He's always got something funny to say."

"He's too funny," observed Elias. He took her arm and led her through the darkness to the hitching rack and helped her into the buggy. Then he untied the horse, gathered up the reins, drew the robe about them carefully, and they started out.

"It's snowing," said Lizzie. "I felt something on my face."

"Yes, I noticed it too. Wish it would hold off for a few more days, until the corn's out."

"We finished yesterday," she declared. "Pa got out the last load at four o'clock. You ought to seen him come drivin' on the yard! He had the horses and the wagon all decorated up with cornstalks, and the team came flyin' on the yard with him yellin' like he was crazy. Ma got excited and hollered, 'The horses are runnin' away with pa,' but when she saw that he was just feelin' good because the corn was out, she got kind o' mad at him."

The boy gave Sadie full rein while they were in town but, after they had turned the last corner, and faced the darkness, he drew her down to a walk.

"Sadie passed every horse on the road coming down," he said, with a touch of pride. "Not many horses can keep up with her."

"No, I don't think so either." Her voice was far away.

He turned his face toward her, but the darkness was so great that her features were scarcely visible. There was silence for a time. A steady push of wet wind coming from the east met them. Now and then the boy could feel the light touch of snowflakes on his cheeks. As they drove past a long line of trees that stood at the side of the road, the low, surging sound of the wind deepened, seemed to him almost articulate, as though it were the voice of God, a living, eternal mystery.

"Lizzie," he said suddenly, "were you mad when I didn't come to take you to the party night before last?"

She did not reply for a moment. Then she answered, and her shoulder pressed his. "No, I wasn't mad about it at all. I sort o' thought that it would turn out that way. I know your pa pretty well."

"You see, I wanted to come," he said, "but it meant that there'd be a lot o' trouble, and I thought maybe you wouldn't care so much."

"Are you goin' to always do just what he wants?" she asked.

Something in her tone stirred him. "Well, I guess *not!*" he said vehemently. "If he keeps pickin' on me, he'll have to do without me some time. I can stand just about so much, and then I quit." The talk of the boys in the bandstand returned to him. "You know," he said eagerly, "I've been thinkin' o' goin' out West next year maybe. Land's cheap out there, I hear, and I'd like to have a farm of my own. Be my own boss, you know."

"Oh," she said softly, "that would be fine! It would be a lot o' fun. You'd have a house, and you'd have to do housekeepin', wouldn't you? Guess you better come over to our house some time, and I'll show you how to bake bread. I'm gettin' pretty handy at bakin' bread now, and ma gives me most o' the cookin' to do."

Again they were silent. The snow, long delayed, now came down steadily. The road suddenly took on character and stretched away, a dim white line, before them. Elias drew the robe more tightly about them. He could feel her body against his. A queer new tenderness came to him. Awkwardly, he placed an arm about her waist. "All right?" he whispered.

In reply, she placed her head on his shoulder. So they sat, silent, while the horse, held down to a walk, thudded along the snowy road. There was not another sound, except for the low, half-audible note of the east wind. To the boy there came a radiance of life he had never known before. This being who was with him in the buggy filled the quietness of the dim white night with loveliness.

"Isn't it fine!" he said softly, with a catch in his breath. "Just you and me out here alone, with the snow coming down. Lizzie, I was thinking—"

"What, 'lias?"

"Oh," he said slowly, "nothing. Just something queer; it didn't amount to anything."

She did not question him, but seemed to be satisfied with silence, and he, too, felt that their intimacy grew with the quietness. The darkness of a grove along the road gave way to the lighter touch of open fields. At last the boy turned the horse's head up the driveway leading to the girl's house. Before they came there, he stopped the horse.

"Lizzie!" he spoke intensely.

She raised her head. He drew her toward him and kissed her. She said nothing, did not move.

Then the horse started once more for the house. He helped her out of the buggy and stood beside her. "I'll never forget this evening," he said. "Never! And some time I'll tell you what I was goin' to say back yonder on the road." He took up the reins.

"Good night, Lizzie."

"Night, 'lias. I had an awful good time."

The horse was weary of the long trip and made, full speed, down the road toward home. The boy sat back, glorying in the wind that fanned his face, his blood singing within him, exulting.

IV

Just before Elias was starting for the barn next morning to hitch up the team, his father stopped him.

"You got home pretty late last night, didn't you?" he asked. "I was up until ten o'clock, and it was quite a while after that before I went to sleep."

"The meeting lasted longer'n usual," Elias replied briefly, and left the house.

It was a miserable day for corn husking. The snow was on the husks, and the boy's gloves were wet and icy. A cold wind, with a few left-over snowflakes straggling through, whined under a lowering, rifted sky. Although Elias tried to recapture the thrill of the night before, the dreariness of actuality soon brought him to the stage where his mind was sodden as the day, aware only of the cold and the wet.

At noon, the man made a few desultory attempts at conversation, but Elias merely grunted in reply. The father glanced sharply at the bent head of his son, and became silent, also.

The afternoon was as raw and bitter as the morning had been. When the first half of the usual round had been completed, the first shadowing of evening was already thickening the gray sky. The boy looked into the wagon box, which was only half full, and then at the sky. The horses, feeling the undecided hand on the reins, started to make the turn toward home. In quick temper, the boy jerked them back, sawing the lines until the brutes, bewildered, and their mouths hurt by the strain on the bits, backed frantically.

"I'll show you who's running this outfit!" the driver shouted at them. "We'll finish the row now if it kills you!" Doggedly he turned them into the other row and commenced husking again.

Before he had reached the end of the field, darkness had come, and it was only by the whiteness of the snow that he had enough light to keep on. When he finished, he drove the tired team to the house. He knew that it was late, and that his father would not expect him to unload that evening, but the acute discomfort of the day had brought a sullen perversity which made him decide to unload first. His body was tired, and his weariness added to the dull anger that had been growing in him all day.

"This is about the way it'll always be," he said aloud, resting for a moment. "I can work like a slave for the old man, and then he'll see to it that I won't have any good times. I'm sick of it. Next spring—" Again he fell to work, and in a short time the last shovelful of corn rattled and rolled into the crib. Then he unhitched the horses, whose heads were bent low in resigned weariness, watered them at the trough, and placed them in the barn. The manger was filled with hay, but there was no grain in their boxes, as the beasts had foraged enough grain in the field. After the harnesses were on the hooks, the boy stepped quickly into the alleyway and gave each of the horses a panful of oats. "Guess it's been a bad day the whole way round," he said, as though he were making apology. He closed the doors carefully and went to the house.

Most of the meal was eaten in utter silence. Then the man raised his face suddenly from his plate. "You took the Dalton girl home last night?"

The boy looked up quickly. "Yes," he replied, half defiantly, "I did."

"I thought so." The man's face became hard. "You remember, don't you, that I said that she didn't amount to much—none of the Daltons do, and they never will—and that I didn't care to have you go with her?"

"I remember what you said," the son replied sullenly. "No use going over it again. I've had all I want o' that."

The man stood up. His eyelids quivered and his face was taut. "You're to stop going with her, do you understand?"

There was no reply. The boy had stopped eating, and his red hands, with fingers outspread, sprawled aimlessly over the tablecloth.

"Did you hear me?" Vaughn spoke sharply. "If you expect to have that girl, you can get out."

"You said that before," Elias replied slowly. "Who'll do your work for you when I go away?" He smiled grimly.

The veins stood out on the farmer's forehead, and he strode up and down the room. Finally he stopped. "Go to bed!" he commanded. "Get out of here!"

The boy leisurely finished his coffee, pushed back his chair, and went upstairs. After the work of the day, even the dull, aching anger could not keep him awake, and he was asleep in a few minutes.

In the days that followed, Elias felt himself in a world of tempest and unreality. His feeling of rebellion became an obsession. He worked day after day, doing things that were not pressing, anything that would keep him away from the house and from his father. And always he brooded over his injustices.

One afternoon, when there seemed to be nothing to do, he climbed to the loft of the barn and stretched out in the hay. A thin gray light filtered in through the single dusty window under the gable. From below came the indefinite sounds of the animals moving about in their stalls. Overhead, on the roof, sounded the light patter of doves walking on the shingles.

All the bitterness that had grown in him seemed to rise for expression. "I'll do what I want to do!" he declared to himself. "He can't run me any more. He thought that just because I used to be easy-going, I'd stand for anything. He's wrong! I'll go with Lizzie if I please. And I'll go to parties and dances." His thoughts went back to that Sunday evening some weeks before when he had last seen the girl, and again a glow seemed to dissipate the weariness of his mind. Finally he got up and stretched his arms. "I'll go my own way," he said aloud, and added grimly, "We'll see what happens."

After the chores were finished that evening, he placed the harness on Sadie. He had fastened the last buckle when his father came into the barn. For a moment they faced each other, without saying a word.

"Where are you going?" asked the man, nodding toward the horse.

"Thought I'd be goin' to town this evening," replied Elias casually.

"Better not," said the man, "and you might as well get it out of your head once for all that you can take the horse whenever you feel like it."

"Then I'll walk."

"Go ahead and walk."

It was Saturday evening, and the boy knew that Emory Reems would be going to town. He walked the mile to his farm and entered the driveway just as Emory was leaving.

"Hello, 'lias," he cried, "what's up?"

"My old man wouldn't let me have the horse, so I told him I'd walk to town," the boy said, with a short laugh. His face was hard, and yet half embarrassed.

"Come along with me. Lots o' room in the buggy," invited Emory.

As they drove toward town, the boy told his companion in disconnected sentences of the trouble that lay between him and his father. Emory was deeply sympathetic and urged him to stand his ground. "He doesn't see that a young fellow needs lots o' rope," he declared. "He'll learn a lot, if you don't give him his way."

Under the guidance of Emory, the boy went to places that night he had never entered before. He followed his companion, rather reluctantly, into a small room behind the General Merchandise store, where a few men in shirt sleeves were playing pool. Jerry leaned on the glass show-case, called the proprietor familiarly by his given name, and bought two cigars. He offered one to Elias, who took it, bit off the end, as he saw Emory do, and lighted it.

"I'll shoot you a game of pool," offered Emory.

"No, I guess not," replied the boy. "I don't know anything about it. You find somebody else, and I'll watch and see how it goes."

Emory found a player, and Elias sat down in one of the chairs along the wall. He smoked the cigar slowly. After a time his head became light. He longed to throw the cigar away, but he knew that Emory was watching him. The clicking of the balls on the table, the stale air, heavy with tobacco smoke, all became unreal and far-away. The minutes seemed endless. At last the players stopped. With a sigh of relief, Elias threw the stub of his cigar away and followed Emory into the sharp outdoor air. He breathed deeply, and the dizziness passed off quickly.

"That cigar was pretty heavy," he observed.

"The first one you ever smoked, wasn't it?" asked his companion, with a laugh.

"Yes," confessed Elias, "but I sort o' liked it, at that."

On the way home, Emory remarked, "We're havin' another party over to our place on Christmas Eve. Want to come over with Lizzie? Guess we can promise you a pretty good time, all right."

"Sure. I'll be there," replied Elias quickly. "And this time there won't be any hitch either."

"Good," his friend said briefly. "We'll expect you." Then he added, "Guess your dad won't let you have a horse, will he?"

Elias was silent for a few minutes. "I can fix it all right," he declared. "The old man will be goin' to church, and I'll wait until he's gone and then take Nance and the old buggy."

They had come to the driveway leading to the Reems yard. Emory offered to drive the extra mile, but the boy refused the offer. As he walked, the snow crackled sharply underfoot. Above him, the stars shone with a sharp brilliance in a blue-black sky. There was no moon. The still air was soundless. He walked rapidly, feeling the blood warming his body. At last the road dipped into a hollow and rose again. Through the dimness he saw the house. The windows were black; evidently his father had gone to bed. Just at that moment, it came to him that this was the first time that he had ever deliberately flaunted the wishes of his father. He remembered the cigar he had smoked, the profanity he had heard at the poolroom, and a lump came into his throat.

With stealthy care, the boy opened the door and made his way quietly to his room. For the first time in years, he could not go to sleep at once. A queer sense of desolation stayed with him. He thought of the man who had spent the evening alone; he decided to throw away his defiance and be on good terms with his father again. Then, inevitably, he thought of his promise to go to the party, and he thought of Lizzie. Well, he couldn't make up with his father and still be able to take Lizzie to the party. He turned first on one side and then on the other. At last he fell asleep.

At breakfast, next morning, the man was talkative. He ate little, the boy noticed, and twice he did not finish what he was saying. Contrary to his custom, Elias stayed in the house after the meal, sprawling back in his chair, feeling comfortable and at ease for the first time since he had had the trouble with his father. The man was busy with the dishes, moving constantly through the door between the dining room and the small kitchen.

"Did you enjoy yourself last night?" he asked suddenly, with an obvious attempt to keep his tone casual.

The boy hesitated. Then he answered frankly, "No, I didn't, Pa." He wanted to say more, but it was hard to say just what he wanted to express.

"I'm glad of that," Vaughn replied ponderously, "because, you know, things can't keep on like this."

"No," Elias responded briefly.

"You won't care much for Emory Reems. You're not like him. You come from better stock, if I do say so myself. It'll go the same way with that Dalton girl. She isn't more than half alive, there's no color to her,—she's, just like all the Daltons. They're not made to get along."

The blood rushed to the boy's cheeks. Without a word, he took up his cap and went outside. So that was what the old man had been driving at all along! He might have known something was wrong when he started out to talk in that friendly way at breakfast. Well, he'd find out how things stood.

Christmas Eve fell on Friday. Immediately after the early supper, the man went to his room and after a short time reappeared clad in stiff black. The boy, sitting at the table in an attitude of reverie, looked up to meet the surprised glance of his father.

"Why, you'd better get into your other clothes, 'lias," he suggested. "We won't have any too much time."

"I don' think I'll go." The boy's eyes shifted away.

"You're not going to the exercises at church?" The man's voice was filled with astonishment. "Why, everybody's going."

"I guess I'll stay home." The son's eyes were fixed on the floor.

There was a moment of silence. Elias, out of the corners of his eyes, saw his father button his coat and unbutton it again.

"Oh, you'd better go with me," the father said. "You never stayed away before. It won't seem like Christmas to you if you stay home from the exercises. Come, better put on your other clothes."

The boy shook his head. He did not look up. After another interval of silence, he heard the man open the door and go outside. He sat motionless. Then he stationed himself at the small window that overlooked the yard. He saw his father lead the horse from the barn, hitch it to the buggy, and drive away.

Before the buggy had left the yard, Elias was in his room, changing his clothes. After a cursory examination of himself in the kitchen mirror, he extinguished the lamp and went to the barn. He threw the harness on the horse, went outside to draw the buggy out of the shed, and then hitched up.

Lizzie welcomed him when he arrived at her home. He accepted her invitation to step in and warm himself at the kitchen stove.

Lizzie's father came in, a large, broad man, whose mop of uncombed brown hair fell slanting over his forehead. He slapped the boy on the shoulder in violent good nature. "So you're takin' our girl away from us tonight, I see," he remarked loudly.

"Yes, that's right," replied Elias, half embarrassed. His face took on a set smile. There was something in this man that he detested instinctively—the small eyes, the flat, sagging cheeks, the wide, loose mouth, all these made him recoil from Lizzie's father. And then, the man was big and awkward, and the sleeve of his coat was torn from the elbow down.

"Oh, Pa, you're scarin' the poor boy!" A small, lighthaired, gray-eyed woman came up and shook hands with Elias. "We thought sure that you'd be goin' to the program at church tonight," she said, her expression suddenly growing sharp with curiosity.

"I'd rather go to a party any old time," Elias said, with a touch of bravado. "I've been to church programs a lot of times, but I've never had a chance to go to many parties."

"I guess that's right too," approved Dalton in stentorian tones. "A young fellow ought to have a little excitement now an' then."

"We was goin' to church this evening, but it's a seven mile drive, and pa always gets sleepy after supper," Lizzie's mother informed him.

The girl appeared in the room in a long white dress bound rather tightly at the waist. There was a touch of color in her cheeks. Her eyes glowed shyly when she met the admiring gaze of the boy. Elias glanced aside just in time to see Dalton smiling broadly at his wife.

"I hope you folks have a mighty good time," Mrs. Dalton said, as they made for the door.

"Thank you," Elias replied with stiff formality. "I guess we will, all right. Good-bye." He closed the door quickly.

When they reached the Reems house, everybody was there. A girl took charge of Lizzie, and Elias was led into another room, filled with young men who were smoking furiously. Emory took his coat and cap and returned in a moment. He touched the boy's shoulder.

"Better have a little swallow to warm you up," he suggested, nodding in the direction of a table in the corner of the room on which stood several tall bottles and a number of wine glasses. Elias hesitated.

"It won't hurt you," declared Emory in a whisper. "Just a glass o' brandy."

Elias saw that several of the young fellows were watching him. "Sure," he said loudly. "Guess I need a bracer."

The fiery liquor seemed to strangle him, and he turned his face away so that his companions might not see the tears that had come to his eyes. More than half of the brandy was still in the glass. Wisely, he sipped the rest of it, holding the muscles of his throat tight so that he would not cough. Emory slapped him approvingly on the back. "Pretty good stuff, hey, 'lias?"

"Fine!" replied the boy. Already he felt a glow running through his body.

"You fellows come on out o' that room!" came a girl's voice stridently. "What do you think this is anyway—an old maids' party?"

After this invitation, the young men straggled out of the room. Elias was the last to leave. He looked about anxiously for a chair. A girl laughed.

"There ain't any empty chairs left, 'lias!" she cried. "Come out here and I'll sit on your lap."

It seemed to Elias in that moment that all of the people ranged along the side of the room were looking at him. The blood began to run hot to his eyes.

"Sure!" he said, smiling weakly. "Why, sure! You bet!"

The girl got up, gave him the chair, and then sat down on his knees. He hoped, in horror-stricken desperation, that she wouldn't notice that he was trembling in uncontrollable fright.

The girl, dressed in white as were all of the others in the room, was a lively companion. Elias found that he rather liked the sprightliness of her expression.

"Look at Bill Jeffries," she whispered.

Elias looked in the direction she had pointed out and saw an uncomfortable-looking youth with his arm about a girl who sat on his lap. Immediately, he placed his arm about the waist of the girl who was with him. She laughed aloud, so that many eyes were turned toward them.

"You'll hear about this from Lizzie Dalton!" she whispered gaily in his ear. "You ought to seen the look she gave me just now!"

A darkness came upon the boy. Suddenly he realized that he had blundered. Lizzie was his girl, and he should have asked her to share a chair with him. He fell into utter misery.

The rest of the evening passed in a blur. Once more the boys went to the adjoining room and poured out glasses of brandy. Elias filled his glass, drank slowly, and soon felt fortified. He felt sure now that he could explain to Lizzie how it had happened.

One of the boys began playing on a mouth harp. The rest formed a large circle in the room, each girl holding tightly to the arm of her escort. Elias felt as though he were swimming in space; his head rang. Half-consciously, he knew that Lizzie would not look at him. They began to walk. Someone was repeating rhymes that seemed to go with the music of the mouth harp. Suddenly there was a slight pause, Lizzie stepped away from him, and his arm was seized by another girl. Again they walked to the music, and again his partner drew away and was replaced by another. Finally he learned the line that caused this change:

The lady steps forward, and the gent steps back,

The player started up another tune, and again they walked to its rhythm. After a time Elias learned the words and sang them aloud with the rest,

Skip, skip, skip the maloo;
Skip the maloo, my darlin'.

He saw with relief that refreshments were to be served. Quickly he found Lizzie and drew her to a chair in the corner of the room. She followed him silently.

"It wasn't my fault," he whispered to her.

"What wasn't your fault?" she asked, turning to look at him. He saw that there were red spots in her cheeks.

"I didn't know any better," he stammered, almost abjectly. "I wouldn't have had Nellie on my lap if she hadn't asked me right out before everybody. I was sort o' excited, I guess."

She said nothing, but he felt that she was mollified.

They consumed the cake and hot chocolate slowly, listening to the conversation going on all about them. To Elias it all seemed a dream. He felt tired, and the ringing in his head had given way to a feeling of sick depression.

The clock on a shelf in the corner struck twelve. Immediately arose cries of "Merry Christmas! Ah, I beat you! Merry Christmas!"

There was renewed talking and laughing. They all stood up. It was time to go home.

Out in the cold night air, Elias felt better. He did not feel like saying anything, and the girl beside him in the buggy said nothing. The sky was clear, and the moon, near the zenith, threw over the still, white world a dusky light that blurred the outlines of things.

"I don't care much for parties," the boy said suddenly, "do you, Lizzie?"

"No." Her voice was tired, listless.

"I guess I'm tired of everything out here," he continued, "mighty tired! Guess I'll go out West next year."

She stirred slightly. He drew her close to him. As the horse walked along over the snowy road, he told her of the trouble he was having at home. She said nothing, but he could look down and see that her eyes were fixed upon his face, wistfully. A great confidence came to him, and with it, a deep tenderness. The horse was plodding along the line of trees that marked the edge of the Dalton farmyard.

"Lizzie," he said suddenly, bending over and looking into her eyes, "I'm goin' West in the spring, and I want you to go along. Will you marry me?"

She continued to look at him, as though she were dazed. Then he saw her lips move. "Yes, 'lias," she answered softly. He kissed her, and knew, without thinking, that he was crying.

On his way home, he remembered that his father would know about this, as he surely must have seen that the horse and buggy were gone. He unhitched the horse, closed the barn door carefully, pulled the buggy into the shed, and walked to the house.

He turned the knob, but the door did not open. Again he tried the door, feeling somewhat puzzled. Then he knew that his father had locked him out. With a defiant laugh, he strode away to the barn, climbed up into the haymow, and burrowed into the hay. His thoughts were running riot, and again it took him a long time to fall asleep.

Next morning he awoke, stretched, and went to the house. The man was at the table and did not look up.

Elias straightened, and a hardness drew his mouth together. Then he smiled. "Merry Christmas!" he greeted the man, mockingly.

The father raised his face, and the stern eyes gazed heavily at the face of his son. He said nothing in reply.

V

The wedding was solemnized late in February at the Dalton home. For days the house had been filled with delicious spicy odors. Early on the morning of the wedding day, Dalton drew Elias aside.

"Will your dad be here, d'you think, 'lias?"

"No, I don't think so," replied the boy shortly. "Maybe he doesn't know about it."

"Do you want me to drive over and tell him? That would give him a chance to change his mind about things."

"I don't care. You may go if you want to, but it isn't any use."

Dalton shook his head. "It won't look right," he declared. "Everybody'll be wondering where your pa is."

"Let 'em wonder," Elias spoke defiantly. "I guess everybody knows that there's been trouble over to our house."

At ten o'clock the guests began to arrive. From that time onward, the events of the day took on a veil of unreality to Elias. As the tall clock on the shelf slowly struck twelve, Lizzie and he walked from the stairway through the living room, which was packed with red-faced people, into the small parlor where, backed off into a corner, an unbending minister, clad in black, awaited them. His words came to Elias from far away, and they seemed to come in an endless stream. Then the man stopped talking, and Elias, half hypnotized, kissed Lizzie. At once there was a scraping of chairs and a clacking of conversation. The two stood close together, their backs to the wall, while a long stream of people straggled up to them, talking and laughing loudly. They pressed the boy's hand and murmured congratulations. Through all of this, Elias was disagreeably conscious that both the men and the women were kissing the bride. Finally the line thinned, and a call came for dinner. Lizzie and Elias were pushed through the crowd and took their places at the head of the longest table, where they sat, almost owlishly, while on all sides the guests gave evidence of gustatory delight.

The afternoon seemed interminable. Toward four o'clock the older people left. Dalton took on a mysteriously jovial expression and went upstairs, followed by all of the young men.

"Guess pa has the wine and the cigars up there," whispered Lizzie. "Maybe you better go, too."

"No," Elias rebuffed the suggestion, "I don't feel like goin' in for that today."

The young men finally tramped down the stairs, and again the rooms were crowded. Their faces were unnaturally flushed, and they laughed boisterously at the least provocation. Another meal was served. The guests ate heartily.

Lizzie and Elias had drawn away to themselves. "Oh, I wish they'd go!" she said wearily. "I'm dead tired. It just seems like I can't stand another hour o' this!"

"They'll be goin' now," Elias assured her. "They never go till they've been fed."

By seven o'clock the last team and carriage had driven from the yard. Mrs. Dalton came into the living room and sat down beside the boy and girl.

"It's sure been a big day," she sighed. "The only thing that I didn't like about it all was that your pa didn't come, 'lias."

The boy was silent. While Lizzie helped her mother clear the rooms, he went outside. Darkness had fallen, and a cold wind drifted from the north. The sky was overcast. Elias stared out into the void, and suddenly he felt that the earth was very old, and very tired. Then the numbness of his mind seemed to slip away.

"I'm married," he said to himself. "I'm married to Lizzie at last." Her face came before him sharply, and a tenderness touched him poignantly. "We'll make it all right," he resolved. He remembered all of the people who had been at the wedding, and the weariness he had felt. It seemed to him that this weariness came only when he mixed with people. Next spring, if all went well, they'd go West! Then they'd be all alone—and happy. His body straightened. Alone out there in the darkness, he felt that he had the strength to mould life according to his desire.

In the morning, as Elias was preparing to leave the house, his wife drew him aside.

"Don't have any trouble with him," she whispered. "Try to fix things up."

He smiled at her. "I'll be careful," he promised. "But there isn't much chance to fix things up. You don't know your new father-in-law."

She sighed. "It'd be so nice if he'd want you to come back," she said.

He looked at her quickly. "He won't have me back," he said positively. "But that doesn't matter. We're goin' out West in the spring, some way or other."

She did not reply. He opened the door and went out of the house.

It was a white, lifeless day. A sheet of unbroken cloud stretched over a frozen earth covered with a blanket of grimy, icy snow. The quietness of suspended animation hung in the cold, stagnant air. Elias walked rapidly between the corn-rows, his hands in the pockets of his sheepskin coat, his face bent downward. An odd, undecided expression haunted his eyes. For once, he was taking stock of himself. He was married. That thought came back to him time after time. After the momentary thrill when Lizzie's face stood out before him, a queer numbness came. All of his bridges had been burned behind him, and with his marriage, all of his youth seemed to be a thing of the past. Already he knew that he would not wish to stay at the Daltons very long—he couldn't like them—and his father was a man of his word. Lizzie and he were alone now. He wondered why his father wanted to see him. If he meant to say anything against Lizzie, as he had done before, there'd be trouble.

Elias had reached the place where the cornfield gave way to the pasture. For a moment he hesitated, wondering if it would not be wiser to go back. Then, in sudden determination, he stepped over the barbed wire fence and made his way to the barn.

When he came to the building, he opened the door and stepped over the sill. The horses stretched their necks over the manger and nickered lazily. He stroked their muzzles for a few minutes, looking over the stall with the deep interest of one who has been away from home for the first time in his life, and for an entire week. Then, with an expression of distaste, he walked over the trampled snow of the farmyard to the house. Outside, he took off his overshoes before entering the storm porch. He knocked at the door.

"Come in!" The voice of his father came from within, with peremptory abruptness. Elias stepped into the living room. His father stood beside the window on the opposite side of the room, half turned from his son.

"Hello," greeted Elias, with what assurance he could muster.

The man did not reply, but seemed to be thinking, as though he were trying to formulate something in his mind. Slowly he turned to his son. His face was impassive, the boy saw, with the mask of smooth grayness hiding any emotion he might feel. He motioned to a chair, and the boy sat down.

"Well," the man said at last, "so you married Lizzie Dalton."

"Yes," Elias spoke evenly, "we were married yesterday, you know."

"I know." The farmer drummed with his thick fingers on the window sill, staring ahead of him with unseeing eyes. "I guess Dalton, your father-in-law, told you that I wanted to see you?"

"Yes—that's why I came."

Again the man drummed with his fingers against the window sill. Then he straightened. "We might as well get down to brass tacks," he said abruptly. "When your mother died, she had some property from her side of the family, and she wanted that it should go to you. It's at the bank now—in money—nine hundred and forty dollars. I'll fix it so you can get it in your own name."

The boy was silent. Half consciously, his eyes stared through the window to a distant line of trees almost indistinguishable against the gray western horizon.

"You left some of your things when you went away," resumed the man, "and I rolled them into a bundle. You can take them along when you go back after a while." He left the room, mounted the stairs, and soon returned with a neatly tied bundle.

Elias stood up. His face was strained and tired. He held out his hand. "Good-bye, Pa," he said quietly.

The man did not respond. Instead, he gazed steadily into his son's face. For a moment his eyes were wide and sick. Then a fierce light came into them.

"It's all over now." He spoke in a low tone. "I expected such a lot from you. We lived here like men ought to live—quiet, without any trouble, and the blessing of God was on us." His voice mounted. "And I thought it would be that way always, that we could stand out against these new things—dancing and card-playing, everything that comes from the Devil. I wanted to leave you the farm—" The words were half strangled in his throat, and he stopped for a moment. The son still stood beside the chair, the lids almost closed over his eyes.

"No use talkin' about it this way," the farmer resumed, and his voice was hard. "You made up your mind to break away and go wild. I thought there was a chance, until you married that girl. I told you that you couldn't marry her and come back here. You remember that, don't you?"

"I remember," Elias said heavily. "I wouldn't have come if you hadn't told Dalton that you wanted to see me."

"Oh, that was just to settle about the money you have coming," Vaughn said impatiently. "What I mean is that you mustn't expect to come back here. I'm through with you, and I won't have that woman on my yard."

"You don't have to be afraid," the boy flared up. "I didn't come here to beg you to take care of us. I can get along." The deep-set gray eyes burned with a steady, slow anger. "You only think of the way you look at things. Haven't I always worked for you like a slave? What did I get out of it? It never was my way; it was always your way. I got sick of it. You don't have to be afraid—you'll never see me back here."

A sneer came to Vaughn's lips. "You talk like a fool," he said, "and that's what you are. Don't you forget it, you'll want to crawl back to the old farm, but I won't have you here. 'Sow the wind, and reap the whirlwind.' That's in the Bible. Just remember that."

Elias's lips were drawn tightly together. He picked up the bundle and, without a word, flung out of the door. His mind was seething. Unconscious of anything about him, he strode swiftly back to the Dalton farm.

When he entered the house, they were ready to sit down to the noon meal, evidently waiting for him.

"I don't want to eat," he said gruffly, and went upstairs. Lizzie followed him.

"You've had trouble, haven't you?"

He nodded, and then advised, "You'd better go down and eat dinner." She hesitated a moment before obeying. But after a short, wistful scrutiny of his face, she turned and went down the stairs.

The room where the boy sat bent over on a stiff-backed chair was cold, but he stayed there all afternoon. After the turmoil of anger, made all the sharper because there moved through it an uneasy sense of the tragedy in the life of his father, he fell into a mood of contemplation. He sat before the little four-paned window overlooking the snowcovered fields, and the gray stillness of the day seemed to draw into him. His mind ranged ceaselessly from the past to the present. He remembered his mother, a silent woman with a brooding face. At twilight she used to push aside the curtain of the west window in the living room and stare out with wide eyes. She never lighted the hanging lamp until it was too dark to see things plainly in the room. His father had been different: he had always worked hard, from morning to evening, and he had lived his religion almost fiercely. The man had seen the thing that stood before him; the woman had always stared at things that were dim with distance. She had died ten years before.

The figure at the window stirred slightly. The past seemed remote now; it was no longer a part of him. His thoughts contemplated the future. Lizzie and he would go West in the spring. He couldn't stay here, where he'd be so near the home farm. And anyway, he felt that life had become old and tired here. This was a land of men who had had their day and their fight. There was nothing for him, no excitement, unless he cared for the things that Emory Reems liked. As he remembered the party at the Reemses, a feeling of disgust came over him.

The gray light in the room darkened. There were quick steps on the stairs, and Lizzie entered. She stood beside him, her arms across his shoulders.

"It's too cold here," she said, almost apologetically. "You better come downstairs."

He stood up. "Lizzie," he said, and a glow was in his eyes, "we're goin' to get out of here just as soon as the weather opens up. We'll go West—you an' me—in a prairie schooner. We'll take our time, an' we'll live easy, like tramps. It will be all new country, and we'll be alone."

She smiled. As he looked down into her face, all of the weariness of the last few days left him. Together they went down the stairs.

The kitchen was almost dark. Through the cracks of the stove the flames showed lines of orange and red, and shadows of firelight played a flickering dance on the low ceiling. Elias and Lizzie stood near it. His arm still lay upon her shoulders. They stared into the dusk with wide eyes, silent.

Mrs. Dalton moved about slowly, sighing now and then over her work of preparing the evening meal. She glanced at them curiously when she lifted the stovelid and shoved a piece of split wood on the red coals.

"You folks are the quietest couple I ever seen," she observed at last.

"Nothing to talk about," Elias replied abruptly, and then, because his voice had been sharp, he added, "Lizzie and I know each other so well that we don't have to talk, do we, Lizzie?"

"Why, no," she said slowly.

"Guess I'll go out and help my new dad with the milking," he observed, with an attempt at lightness.

"Oh, there ain't much chores to do," Lizzie looked up at him, and he knew that she wanted him to stay with her.

"Sure, go ahead and help pa." Mrs. Dalton agreed heartily with his proposal. "He's always glad to get a hand."

Dalton was on the stack of cornstalks, throwing fodder into the yard for the cattle. Elias heard the swish and crunch of the animals as they tore the husks aside and broke off the ears. Dalton's figure stood outlined against the gray of the evening sky, black and rather squat. He descended in a few moments.

"Oh, you got the milk pails!" he observed in a pleased voice.

"Yes, I thought maybe you wouldn't care if I milked a few cows for you. If you don't like it—" Elias laughed.

"I guess I can stand it all right," Dalton remarked cheerfully, as they walked to the barn. "I've had enough of it, as far as the fun o' milkin' comes in."

The lantern was hung on a nail behind the row of cows waiting to be milked.

"You milk Old Whitehead," the older man directed. "She's so tough that I feel like I done a day's work when I get through with her. You're young, and you ain't had to milk her mornin' and night for the last two years."

"Sure," agreed Elias. "I guess I can handle her."

For a time there was nothing but the rhythmic sound of the milk as it streamed against the sides of the pails. Then, when the bottoms of the milk pails were well covered, the sound became dulled, a steady, soapy bubbling.

"You know," Dalton said, in the tone of one continuing the thread of his thoughts aloud, "farming is a pretty poor business. Whenever I go to town and see how they live there, all slicked up, finished with work for the day 'bout the time when we're gettin' ready for the evening chores, and snoozin' in bed when we're slavin' at the mornin' chores, it makes me kind o' sick of it all. Here I've been on the farm all my life, and there ain't such a lot to show for it. One year there's fair luck, and the next year there's bad luck, and you got to work just as hard for the poor years as for the good years. When ma and me got married, 'bout twenty-five years back, I rented a farm. And I'm rentin' a farm now." He had finished milking the cow and, breathing deeply in his disgust, approached another.

"Well," Elias declared, "I guess it isn't the easiest kind of life, but you can't find many jobs anywhere that will let you be outdoors and be your own boss, too."

"Give me a nice warm place inside, and you can have my share o' outdoors," the man returned, complainingly. "I've had all I wanted o' freezin' and roastin'."

The younger man did not make a reply to this. They worked in the feeble yellow light, surrounded by darkness filled with the warm smell of the animals.

"By the way," Dalton began, in a casual tone, "what did your dad want to see you about this morning?"

"Oh, nothing much. There were some o' my things that he had packed up for me."

"Then he didn't ask you to come back?"

"No."

"You and your dad are built about the same way," Dalton asserted impatiently. "Why didn't you make up with him? You didn't have anything to lose by it, and everything to get out of it. If I had a chance to get on a farm and know that it was comin' to me, I tell you I could put up with a lot, and glad to."

"Well, I won't. He doesn't care to have us there, and he couldn't get me to go back now, even if he wanted it."

"See here, that's no way to talk. What do you expect to do? O' course, we like to have you an' Lizzie with us for a while, and all that, but there ain't work for two men here. We thought that the trouble would blow over when you got married and that you'd go back. You can't afford to be so high and mighty. What'll you do?"

"We'll get along. Don't worry," Elias assured him coolly. "We're goin' out West in the spring, Lizzie and I decided this afternoon, just as soon as the weather opens up. We'll buy land there."

"If you got the money to buy it with."

"I have. Ma left me something—enough to start out on."

"How much?"

"Oh, enough, I guess."

They had finished milking. The stools were thrown into the corner. In silence the men walked to the house.

VI

The heavy, lumbering prairie schooner rolled protestingly over a winding, indistinct trail leading to the west. The sun stood at the quarter mark in the eastern sky, shining out of the cloudless void upon an empty land touched with the first misty green of spring. Near at hand the grass rose in stiff bunches from the mat of dead growth, light green against a washed-out brown. Farther out, as the land swept away in long undulations, the green was lost in the flow of strong light and became a shimmering shadow upon distant slopes until at last the earth became a vast level, cut off by a sharply etched horizon. The breeze was soft and mellow, coming out of the south, scarcely strong enough to ruffle the thinnest spindles of new growth.

Behind the wagon, a red-and-white spotted cow pulled obstinately at the rope that forced her to keep up with the pace of the horses. Now and then the animal turned her head and lowed mournfully to a half-grown calf that answered the summons by deserting some juicy clump of grass and galloping up to the wagon in stiff-legged friskiness.

Elias sat on a board at the front of the wagon, staring out into the distance. When the trail dipped down, he tightened the reins, and the horses obediently pulled back on their collars, steadying the wagon; then, when they were past the strip of level ground at the bottom of the slope, he clucked encouragement to the horses and they, with bent heads, toiled heavily up the rise.

Just two weeks before this they had set out from the Dalton farm. Even now, feeling eased and refreshed as his eyes traveled over miles and miles of virgin prairie unscarred by any sign of habitation, he recalled with vague discomfort the morning of their departure. Lizzie had cried a little, and the sight had shocked him.

Her grief had been soundless; only the tears on her face had given evidence of her emotion. Mrs. Dalton had wept, and her grief had not been silent. Finally, however, they had climbed to the rough seat of the wagon, and the last thing they had heard was an admonition from Dalton to "stick it out." At first they had traveled north for two days, trying to avoid the towns where people had stared at them and stopping only at night on little-traveled roads, at places where there was water for the stock.

On the evening of the second day they had reached a small town that rejoiced in the name of Calliope, situated on the banks of a slow-flowing river. Elias pointed to the rolling country on the other side of the stream. "Out there's the kind of country we're looking for, Lizzie!" he had cried in excitement. "After we get over the river, we're really in prairie country. But we won't stop for a long time yet. We want to get far out." He had stopped the horses on the outskirts of Calliope, even though the hour was early, and they had spent an hour at the one store at the town, buying a few last necessaries.

On the morning after that, they had crossed the long wooden bridge. Lizzie had looked back often from the rear of the wagon. Elias had shouted gaily at the horses, who had stepped briskly out on the road that twisted away to the west. The poor cow tied to the rear of the wagon had been forced into a reluctant gallop to keep herself from being throttled, and the calf, in its usual morning spirits, had dashed head down and tail up. From that moment, it seemed to Elias that a sense of freedom had come to him.

Now they had drawn so far from settled country that it already seemed as though the things which they had left were unreal. He did not wish to think of the past. Odd scraps of song came to mind, especially a tune which he had learned from a hobo who had stopped to work for his father one summer during harvest:

"Then beat the drum slowly, and play the fife lowly,
And play the dead marches to carry me on;
Take me to the valley, and plant the sod o'er me,
For I'm a poor cowboy, an' I know I done wrong."

He sang lustily, his eyes sparkling. Lizzie, who had been folding things into place in the wagon, took up a seat beside him, without saying a word.

At noon they halted for an hour and a half to give the horses a chance to crop the grass and to rest. After the hearty meal, Elias lay out full length upon the ground while Lizzie gathered up the remnants of the meal and replaced them in the wagon. Once more the horses were hitched, and again the prairie schooner crawled along the trail through a sunny silence. The afternoons brought a warm haze into the air that softened the clear light of the horizon into purple. They were beset by strangeness and silence, caught up in the loveliness of blue sky and shadowy distances.

They did not talk more than was necessary. Lizzie sat beside Elias on the seat, crouched down, her thin face faintly wistful, her eyes wide. He turned to her once, and found that she had fallen asleep. He drew her body against his, so that she might rest more comfortably.

Slowly the sun drew into the regions of the west, growing larger and larger as it dipped downward. The sky flushed into yellow and red and orange. Against the glow, the edge of a distant rise stood black and murky.

The trail struck down more sharply than usual. Ahead, a twisting line of dark growth marked the course of a prairie stream.

They made their camp on a low ridge, well away from the creek. The woman commenced preparations for the evening meal while the man unhitched and led the horses by halter ropes to the water. Directly below the camp a gap in the thick growth of willows gave access to the stream, which was a thin sheet of water flowing blackly between mud banks. The horses sank deep into the ooze and sucked the water into their mouths eagerly. The man looked downstream. The black line of willows writhed out and away until it was lost in the shadows of the east. Farther out, the water came into view again, touched with the sombre flare of sunset.

Finally the horses satisfied their thirst and pulled themselves out of the mud. Snuffling contentedly, they docilely followed the man back to the camp, where he staked them out with long ropes. Then he carried water from the stream for the cow and calf and found a grazing place for them. By this time, only a narrow line of dark red in the west remained of the day, and the light of the campfire flickered strangely against the canvas top of the wagon.

Seated on blankets spread near the fire, they consumed their simple meal of bread, meat, and coffee in silence. They ate with hearty appetites. When the supper was finished, the woman poured boiling water over the dishes, dried them, and returned them to the wagon, while the man lay back on the blanket and looked up into the night sky. After a short time she joined him.

The fire had burned down to glowing coals that radiated a slight but welcome warmth over them. He turned his face toward her when she sat down beside him.

"This just seems great to me, Lizzie," he said in a deep, contented voice. "I don't know that I've ever felt like this before— so sort o' satisfied. This is wild country. You can just feel it in the air. Ain't you glad that we came out here?"

"Yes, 'lias." Her voice was not colorless as it usually was, but held a quiet intensity. "It seems strange out here—it's so still,

and there ain't any people around—but I'm awful glad we came."
She was silent for a time, then continued, speaking rapidly, "I'm
beginning to feel like I amounted to something again. You know
how it was back home. I was all right, but I was just one o' the
Daltons. Pa ain't made a go o' farmin' and he takes things easy,
an' so we got the name o' bein' shiftless. That's what your father
thought, an' I guess that's the way everybody thought. I was sick
of it. It just seemed like there wasn't anything to do but just live
through with it. Then, when you started goin' with me, it seemed
like I was startin' to live again, in a new way. But—" Her voice
trailed away.

"What?" he prompted her, quietly.

"If you hadn't gone an' married me, you could 'a' stayed on
the farm. Your pa didn't think I was good enough for you. Maybe
I wasn't, either. I just keep thinkin' that. We ain't the same kind o'
people. You can think o' things that never come to me, and when
you say 'em, I can think of 'em, too. At home we just went along,
workin' an' eatin' an' sleepin'—an' that's about all there was to it.
Your family wasn't like that. I don't know—"

"We ain't going to talk about the folks back home any more,"
he announced shortly. "And there isn't a lot o' difference between
us, not more than there is between other people." His eyes, dimly
visible in the glow of the dying campfire, were alight. He reached
out and placed his hand in hers.

They were silent. Elias turned his face upward again. The sky
was without a moon, but it was not dark. The stars shone in a field
of hazy blue light. The wind held from the south, adventuring
lazily through the night, now and then freshening to a cold breeze.
From the stream, invisible at the foot of the slope, came the
croaking of frogs in rusty chorus, the only sound in the silence of

the prairie, except for the occasional movement of the horses, some rods away in the darkness. Beside them, a dim, uncouth outline, stood the wagon.

"'lias, wake up!"

He stirred sleepily. "Guess we better go to bed," he yawned. "I didn't know that I'd gone to sleep."

The next day, the trail swung to the north, evidently avoiding a river whose course was marked to the west by a broad strip of marshy lowland ending in a line of black where underbrush grew on the bank.

"We'll be coming across people soon," Elias observed. "In a day or two we'll strike Junction City, where we can stop for a while and look over the country before we decide where we'll have our farm."

"Oh, I'm glad," she said. "It's been so long since we saw any people; it seems like a year to me."

"Just a little more than two weeks," he assured her, laughing. "I wouldn't mind having a year of it, though. We'll remember this trip for the rest of our lives."

"Yes," she assented. "But it's nice to have people around, anyway."

Toward evening the wind shifted to the east, and the sky thickened. The river was nearby, cutting to the northeast.

"We'd better not try to cross the river today," declared Elias. "It looks like the ford would be somewhere near, but it's coming on rain, and if we stop where the ground's high, the mosquitoes won't get at us so much."

It was early and, after unhitching the horses, he walked down toward the river. A half mile from camp the trail ended on the bank of a wide stream. Elias noted the swift current rather dubiously. The crossing looked decidedly unsafe. However, the trail stopped here,

and if others had made the ford, he could. He walked back to the
wagon.

"Did you find the place to cross?" Lizzie asked.

"Yes; the crossing's straight down from here."

"Is it a big river?"

"No," his tone was reassuring. "There's a ford that everybody
uses. We won't have any trouble."

"Something like that scares me." She looked to the north,
where the grayness of nightfall made the black line of river bank
portentous, and she shivered.

"Oh, Lizzie," he cried, as though he were mocking her fear. "It's
nothing at all!"

A thin drizzle set in. Before they had finished a hasty meal
at the campfire, this thickened into a steady rain. They quickly
placed the things under cover; and then climbed into the wagon.
There was nothing for them to do but go to bed, in spite of the
earliness of the hour. The rain beat against the canvas of the wagon
in soothing cadence. Elias lay awake for a long time, listening to
the soft roar of the rain. Now and then, faintly, he heard the quiet
breathing of the woman beside him. Outside, one of the horses
whinnied. The wind came in a sudden gust and drove the rain
against the canvas so violently that the interior of the wagon was
filled with a fine spray. Through the slight opening at the rear of
the wagon, a breeze straggled in, filled with the smell of a wet,
green earth. Then the sudden flurry passed, and the rain pattered
softly again on the canvas.

Elias fought off the sleep that tugged at his eyelids. The sounds
of the wind and the rain brought to him a strange mood of
exaltation. Through it all he could sense something sprightly and
free, something wild and lawless. He almost wished that he could

be abroad in the night, facing the wet wind. He thought of the days that lay ahead. There would be rainy days and bright days, and they would be filled with this intimate sense of the earth. He thought of Lizzie, and the little house he would build for her. She liked this sort of life all right, but be wished that he could tell her just how he felt about it; if only he could find the words for his feelings, she would know that this was her country, too.

At last he fell asleep.

They were up betimes in the morning. The rain had stopped, and the sky was rifted with blue in the northwest. They ate an uncomfortable, cold breakfast. Lizzie glanced often toward the river.

The horses were harnessed and hitched to the wagon, the cow and the calf were both tied securely to the end of the box, and they started.

Elias drew up at the river bank. The water was higher than it had been the preceding evening, and the swift, boiling current made the crossing look treacherous.

"We can't go through this!" the girl cried in fear, clutching the arm of her young husband. "I don't dare!"

"It isn't deep," he said. "Not much chance of any trouble. Besides, the river will be getting higher all the time."

"I won't go!" she declared, her thin face white with fear. "I can't do it!" She started to descend from the wagon, but he drew her back.

"Oh, yes, you can do it," he said, rather shortly. "You must, because I'm going to drive through right now."

She stared at him with hunted eyes, but she said nothing more.

The team refused to enter the water. Elias jumped from the seat, cut as heavy a willow stick as he could find, and once more climbed into the wagon. He struck each of the horses sharply. They sprang forward. Half consciously, Elias heard the frightened bawling of the calf as it was drawn into the water. The horses, finding the stream shallow, recovered quickly from their panic and straightened obediently at the tugs. Elias was bent forward, his eyes fixed on the horses. Suddenly the river bed became deeper. Water swirled madly around the wagon. The horses stepped forward cautiously. Then one of the team lost his footing and fought madly. The mate, after a vain attempt to pull him up against the sharp sweep of the current, also lost her footing. The animals struggled furiously in the current. Because the wagon was heavy, the water could not budge it. Slowly, however, as the rushing stream drove the bottom from under the wheels, they sank deeper and deeper. Elias pulled steadily at the reins until the horses, somewhat quieter, regained their foothold. Then, carefully, he brought them once more into line with the wagon. Again he tried to start them. The brutes would not move forward, but backed against the wagon. Taking up the stick with his free hand, the man struck them with all his strength. The tormented animals, desperate, plunged forward once more. The wagon was lifted out of the sand into which it had bedded, and in a few moments the water became shallower. Only after they had drawn up on the bank did Elias suddenly realize that the danger was past. Beside him, her eyes staring in horror, the woman sat crouched forward. He quickly jumped to the ground and walked back to see how the cow and the calf had fared. The cow had a look of abject misery, but had suffered no apparent harm; the calf seemed half drowned. He untied the ropes that bound the creatures and they immediately settled down in their tracks. Then he returned to his wife. She was in the same huddled attitude.

"Don't look that way, Lizzie," he said, putting his arm about her. "That was pretty bad, but we got through all right."

Then she began to cry, not aloud, but in a silent paroxysm that racked her frail body. Her breath came sobbingly; tears rolled from her eyes; she clung to him in nervous fear.

He tried awkwardly to soothe her, his face full of tenderness. "Don't cry, Lizzie girl," he repeated. "It's all over now." He smiled down into her eyes. Slowly the woman grew calmer and at last smiled faintly. She said nothing.

"We'll all rest up for an hour," he declared cheerfully, "and I guess we all need it. The calf looks like she tried to drink too much of the river and it didn't agree with her a lot." Then he added, "You lay down and take things easy while I try to start a fire, and we'll have a little something to eat. After that, we'll feel better."

With much ado, he found enough dry weed stems to start a fire and soon had the coffee boiling. While they ate and drank, he talked a great deal. She said nothing, but he saw that her eyes looked up at his with an expression of fear.

"Maybe I acted sort o' rough to you, Lizzie," he spoke apologetically. "You see, we simply had to get across the river."

She shivered. "I wish you'd shave," she said in a low tone. "When we were goin' through the deep part, when you was hittin' the horses so, you looked like you was half crazy, just like you'd kill everything if you didn't have your own way. And you was swearing all the time." The hunted expression came back to her face.

"Why, I don't remember anything of that," he said, contritely. "But you see, I had to do that. If I hadn't hit the horses the way I did, we might all have gone down. There was deep water on the other side, and I knew we wouldn't have much chance there. You mustn't think about it any more. And I don't know why I was swearing; I don't swear other times."

The rifts of blue in the sky had grown larger, and now huge masses of loose clouds were being driven by a fresh northwest wind. The sun shone out warmly upon a land of newly washed green. After an hour they took to the trail again, the wagon creaking heavily up and down the long swells of the prairie to the north.

VII

They traveled long that day. When the wagon drew creakingly to the top of a ridge, Elias looked eagerly toward the next hollow, hoping that there might be a stream, so that they could make camp, but each time they were disappointed.

They came to another ridge, and a long scrutiny failed to show any signs of a stream ahead of them.

"Guess we'll have to stop," the man grumbled. "We'll have water for ourselves, but the stock will have to go without. There'll maybe come a heavy dew, and so the animals won't have it so bad. Funny that we didn't strike any crick."

"Oh, 'lias, look!" The woman grasped his arm excitedly. "Ain't that a farm 'way out there ahead of us?"

His eyes followed the direction in which she was pointing. Far away, a small patch of black made an irregular blot against the uniform duskiness that evening had thrown over the prairie.

"It sort o' looks that way," he agreed. "It's hard to tell, looking against the sun. Well, we'll go along for a while, and then we can see."

The horses reluctantly straightened the tugs, and the monotonous squeaking of the wheels began again.

"Oh, I hope that it will be a house!" exclaimed Lizzie.

"If it's a farm, we can water the stock," he replied. "If it wasn't for that, I wouldn't go out of my way to stop at a house. It's more fun to camp."

The tawny glow in the west drew into a thin strip that edged the western horizon with a deep, almost stormy red. Suddenly one of the horses raised his head and whinnied sharply.

"Guess it's a farm all right," observed the man. "It's too dark to see the place until we're right up to it, but it can't be more than a quarter of a mile away."

A slight turn in the trail brought a light into view, a short distance ahead. The horses were stepping briskly and soon drew up before a small frame building, from one window of which a light shone.

The door of the house opened, and the figure of a tall man stood against the yellow light of the interior. "Hello," he spoke loudly.

"Have you got room for us?" asked Elias. "We've been looking for water and couldn't find any, so we decided to keep on and see if you could help us out."

The man had come up to the wagon. "Sure," he said, hospitably, "we can put you folks up all right." He turned toward Lizzie. "You go right on in, Missus," he directed. "You'll find ma in the house. I'll help unhitch."

Lizzie descended, unhelped, from the wagon and slowly walked to the door, which had remained open. Evidently the woman inside had overheard the conversation, for Elias heard a hearty greeting before his wife had entered the house.

"You can put up the horses in the barn, if you want," offered the stranger. "Guess they can stand a little hay and corn if you've been keepin' 'em on grass."

"They've had some grain," replied Elias, "but we didn't have room for hay."

The barn was a tiny makeshift, with a low, strawthatched roof. While Elias drew the harnesses off, the stranger filled the low manger with hay and placed corn in the boxes. Then, together, they walked through the cool darkness of the evening to the house.

"By the way, my name's Hartmann," volunteered the farmer.

"I'm Vaughn—Elias Vaughn."

They shook hands.

When they entered the farmhouse, Elias saw that Lizzie was placing the food on the table. He noted that her face was flushed.

"Mrs. Hartmann wanted me to sit back in a chair and be company," she declared gaily, "but I told her that I wasn't brought up that way."

"Ya, I don't want her to help with the work after she's been bumpin' around in a wagon all day," declared Mrs. Hartmann, a tall, middle-aged woman with prominent cheek-bones. "But I guess she's like me—she can't be sittin' around when other folks are workin'. Well," she continued, placing a large tin coffee pot on a piece of shingle beside her plate, "supper's ready. We ain't got so much, maybe, and it's plain, but there's enough to go 'round."

They pulled up their chairs, and then there was a short silence. Hartmann nodded solemnly and meaningly at Elias, whose face became a brick-red. They all bowed their heads over their plates while he prayed, in awkward, disjointed sentences, for a blessing upon the food. When he had finished, he kept his eyes turned toward his plate for a few moments.

The meal consisted of bread, boiled potatoes, hot fried pork, and coffee. They ate heartily, and there was little conversation, except when Mrs. Hartmann urged them to help themselves, as it would be a long time till morning. Finally they all sat back in repletion. Hartmann reached up to a small shelf above his head and took down a Bible.

"I heard a man sayin' once that people ain't readin' the Bible no more after meals," he announced, "but that don't make no difference with us. We wouldn't feel right if we didn't do it, would we, Ma?"

"No, I guess not," she replied, "and anyway, we aim to read through the Bible every year. Just now, pa's in a kind o' hard place, where there's a lot o' names o' kings, and it don't say much about 'em, but he gets through some way."

"Here," said Hartmann, handing the open Bible to Elias and pointing to the chapter to be read. "You read. You got better eyes than me, and I guess you can read better. It'll seem sort o' good to have somebody else read, for a change." He lifted the lamp from the middle of the table and placed it at Elias's elbow.

The chapter dealt with the succession of the kings of Israel, and Elias read slowly, the words conveying little meaning to him. Then, feeling that his auditors would not know if he mispronounced, he read more rapidly, and with growing assurance.

"Say, I wish I could rattle off them names like that!" Hartmann, who had tilted his chair back against the wall, spoke in a tone of admiration.

"It must be nice, all right," agreed Mrs. Hartmann. "When pa reads, it don't sound that way at all. I guess he just sort o' makes up sounds."

"Well," expostulated her husband. "It ain't that bad. You see, we ain't learned the thing in the same way."

The meal was concluded with a prayer, spoken in German, by Hartmann.

While the women cleared the table, the men leaned back comfortably in their chairs.

"Smoke?" queried the farmer.

"Sometimes. But I haven't got a pipe."

"Well, I guess I got one for you." Hartmann fumbled in the pocket of a coat hanging on a nail near the door and brought out a short black pipe. He took down a tin pail from another nail, placed it between his knees, and pulled off the cover. Putting the bowl into the tobacco, he pressed the long-cut into it. Then he passed the pail to Elias, who filled his pipe as he had seen the other do. Hartmann scratched a match on the chair, held the flame over his guest's pipe, and then lighted his own.

"You men will have to sit in the dark for a while," declared Mrs. Hartmann. "We need the lamp in the kitchen."

"Go ahead," her husband replied. "We're makin' our own light, hey, Vaughn?"

"Yes."

They smoked in silence, the glow of their pipes deepening and dying in the gloom at regular intervals. In the kitchen the women were talking with animation.

"It's like this," Elias heard Mrs. Hartmann say. "You like it out here, or you don't like it. You don't just sort o' like it. Now, both Hendry and me always lived on the farm, and we liked to be alone, too. Even at that, I tell you we went through some times here that would 'a' scared me if I'd 'a' known they was comin'."

"In what way do you mean?" Lizzie asked, in a small voice.

"Oh, it's kind o' hard to tell," Mrs. Hartmann hesitated for a moment, and then continued. "O' course, there's hot weather in summer, and bad snowstorms in winter—but it ain't them so much either. It's the waitin' for things to happen, I guess. Lucky we ain't nervous, or we might 'a' gone crazy. Out here you got to watch weather a lot more than back East, and sometimes, when you're all alone for a long time, things just seem to get tighter an' tighter in you. Oh, I can't tell you what I mean."

For a short space of time there was no sound except for the slight rattle of the dishes. Elias knew, by the attentive tilt of Hartmann's head, that his host also was listening.

"It must be pretty bad?" Lizzie asked at last, in a low tone.

"Yes an' no," Mrs. Hartmann said slowly. "Even if we had the money, I guess we wouldn't go back East. But you'll find out what I mean all right. Most folks who come out here don't last more'n a year."

"Ma, you quit talkin' that way," Hartmann's voice, half serious, half amused, bellowed heartily in the gloom.

"Well, ain't it true?" the woman retorted. "You men don't never see the woman's side at all. I ain't complainin'; I'm just tellin' the truth."

"If the right people come out here, things'll be better," the man growled. "This ain't no country for slick city fellows or for them that are lookin' for a soft snap; but I say it's the right place for people who can fight it out." He drew vigorously at his pipe, so that the smoke became bitter and rank. He turned to Elias. "You take my word for it," he declared emphatically, "this is goin' to be the best corn an' wheat country in the world! You just mark my words!"

Elias nodded in agreement. "We'll stay by it all right," he said positively. He placed his pipe on the window sill.

"How d'you like the tobacco?" asked his host.

"Pretty well—but I'm not much of a smoker, and it seemed a little strong."

"More'n a little, I bet!" chuckled Hartmann. "That was raised right out here, and if you ain't use' to it, it'll take the hide right off your tongue."

The two women re-entered the room with the lamp. Mrs. Hartmann washed the boards of the table with a wet rag and then seated herself beside Lizzie, opposite the men. Elias glanced at his wife. Her face had a downcast expression, and he felt that she was worrying about the things that Mrs. Hartmann had said. He almost wished that they had not stopped at the farmhouse.

"Well," asked the man. "Where are you folks expectin' to settle?"

"I don't know for sure." Elias turned to him. "We thought of stopping off at Junction City and buying at the railroad land office."

"You better look around good first," advised the other. "You see, there's quite a lot o' people been comin' in, so you'll have to get pretty far out."

"Oh, it doesn't matter if we're far out, for a while," Elias remarked. "By the time we get things going so that there's some hauling to do, the country will have more towns. The only thing I want is good land."

"But we don't want to be too far from other people, do we?" Lizzie broke in quickly.

"Oh, we'll have near neighbors in a few years wherever we go," Elias said reassuringly.

Lizzie turned to Mrs. Hartmann. "We didn't see a single farm from the time we left Calliope until we got here," she said, in a troubled tone. "I didn't know there could be such empty country."

"That's because you followed the old trail that sticks to the sandy bottoms country," Hartmann volunteered. "The good land starts about ten miles away from the river. If you'd turned off, you could 'a' seen farms every day, I guess." He laughed, and added, "Ma's been scarin' you, that's all. There's people here, just like everywhere, but not so many. An' anyway, you c'n learn to do without neighbors most of the time."

Mrs. Hartmann looked up, as though she were about to speak, but remained silent.

Elias yawned. "Guess we better go to bed," he announced sleepily. "We got to have an early start. How much farther is it to Junction City, Hartmann?"

"Forty-seven miles, as the crow flies—'bout fifty-two by trail."

"Are there any more rivers to cross?" asked Lizzie.

"No; just a few little cricks."

"Let's see; we can make it in a couple of days. It'll take a few more days to get the land we want, and then we'll be ready to settle down." The young man's face lighted up, and a certain excitement came into the gray eyes. "This is the country for us, all right!" he declared.

The talk died into silence. Then Hartmann led the way to the wagon, carrying the lamp. After a brief "Good night" he returned to the house. Lizzie crawled into the wagon at once, but Elias stood a minute or two, looking about him. The night was peculiarly dark, with only the faintest glints of starlight. It was so quiet that he could hear the horses eating their hay in the barn. He stretched out his arms, tensing and relaxing his muscles. Then he, too, crawled rather awkwardly into the wagon.

VIII

Lizzie stayed at the ramshackle frame building which served as a hotel at Junction City while Elias drove from morning to night for several days with a guide under the employ of the railroad. The men started out early in the morning and did not return until late at night.

On the first day they struck out to the southwest. In this direction the country grew rougher. Harris, the guide, commented briefly on the new farms, which were marked by occasional board shanties standing starkly on the treeless expanse of prairie.

"Somehow, this doesn't look good to me," Elias said, upon their return that evening. "I'd like to see smoother land."

The next day they traveled to the northeast, but here the country became sandier, and Elias, forewarned against a light soil in a country subject to drought, stubbornly refused to consider it.

That evening, when they returned after dark, he found Lizzie waiting for him on the small porch that faced directly upon the street.

"You didn't find what you wanted, did you?" she ventured.

"There's country I like pretty well," he answered, "but I'm going to see what there is to the northwest of town. Better take time to look things over now than to be sorry later."

She nodded.

Opposite them, yellow lamplight blurred against dusty store windows. The streets were unlighted, and the presence of human life was betrayed only by the sounds of advancing or retreating footsteps, or by the creaking and bumping of a wagon as some belated farmer started out for home.

"Did you have a good time all by yourself today?" Elias asked, looking down into the indistinct face beside him.

"Oh, I got along all right," she answered. "There's always something going on—and I kind o' like to be near people."

"Well," he said briskly, "I wonder if I can get some supper here. I'm pretty hungry."

They went inside, where they found two weather-beaten old men playing cards by the dim light of a kerosene lamp. Elias had to wait until the game was concluded, and then the proprietor, with a sigh, retreated into the other room, from which came, after an interval, the smell of boiling coffee and frying meat. The landlord shuffled in and out of the kitchen rather disconsolately, until finally the meal was ready.

"Supper's ready," he announced gruffly, "and if there's anything y' want, just yell. I'll be out on the porch."

Elias ate voraciously. Lizzie sat beside him, her elbows on the table, her hazy blue eyes wide and reflective. When his coffee cup was empty, she filled it.

The young man sat back in his chair at last. "Say, that supper tasted good!" he exclaimed. "I tell you, this air gives me an appetite." Then, noticing her attitude, "What's the matter, Lizzie? You're not homesick, are you?"

She tried to smile. "It's so different," she explained wistfully. "I just keep feelin' that we're only visiting, and then, when it comes to me that we'll always be here, somethin' seems to go through me. It's all right when you're around, but I don't like to be alone. It makes me feel queer."

He smiled at her. "You've got a touch of homesickness, I guess," he declared. "And it's no wonder—you've never been away from home before, have you?"

"No, not farther than ten or fifteen miles. Oh, it'll be fine when we have our little house and can settle down."

He kindled at that, and they spent half an hour planning their home on the prairie.

"We'll find something tomorrow," he spoke confidently. "Harris told me we'd strike good land northwest o' here. It ain't settled as well, but I just got a kind o' feeling from what he said that we'll find a place I want." He yawned, stretched his arms above his head, and sighed comfortably. Then they ascended the steep, narrow stairway to their room.

The next morning, after a hearty breakfast, Elias found Harris waiting for him.

"You've got another team this morning," Elias remarked, as he stepped into the buggy.

"Yep," responded Harris, "we're gain' to make a big day of it, and we'll keep gain' till you find something you want."

"Guess I'm hard to suit," Elias confessed. "But I sort o' had something in mind—you know how you can have a place figured out before you see it—and that's why I've been holding off."

"That's all right," Harris said good-naturedly. "It's a lot better to go at it in your way than to grab the first piece of land you see, like some o' these new settlers do. An' they're the fellows that go chasin' back East as soon as things don't pan out the way they want 'em to, and give this country the black eye." He launched into an extended denunciation of these "would-be" farmers. "This country's all right," he argued. "It's just got to get the newness worn off. Funny, that is, but it works the same way with all new land. At first it seems like there's either too much rain or not enough, the storms are bad, and then, when the country begins to get under the plow, the whole thing changes. After that the land is tamed, and there's just enough rain, and the storms ain't so bad."

Elias listened eagerly. "It comes to this," he stated. "The ones who stick it out are the ones who make out big at last—isn't that right?"

"Sure, that's right."

The team, a pair of well-matched ponies, kept up the same even trot. Under the wheels, the two ruts, with grass growing between, were soft and springy.

The morning air, unstirred by a breeze, was cool and exhilarating. As Elias looked out at the long reaches of gently rolling prairie, a glow came into his deep-set gray eyes. This was the country he had dreamed of, this was his Promised Land. It was so wide, so free; the small farm houses, miles apart, each with its tiny cluster of buildings, only served to accentuate the feeling of vastness. To the young settler, there was something remote and magical in these dwellings, as though they were under the spell of a pervading, sunlit silence. On all sides stretched the prairie floor, gray-green with a carpet of unnumbered grasses. Now and then, a soft blurring of green into purple or yellow marked a bank of wild flowers. At such times, if he had been alone, Elias would have stopped to look more closely, but he was ashamed to have his companion know this. And there was no hurry; there were years and years ahead to revel in all these things; there would be a new delight for each day—a new fragrance, a new possibility. He thought of Lizzie, and wished that she were with him.

"I like the lay of land around here." Elias could not keep still, and turned to Harris.

"Well, we've got land out here that's good, but I want to show you the country north o' Hayes," Harris replied. "Hayes is just a store, a church, and a blacksmith shop, and the land is well north o' that, pretty well out, but it'll suit you, I guess. It ain't as well settled as here, but it will be, in a couple o' years. People are comin' in fast."

After the lapse of an hour, Harris pointed to the northwest. "See those buildings out there?" he asked. "That's Hayes. It's old, for this country. Two trails cross there, one from the east and one from the south, and in the old days there use' to be some big doin's there."

Seen from a distance, the town seemed incongruous. The tiny huddle of buildings, appearing black at this distance, were set on the top of a high point of land, infinitely small against the void of deep blue sky behind them.

They drove through the crossroads hamlet without stopping. The ponies kept up the same pace, up-hill or down-hill. Finally, where a stream crossed the trail, they stopped. Harris squinted at the sun.

"About noon, I guess," he stated. "What say we eat here and give the horses a rest?"

The horses were unhitched and tied to the rear of the buggy, where they could eat their hay from the box. The men squatted on the ground and ate their meat sandwiches to the last crumb. Then, after a long drink at the stream, they lay down on the grass. Harris smoked his pipe, and Elias, who caught the tantalizing aroma of the tobacco, decided that he would buy a pipe when he returned to town. He lay back, half drowsy under the mellow warmth of the sun, his mind aimless, his body comfortable with the food he had eaten. He had almost dropped off to sleep when he was aroused by Harris, who rose with a sigh and remarked, "Guess the horses have cleaned up the hay, and we'd better get along."

"Look around good," advised the land agent, after they were once more on their way. "This is railroad land, even though there ain't a railroad anywhere around. Must 'a' got it on a trade, I guess. Anyway, it's as good as the best."

Elias, fully awake, took in every feature of the country through which they were passing. Finally, where the stream they had crossed at noon swung in from the east, he called a halt.

"This looks pretty good to me," he said. "Let's take a look at it."

The longer he considered this place, the more it pleased him. The house would be set pretty well above the stream, and not too far away. Harris found the stake that marked the section corner, set under a stone years before when the government surveyors had gone through. From this corner they paced out, by compass line, a half-mile to the north and a half-mile to the east.

"That will give you just what you want," declared Harris. "You get the stream in the corner of the land where it won't bother you, and every acre of this quarter can be farmed; there ain't an acre in the piece that won't pay you big interest on your investment."

They talked over prices and terms. Finally Elias straightened. "I'll take it," he said. "Seven dollars an acre, half down, the rest in ten years at eight per cent."

"That's right."

It was mid-afternoon when they started back, and in all of the trip they spoke scarcely a dozen words. Elias was preoccupied with plans which were hardly formed before they were replaced by others. When they reached Junction City, it was after midnight.

Elias mounted the stairs rapidly, entered the room, and lighted the small lamp. The figure in the bed stirred.

"Well, I bought a quarter!" he exclaimed. "I'll sign up for it at the office tomorrow morning."

Lizzie sat up and regarded him with dazed, blinking eyes. "Oh," she smiled, sleepily, "that's awful nice." Then, more fully awake, she became almost excited, and he told her all of the details of the day's trip, showing her the place as he saw it in his mind. Her face grew brighter. It was only when they heard uneasy sounds on the other side of the partition of their room that they desisted from their talking and finally composed themselves to sleep.

IX

In the following month Elias worked from early morning to late night. Each load of building material had to be hauled from Junction City, and such a trip took two days. In the meantime, Lizzie stayed with Mrs. Anderson, wife of the man who owned the General Store at Hayes—a woman, Elias noted, who did not mind if a conversation resolved itself into a monologue so long as she was the one who conducted it.

The small house took form upon the knoll. It was made as weather-proof as the rough lumber would allow and contained three rooms. The dining room and the bedroom were moderately large, as rooms went in that country, and made up the side of the house which faced the west. The kitchen, a low-ceilinged extension on the east side, had the appearance of an afterthought. As soon as the roof was on, Elias hitched the team to the wagon and set out for Hayes. He arrived there shortly before noon. As he drew up the team before the hitching posts, that marked, rather indefinitely, the boundary of the yard, a short, plump woman hurried toward him from the house.

"You got to have dinner with us, Mr. Vaughn," she shouted hospitably.

"Why, there's a lot of work waiting for me," Elias hesitated, "and I thought we could just as well eat something as we drove on the way back."

"No, you put your horses up in the barn and give 'em a respectable rest," the woman commanded, her round face wrinkled with good nature. "My man will be comin' home from the store in a few minutes, and you ain't so busy but what you can take off for an hour. Why, we ain't had a real chance to get acquainted yet!"

"All right, Mrs. Anderson," Elias replied, as he started to unhitch the team, "I guess I'm only too glad to get a square meal. You see, I've been having pick-up meals all this week, and it'll seem pretty fine to get something hot."

Lizzie had come up before this and walked beside him as he led the horses to the water-trough. "It's nice here," she confided, after he had pumped the wooden trough full, and the horses were drinking, with their muzzles deep in the water, "but I'll be glad to get into our own house. I guess I like to feel that I'm boss of the house I'm in."

He nodded. "From now on, we'll have our own place," he said. "Of course, the house isn't much, when it comes to size, but it'll keep out the weather, and we'll be snug."

By the time the horses were fed and the Vaughns had returned to the house, Anderson came in, slamming the door behind him. He was not much taller than his wife, but very much leaner. His hair was edged with gray. The eyes had a curious expression, half quizzical, half disconsolate, and a ragged scrub of young beard covered most of his face, which was as brown as worn leather.

The men shook hands and immediately fell into a desultory conversation concerning weather and crops. They were interrupted by Mrs. Anderson who, with Lizzie's help, had placed the food on the table in the dining room.

"You sure got a place pretty far out, Vaughn," remarked Anderson, after they had begun the meal. "I guess you folks don't care much for company."

"Oh, yes, we do," broke in Lizzie. "You can just call yourself invited any time you want to come."

"We want lots o' company," agreed Elias. "I took that place because I liked the looks of the country there."

By the time they had finished the meal, they had become the best of friends. Anderson brought forth cigars from his vest pocket.

"Have a smoke, Elias," he offered.

Elias placed the cigar in the pocket of his shirt. "I'll keep it for the drive home," he said. Then, turning to Lizzie, "We'd better be getting along."

Lizzie hesitated. "I hate to leave Dora with the dishes," she said.

"Oh, get along!" cried Mrs. Anderson, with a jolly laugh. "I guess I can take care of a few dishes."

The men hitched the horses to the wagon and then waited.

"Womenfolks don't know what it is to hurry when they're visiting," growled Anderson, noticing that the young man looked toward the house. "They're never talked out."

They came finally. "You folks got to be sure to come to church," Mrs. Anderson called as they were about to drive away. "Our minister comes every two weeks, and every body goes to church then. Come over and make a day of it; you can always stay with us, if you can stand the board."

"If it's always the way it was today, I guess we can stand it," Elias replied gallantly. He took up the reins, slapped the horses lightly with them, and the wagon rumbled out to the road that led past the store and to the north.

It was a holiday for Elias. There was no hurry, now that he had given over the idea of working any more that day, and he held the reins loosely in his hand. The thudding of the horses' hoofs on the soft turf and the rhythmic squeaking of the wheels sounded restfully in the universal silence. The sky was of a deep, solid blue, going down from zenith to horizon almost without gradation of color. On all sides of them, as they advanced, there were scurryings and flutterings among the grass clumps. A bird flew up and, after a short, rapid, sailing flight, settled down upon a tall dead weed. Immediately the air seemed to ring with the zest of its song, the clear notes lingering on into the silence that followed. Then, from far away, came the answering song of its mate, faint, but still clear.

"What is that bird?" Lizzie asked curiously.

"Meadow lark," replied her husband. "You ought to hear 'em in the morning! And it's funny, but they always sing facing you, just as though they wanted you to listen. Did you see that black spot on the bird's throat? There's yellow all around, and it looks nice, I think." He turned eagerly toward her.

She nodded.

They did little talking. The horses made steadily for home, trotting heavily when the trail dipped, walking when it climbed to the next rise. The sun grew larger and larger as it moved into the west, and the long miles of green became brown, almost black, far away. High overhead a large bird soared lazily. A cool breeze stirred up eddies in the grass, sweeping away the warmth and languor of the afternoon.

Lizzie stirred uneasily and sighed. "I'm getting kind o' tired, 'lias," she said.

There was something child-like, a comfortable complaint in her tone that touched him. "Here," he directed, putting his arm about her waist and almost lifting her against him, "put your feet on the seat and snuggle up to me."

She did as he had told her. His arm supported her easily; her head lay relaxed against his shoulder. He looked down at her and saw that her eyes were regarding him wistfully. For a moment their curious, wondering gaze held. They both smiled slowly, intimately. Then he looked away. Later, when he glanced down again, he found that she was asleep. A subdued gaiety touched him. It was pure Adventure to be high up on the spring seat of a wagon riding through a silent land, taking a winding trail that was lost in the flaring shadows of sunset. And they were on their way home.

Slowly the last light of day seeped away and then, as it died into darkness, night came, and starlight. Coolness drew up from the ground in the hollows, but on the low crests of the ridges the wind was warm.

One of the horses whinnied. Indistinctly outlined against the night sky, aloof in the darkness, was the house.

"Whoa!" cried Elias. Then turning to the woman, who had awakened, "We're home, Lizzie!" He jumped from the wagon and extended his arms.

"Jump!" he commanded, "and I'll carry you into the house."

Hesitating, she released her hold, and he carried her as though she were a child. Inside of the house, all was jet black. He set her down and lighted a lamp. The yellow flame revealed a rather bare room, containing nothing more than a few chairs and a board table. The smell of new lumber pervaded the place.

"Isn't it fine?" he asked, smiling.

"It's ours," she said quietly, and a light was in her eyes. "This is our place, ain't it, 'lias?"

"Yes," he agreed. "It's the nicest place there can be for us. Do you like it?"

"It's fine," she answered. "Just fine!"

What with putting up the horses, preparing a meal, and placing things to rights, it was late before they went to bed, utterly tired and happy.

Sometimes, in the weeks that followed, Elias felt that the work of getting settled was endless, so great was his eagerness to get a start with actual farming.

"There's so much to do," he sighed one evening, when he came into the house after dark. "The house is in shape so we can live in it, and the finishing touches can be put on in the fall, but these trips to town take a lot of time. We simply have to get things to work with—we can't get along without machinery, and that makes heavy hauling."

"Work won't hurt us, I guess," she said cheerfully.

He smiled agreement. A pleasant weariness made him reflective. He watched his young wife as she went about her evening's work. She looked happier, he thought, than she had when she was at home. No wonder, either, considering that her folks didn't care much about anything at all. Her cheeks had more color now, and there was a touch of gay defiance in her talk with him. Then his mind went on to plans for the work that lay ahead.

"I'm going to start plowing tomorrow, Lizzie," he declared. "The rest of the work will have to wait. It's too late for much in the way of crops, but I can put in corn for fodder, and some millet. Then, after that's done, I can keep right on getting ground ready for winter wheat and rye, and get them in about August."

"Yes, and you'd better start out with a garden," she informed him. "We have to plant potatoes right away and a lot of garden truck. How'll we live next winter—on fodder and winter wheat? You men always think of field work and you don't seem to know that a garden does a lot more to keep you fed."

"Well," her husband replied mildly, "I never took to gardening, but I guess we can handle it." He smiled gaily at the tone she had employed; she had spoken in fun, but she had meant it, too. "I'll get the garden ready," he promised, "and I guess you'll want to take care of it."

"You get it planted, and I'll see to the rest. I'll get as good a crop from the garden as you get from the field."

"All right," he accepted the challenge. "We'll just see about that."

The work of plowing went along slowly. There had been no rain for more than a week and this, coupled with the fact that the virgin sod was very hard to plow, made it necessary to rest the horses often. Day after day, however, the strip of grayish-black soil grew wider.

The first field was being laid out at some distance from the house. On the third morning after he had commenced plowing, Elias saw his wife coming toward him.

"I got so tired of being in the house," she said. "There was nothing to do, so I made some coffee and fixed up some bread."

"Fine!" he exclaimed, pleased. "We'll have a party right here."

He talked about the work, as always. It was a clear day, rather hot. She didn't seem to be listening to him.

"I'm going to come out and watch you work every day," she declared. "It feels kind o' lonesome in the house, especially when all the work's done up. When I ain't got any thing to do, I just get restless. It makes me feel queer to look out of the door and see no trees or farms anywhere, like it was back home. I guess I need company."

"Come around any time you want," he replied. "I like your company fine, and I like your lunches, too."

The horses had enjoyed a long rest. He placed the knotted reins over one shoulder and under the other arm, and started out, while Lizzie walked along behind him in the soft black furrow. The horses strained heavily at the tugs; the sod turned over in one long unbroken ribbon.

The sun was hot. When the horses needed another rest, the woman pointed back over the plowed land. "See how the heat just seems to be boiling in the air?" she asked. "It's getting time for another rain."

"It *is* pretty dry," he admitted. "We'll probably be getting a good soaker soon. It wouldn't hurt the plowing, that's sure."

"People out here are afraid of dry weather, I guess," she ventured, "at least, everybody I've talked to since we left home had something to say about it."

"Oh, there's dry weather here just as there's dry weather at home now and then. It isn't any worse here than most other places, I guess," he replied easily. Then he added, "We can't afford to have dry weather this year, Lizzie; we won't have big crops anyway, and we'll need everything we can get so's to pull through the winter in fair shape." He smiled. "It's a kind o' gamble—starting out farming. But we'll make it."

X

The weather continued hot as day followed day. The sky was always clear, of a deep, clean blue in the mornings, thinning out into haziness as the sun attained the zenith. Now and then, toward afternoon, huge, billowy clouds with ragged white edges sailed up out of the southern horizon, becoming darker as they climbed higher. They passed over silently, marked by fleeting shadows on the earth and swam away into the unknown regions of the north.

The young farmer worked his horses more carefully now, as the poor brutes could hardly pull the plow through the dry, flinty soil. While they rested, his eyes turned often toward the horizon; out of the shadowy purple there a bank of cloud would have to grow soon. On all sides, the face of the prairie was burned to a thin brown. The heat struck back from the soil almost fiercely and quivered upward to the empty white sky. Again the man's eyes were drawn to the horizon, and still there was nothing but the thin purple haze that shielded the distances.

At first Lizzie came often to where he was working. She followed his glance. "Do you think it looks like rain?" she asked, in an unvarying formula. And always he replied, reluctantly, "Not much, I guess."

The horses, what with scanty feed and the strain of the heavy work, were becoming so lean that their hides were stretched tightly over their ribs. Elias decided that he would work them only in the mornings. After that, they were allowed to find what grazing they could. The animals always went to the lower land along the creek where the grass was green.

In the afternoons, Elias managed to find work to take up his time. There was much to do about the house, and the garden had to be fenced. His wife, who had become more silent since the hot weather had set in, now became more cheerful and was with him all of the time that he spent near the house.

"Elias," she said one morning at breakfast, "tomorrow's the Sunday for the minister to be at the church. You know, we promised we'd come. I thought," she spoke apologetically, "that if we'd take the whole day for the trip and have dinner with the Andersons, it wouldn't be too hard on the horses."

"Sure," Elias spoke heartily, "we'll go."

After the meal, he went to the small barn, where he was building a makeshift addition in which to house the poultry they expected to purchase in a short time. Once out of sight of the house, he stared anxiously at the sky. Not a cloud! His face seemed older now, with its uneven growth of beard, but there was the wistful look of the boy in the gray eyes. The wind held steadily from the southwest, already warm, although it was early in the morning.

At mid-morning Lizzie came with the lunch. "Did you see that bank of clouds in the north?" she asked excitedly.

"No." He walked quickly out of the shed. She joined him. Low on the northern horizon, large, puffy thunder caps seemed to have fallen in together and were rolling rapidly higher. Below them, there was a broad belt of black.

The man laughed delightedly. "Now that looks like rain to me!" he exclaimed. "Didn't I say it would rain soon? It isn't too late for us. A good shower will just make things start fine in the new ground."

"Well, it hasn't rained yet, so far's I can see. I'll celebrate after it's wetter than it is now."

He looked at her in mock reproach. "You'll see," he announced happily, "it'll just pour down." Then he added, "Let's go inside and have the lunch, and when we get out again, it'll be a sort o' surprise to see how high the storm is."

They said little while they ate the thick slices of bread and brown sugar, and drank their coffee. Elias raised his head in a listening attitude. There was a far-away muttering that grew alternately stronger and fainter but never quite died away. "It's thunder!" he exclaimed. "Now we'll have rain sure. Let's go outside and look." He almost dragged her behind him through the low door.

The storm had risen swiftly and its base, though no longer black, was broader, and of a solid gray. The advance guard of broken, rolling clouds was almost at the zenith, its edges clear-cut against the sunny blue sky. The grumbling thunder grew heavier. The clouds reached the sun, rolled over it, and the world was plunged into a twilight. Now swift patterns of lightning thrusts played constantly against the dark northern sky. Broad belts of mist appeared against the face of the storm, lengthening out to the earth.

"It's raining out there!" cried Elias.

The wind had died down in the early part of the morning. Now it suddenly came to them from the north, in short, sharp gusts, cool and wet. The lightning cut more sharply, the thunder rolled more ponderously through the sky. Suddenly lightning crackled all around them and a terrific crash of thunder followed immediately. As though this had shaken the clouds, the rain came down, in large splashing drops at first, and then in level sheets that sent the man and woman flying to the shelter of the house. They stood at the open door and watched the downpour. Thunder roared above them. The breeze had become a lashing tempest that drove the rain almost horizontally.

The thunder became more distant as the shower drew over and advanced to the south. The rain subsided, came back with a sudden burst, and then stopped again. The horizon in the north showed a widening rift of clear sky. In a short time the sun reappeared, shining down with an amazing light upon the wet earth.

"It looks greener already," Lizzie declared.

"Just wait a few days, and then we'll see what this has done to our crops," declared the man. Hand in hand, like two children, they walked outside past the barn, out upon the prairie. The very air was joyous. Near and far the song of meadow larks rang over the refreshed land. The birds flew in low, beating flight from one tall weed to another, where they perched precariously long enough to fill the air with an utter abandon of melody.

"It's funny, maybe," Elias said quietly, "but there's something in this that makes me feel almost—well—queer." His face was rapt. Then he looked down, met her serious gaze, and smiled.

"You say sort o' funny things sometimes, 'lias," she said, her blue eyes fixed curiously on his face. "I guess it's because the rain makes you feel good just now."

"Yes," he replied. "Sure it is."

As they walked back to the house, the woman ventured, "Are you going to plow this afternoon?"

"Yes. The rain will be pretty well soaked in by that time, and there's as much to plow as I can handle." Then he paused, and asked abruptly, "Why?"

"Oh, you see," she spoke diffidently, "I guess the horses can't stand the trip to town tomorrow if you use them in the field this afternoon."

"No, that's right," he agreed. He saw the disappointment in her face. It struck him suddenly that there was much of the child in her. She could not conceal her emotions, and her face, although often wistful to the point of blankness, yet betrayed her.

"Well," he said noncommittally, "there's a lot of other work that can be done, too, and plowing can wait. I promised you we'd go to church tomorrow, and we'll go." His face brightened. "I'll tell you what we can do!" he exclaimed. "You can do some more planting in the garden, and I'll dig up cottonwoods along the crick and set them in near the house. We want to get the trees started just as soon as we can."

It was a way of making work seem a game, and she smiled in happy agreement.

By the time dusk came on, ten trees had been planted so that they made a square about the house. They seemed nothing so much as tufted sticks stuck into the ground. Beyond, to the south of the house, a carefully leveled section of the plowed ground showed what had been done in the garden. They went to bed when there was still a last touch of red in the west.

It was at an early hour next morning that the wagon rolled down the slope from the house to join the trail. After they had traveled a quarter of a mile, they came to the shallow ruts which marked the trail, and turned south. The woman sat beside the man on the high spring seat, her feet resting on the edge of the wagon-box. The early morning breeze was cool, and her thin face, under the little, black straw hat with its straight, narrow brim, took on a tinge of color. Beside her, also with his feet resting on the wagon-box, Elias gave his attention to the team, which responded to the freshness of the morning and the long rest they had enjoyed by breaking into an awkward gallop now and then. The man's face, freshly shaven, was a deep, burned red. His felt hat was set forward at a slight angle.

The sun had not risen when they started, and a soft grayness lay over the prairie. The thudding of the horses' hoofs was muffled now, as the ground was springy after the rain. Slowly the grayness in the east became whiter and paled into a thin blue at the zenith. There was a sudden rushing sound, and one of the horses swerved slightly as a prairie chicken sprang into the air and, alternately sailing with stiffly set wings and then rising as its wings beat frantically, flew away to the west. The band of light in the east became a soft pink, deepening into orange until the edge of the sun appeared above the low crest of a far-away ridge. With the light came life. The song of the meadow lark sounded in the air. The wind seemed to lose something of its steadiness and swirled here and there among the stiff prairie grasses.

When they were halfway, the trail suddenly became dry.

"Guess we were pretty lucky," remarked Elias. "It didn't rain a drop out here."

It seemed that the day became hot at once. Once more the prairie took on its aspect of unrelieved, withered brown.

The Andersons greeted them heartily upon their arrival. The horses were placed in the barn, and then the four made their way to the white church which stood a short distance up the road.

There were some twenty-five people in the church. Their stiff attitudes seemed spectral in the dim light that came through the leaded windows, stained at the top. All turned, however, and watched the strangers advance up the aisle.

The minister, a tall, lean man, rose abruptly from his chair behind the pulpit, and the services began. First there was the singing of a hymn, followed by a long, dolorous prayer, and then, for almost an hour, the sermon.

Irresistibly, Elias thought of the church at home, and of his father. The man would have the family pew to himself now. Elias abruptly turned his attention to the preacher, but his mind wandered. The quietness of the church, the dimness, the new faces about him—all these quickened his imagination. Lizzie and he hadn't gone to church for quite a while, he thought to himself, rather seriously, and maybe they'd better go regularly after this. Of course, his father had been a crank when it came to church going, but that was all over now. It was fine to sing the hymns, and he felt restful here, even though he didn't listen to the preacher.

After the services, Sunday school was held, and as the Andersons attended, Elias and Lizzie followed them. In the interval, they met the other people. The introductions were made casually, but the responses invariably were hearty. The minister was particularly friendly.

"You folks come out every time we have church," he urged. "We need you here."

"Oh, we're going to, every time, ain't we, 'lias!" Lizzie replied quickly, looking at her husband.

His face was impassive. "Yes, if the weather stays good," he answered in a matter-of-fact tone. The minister smiled benignantly at him. Then, as he was teacher of the class, the preacher took up his position in front of the members.

The teacher taught by asking questions and by answering them himself. To Elias, the questions seemed absurdly simple, and the fact that the others could not answer them gave him a feeling of superiority. When the minister asked him a question, in a perfunctory tone, he answered it at once. There was a stir of surprise, and the teacher seemed quite taken aback. A warm glow went through Elias.

He saw that Lizzie's face wore a pleased expression. It gratified him; and yet, it was irritating. She shouldn't show what was in her mind so easy. A few moments later, when another member shook his head mutely to a question, the minister turned confidently to Elias, who answered correctly again.

"Gosh," observed Anderson in a low tone as the class was dismissed, "you sure know a mighty lot about the Bible."

"You certainly must come every time there's services," insisted the minister, shaking hands again. "You'll be a real addition to the flock."

Lizzie took her husband's arm with a certain attitude of proprietorship that made him draw away slightly. "We'll see, Mr. Miner," he said uncomfortably. "We'll be here when we can."

Outside, in the hot sun of noon, the men formed in one group, and the women in another. Among the men, the talk was all about the weather. Elias talked freely with them. Finally the groups broke up. Elias and Anderson walked down the road to the house, followed by the women.

After the Sunday dinner, while the women washed the dishes, the men took chairs out on the small porch and smoked. Later, the women carried out chairs and joined them.

"Everybody's gettin' all wrought up about the dry spell," observed the storekeeper, lazily drawing at his pipe.

"It's that way every summer, seems to me," said his wife placidly. "Even the folks that's been here quite a while keep on talkin' weather till they're blue in the face. I can't see what's the use. Talkin' won't make things go along any better."

"Maybe not, but weather's the thing that makes or breaks people out here, and they got a lot of respect for it. Just see how it is now: one more week o' this and not one half of the men who was at church this mornin' would have enough laid by to get through the winter in halfway decent shape, and those that did have something would light out for the East. That's the way it's been gain' for years and years. And in a way I pity these people like all get-out." His voice rose. He knocked the ashes from his pipe vehemently. "This ain't much of a life," he said gloomily. "You know mighty well, Dora, that if it hadn't o' been that I just kept on lendin' money in dribbles to the down-an'-outers so that we never had anything ourselves, we'd not be here today. It's a doggone country."

There was a silence.

Elias cleared his throat uneasily. "Why, we had a fine rain yesterday," he said, trying to make his voice cheerful. "I guess the dry weather here won't last either."

"You were lucky," returned Anderson. "But the summer ain't over yet."

"Don't listen to him!" cried his wife. "He's always like that— always doggoning the country, and if he had a good chance to go away, he'd stay right here."

The conversation turned to other matters. The women drew their chairs to the other end of the porch and talked in low tones. Anderson watched them for a time, then glanced at Elias, and smiled. The young farmer smiled back perfunctorily.

They started back home early in the afternoon. As usual, they did not talk much, but when they came to the country where rain had fallen, Elias said vehemently, "Carl Anderson only sees the dark side of things! Why, just look around and see how green everything is after there's been a shower."

"It's fine when it rains," Lizzie agreed uncertainly. Then she added, "If it gets bad, maybe your pa will get over being mad about us marrying and will want us to come back home."

"No!" Elias exclaimed sharply. "I told you before that we'll not go back. For one thing, he'll not want us on his farm and, for another, I'll not go back. We're going to stick it out here. Let the dry weather come! It'll take a mighty lot o' hard luck before I'll get down and crawl back. Anyway, rain or not, I like this country better all the time, and we're going to stay here. And," he finished, as sharply as he had ever spoken to her, "I wish you wouldn't bring in my father again. We haven't anything to do with him."

She did not speak once for the remainder of the trip.

The horses plodded heavily along. The air was warm and still. Over the horses, swarms of gnats eddied, now and then swept away by a random breeze. At last the house came into view.

That evening he said to her, "You mustn't care so much about what I said this afternoon, Liz. I meant it, but I just wanted you to know that we were going to see it out here, and that we wasn't going back."

Her face remained troubled. "It may get to be pretty bad," she said, looking away from him, "and we're all alone. Anything could happen to us, and nobody'd know about it."

He laughed reassuringly. "Nothing so awful terrible can happen to us that couldn't happen anywhere else," he railed. And then, awkwardly as ever, he bent down to kiss her.

XI

For a week after the rain, the green marvel of spring lay on the prairie. The days were hot, but the heat seemed to be gathered into the soft carpet of grass and did not strike back. The distances, which had been hard and purple white in the time of drought, again became mistily blue. A new life had come up out of the soil; birds flew from the willow thickets at the edge of the stream to feed in the upland country. Noondays were no longer sullen, but the hour when the sun stood at the zenith had the silence of a dream, full of color, faintly touched by a universal chorus of humming insect life. Through the long afternoon, there was nothing to mark the passage of time but intangible shading of tint into deeper tint as the sun imperceptibly moved on into the west. The vividness of the morning passed into the drugged whiteness of noon, and then, with the coming of early evening, all the color came back to the earth, not sparkling, as in the morning, but subdued and sleepy. As gray misted the east, clear green entered the field just vacated by the sun. Afterwards, when the sun halted for a time on the black edge of the world, a flush swept up into the sky, drew back slowly into a line of red on the horizon, and finally died away.

Two weeks passed, and no rain came. The grass was no longer green, and a thin brown covered the earth. Day after day passed, and the heat seemed to feed itself, so that a hot day was the prophecy of a hotter morrow. The silence deepened; the comradely birds were gone; only the rising and falling cadence of crickets in the narcotic heat gave a pulse of progress into what, otherwise, would have seemed nothingness.

The man had not shaved since the time they had been in town. A heavy, but uneven growth of dark stubble, burned to a black-red, added a new element to his face. The gray eyes seemed to be set deeper into their sockets, and as dry day succeeded dry day, they took on a troubled stare.

What color and charm there had been in the woman faded quickly. For hours her face was blank. While the man kept up a useless pretense of work, she stood framed in the little doorway of the house, immovable, staring out always to the east. The birth of a cloud at the horizon was watched eagerly, almost furtively, and then, when it attained its size and sailed away from its earthly moorings and moved, mockingly, into the sky, the old weariness returned to her face.

And yet, they did not talk about the drought after it had once resolved itself into reality. The business of life, reduced to mere existence as it was, a marking of time, went on. They got up early in the morning; they worked, if any possibility of work presented itself; they ate their meals; and then they went to bed again.

Now and then there was a promise of rain. Swift prairie storms formed on all sides, and twice the clouds reached past mid-heaven before the perverse wind, sweeping down at right angles to its course, spattered a few large drops down in derision, and shouldered the storm away.

"It's raining somewhere," the farmer remarked with a queer laugh, the second time this occurred, "some place where it can't do any good."

She simply looked at him, bewildered when he laughed, and he strode away.

That evening, after they had finished supper, they stood outside as the sun went down. The sun flared redly between the black fragments of the afternoon's thwarted storm. The air was heavy and murky. Monstrous cloud-dragons were drawn against the smouldering fire of the sunset, phantasms without being, remote, vaguely threatening, finally blurring away.

Their faces were set to it sullenly. The woman turned toward the man and placed her hand on his arm. He turned quickly.

"Let's go back, 'lias," she said, and her voice was that of a child that knows its wish can be granted easily if only the parent will be kind. "I can't stand it here. I'll go crazy. Day in and day out I stand looking around, trying to see something, and there's nothing to see, except the sky. It'll make me crazy. If there was trees, or houses,— or anything, why, it wouldn't be so bad. Let's go back home!"

At first his face had been without expression, half averted. When she finished, he turned to her. The dimming light showed the burning anger in his face, an anger made more primitive by the dark growth of beard and the whiteness of his staring eyes.

"Oh, stop your whining!" he commanded in a heavy voice. "Do you hear? Stop your whining! Haven't I got enough without having you act like that? All day long you're nothing but so much wood. Why can't you be alive!" His voice rose. He stepped closer to her, so that his face was near hers. "I told you once that I wasn't going back, not if all Hell tried to bake me out o' this. Now, d'you hear?" There was sick hate in his eyes; they ached in his head. Her face was stupid. He could have struck her. Then, slowly, an expression of awakening came into her eyes; there was hate mirrored there— hate and utter horror. His own hate seemed to draw out of him in a wave. He felt nauseated and sick.

He took her arm. She flinched back. "Don't be scared," he said gruffly, and then he added, "We won't get anywhere by being fools."

They returned to the house. He lighted the lamp, and they seated themselves on the two straight-backed chairs, one on each side of the little table. He rested his elbows on the boards, his face pressed on the upturned palms of his hands. After an interval he looked up at her. His eyes were wide and bloodshot.

"You better go to bed," he directed, as though he were speaking to a child.

Tears rolled down her cheeks, and she cried whimperingly. He crossed over to her.

"I've been sort o' wild, Liz," he spoke in a low tone. "See, I promise you never to be that way again. It's not worth it. We—I was just excited and I didn't know what I was doing. You just forget about it and go to bed. Everything will go all right."

Again the strange impassiveness that was a natural mantle over her was drawn away, and she clung to him. When she was aroused, she was like a child, he felt. "There, there," he said soothingly, "there, there, don't carry on so. I'll be good to you, Liz, after this. I'll make it up to you some way or other. Now you better go on to bed. I'm going to stay up for awhile. I don't feel like sleeping."

Smiling, he picked her up in his arms and carried her, unprotesting, into the adjoining room.

Before he left he said, in a new, gentle voice, "You're not mad at me now, Liz, are you?"

"No," she whispered, after a long silence. "No, 'lias, but I don't know what to think any more."

They stood there without saying a word, her head against his shoulder. At last he said, "You better go to bed now. You're tired. I want to stay up a while longer, just sort o' think things over."

She sighed submissively, and he left the room.

Once again he took his place at the table. The room was still. The dim yellow light of the lamp brought only duskiness to the bare walls. Against the black windows, heat lightning flickered and died. The air was heavy and motionless. The man had gone to his former position, his body sagging, his face hidden in his hands.

It seemed to him there, with his mind tense, racing aimlessly, that all the world had narrowed its confines to this new land, and all the miles of empty, sweltering prairie came to a focus in this small house. There was a fever in his blood, a slow burning that pervaded his mind with blackness. "What's there to do?" came again and again, a monotonous refrain. There was no escape from the maze into which he had wandered. He'd never go back East, never! And when he had reiterated that, his mind had nothing more to grasp. All that was left was to stay here. But what about Lizzie? There was no irritation now when he thought of her, only a queer dumb wish that she might be different in some way. To himself, he thought, "I wish there was something of the man about her." She got weak when she ought to get mad. So his thoughts wandered on, now stowing down to dull discomfort, now racing on to maudlin, desperate situations.

The lamplight was dying down; the room was filled with the smoke of a charring wick. Elias arose heavily, blew out the sickly remnant of flame, took off the chimney and extinguished the glowing edge of smouldering fire with his thumb and finger, and then stood, undecided, in the darkness. No use to go to bed, he decided, and after listening intently for any sound from the adjoining room where the woman was, he slipped quietly through the door into the night.

It was cooler out-of-doors. There was no wind, but a latent freshness came up from the ground. Out in the west and the south, faint broad lightning played ceaselessly, illuminating loose masses of spectral cloud.

He knew the ground thoroughly and walked forward in long strides. Instinctively, he wanted to get tired, so tired that he couldn't keep on thinking of this crazy tangle. But his mind would not be diverted. Always came back the question, phrased curiously, as it had been when it first came, "What's there to do?" Then, with weariness, a stubbornness grew in him. There was nothing for him to do; it was simple—all they had to do was to keep on and not get excited. He didn't want to leave.

The walk was beginning to tell on him. He breathed deeply, and the intolerable weight seemed to be lifted from him. Slowly the mood faded out, and he felt a queer wonder at what had passed. It all seemed fantastic now, incredible. Why, nothing was wrong. How could he ever have acted that way? He sat down, almost cheerful, and stretched out on the ground.

The lightning became weaker and weaker. A fitful, wandering breeze, filled with an exhilarating coolness, touched him now and then. It was from the northwest. "It'll be better tomorrow," he thought happily, "more livable." The breeze steadied into an even pressure of wind. The sky, which had been murky, now suddenly grew lighter, crisper. Stars stood out more sharply, white points in a light blue dusk. It was fine now, he thought drowsily.

When he awakened, it was still dark. For a moment he was bewildered. Remembering, he walked toward the house, with the drunkenness of sleep still upon him. When he entered the room where his wife was, her regular breathing told him that she had not known of his absence, and in a few minutes he was beside her, asleep.

The drought continued, but the weather had turned cooler. August noons were hot, but the nights were refreshing. Day after day wore itself out. There were things to do. The horses were able to turn over a few long strips of the virgin sod now and then, and the work could be drawn out, so that the time passed. The woman did what there was to do in the house and, as before, stood often in the doorway.

The life had a curious effect upon the man. During the long rests he gave the horses when plowing, queer thoughts came into his mind. One day, unbidden, the words of his father returned. "Sow the wind, and reap the whirlwind." He wondered about it hazily. How could he have sown the wind? It wasn't wrong that he had married Lizzie, was it? That was all that he had done. And this dry weather wasn't his punishment especially. All the people in this country were going through the drought. This train of thought came back again and again. There was something about it that suited his frame of mind. It was as though he were guilty of something he did not know, and that something dark impended, a whirlwind. In the evenings, his mind turned into these channels of speculation. He and Lizzie rarely talked; there was nothing to say. While the woman sat idle, with hands folded in her lap, he tried to work out the matter in his mind. He sat at the table, his face pushed forward, his eyes wide, as though he could clarify the mystery by physical exertion. One night he went to a box in the bedroom and brought out a Bible. He read it for a long time. After that, every evening, he spent his time in this way.

Twice in that month there were rains, but they were light, and the water simply steamed away. The man and the woman went to town once to get a load of supplies. Anderson told them dreary stories of families that were "up against it." The whole country seemed to be burned out, and many people were leaving, that is, those who had enough money to go back. Anderson had looked at the Vaughns with speculation.

"You still think you'll stick it out?" he asked.

"Sure," Elias replied. "We came here to live—and we're still alive."

Anderson appeared to be irritated. "You're alive all right," he agreed, "but both of you look about ten years older than you did when you come."

"It was time for us to grow up, I guess," Elias replied imperturbably. "We'll look better after we have a whalin' big crop next year."

Anderson smiled cynically but said no more. He helped to carry the things to the wagon and invited the two young people to spend the following Sunday at his home. Lizzie accepted the invitation eagerly.

As they were unloading the wagon upon their arrival at the house, Elias said, after a long, preoccupied silence, "Well, if it comes to a pinch, we can get through the winter on what we have. We won't starve."

"Is our money all gone?" his wife asked, in a frightened voice.

"No, but it's going pretty fast," he replied. "You see, I've got to keep something to finish paying for the land. If next year pans out good, we won't have to think so much about money."

Summer waned imperceptibly. The face of the prairie was always the same; the cold nights, with a touch of frost, could not alter the brown slopes; the drought had already accomplished destruction.

It was on a morning in late September that the man went to the creek and found the pool from which he had been getting water so low that he had to dig a pit in the sand of the creek-bed. The water in it rose slowly, until finally there was enough to fill the pail. As he walked up the slope, his mind was busy with plans for digging a shallow well near the creek so that there might be enough water for the stock. As he came to the head of the slope where

the house stood, he saw that a thin haze was drawing up from
the north. This struck him curiously, for it had been a cold night,
and the crisp northwest wind held no suggestion of rain. He went
inside and placed the pail of water on a rough-hewn bench under
the east window.

After breakfast, he remarked casually, leaning back in his chair,
"The water's about gone out of the crick, Liz; guess I'll have to dig
down for it. That is," he added, "if it doesn't rain. When I came
in the house the sky looked sort o' funny in the north—it looked
just like a fog coming up. Guess there isn't much chance of getting
wet today, though." He scraped his chair back, got up, drank a
dipperful of water, and went outside. At his sharp exclamation, the
woman joined him.

The haze in the north had deepened to a dull gray wall that was
advancing rapidly. A stronger sweep of wind from the northwest
brought the acrid smell of smoke.

"The prairie's on fire!" the man exclaimed sharply, "and the
horses are out along the crick somewhere. You stay here, Liz, and
I'll go after them." He ran down the slope toward the stream, while
the woman stood stock-still where he had left her.

Fortunately, Elias knew that the horses would be just below
the bend of the stream, where the grass had attained a fair growth
before the dry weather came. They ran before him docilely. When
he had driven the animals into the barn, he closed the doors
without putting on their halters, after making sure that the cow
and the calf were on their side of the board partition.

The woman was standing near the house, her face to the north.

The smoke was heavy in the air now and was already shading
the sunlight. For a moment the man stood beside her. The gray
wall had become darker and no longer looked like fog. It seemed

to puff forward in great billows that rolled sullenly upwards. When the pall thinned now and then, as the wind grew stronger, the gray was tinged with yellow.

"You get all the sacks you can find," he commanded the woman, "and have them wet. I'll try to start a back-fire."

He lighted the grass in a dozen places to the north of the buildings, but these fires moved slowly. As he worked, with his head down, he felt the increasing heat in the wind. Then, when he straightened up, to find his efforts to start a back-fire unavailing, he found the woman beside him.

"Guess we're in for it," he said calmly. "Maybe you better go in the house."

She shook her head. "No," she said in a strained voice. "Let me stay here. Tell me what to do, and I'll help."

"We'll try to stop the fire on the west side of the plowed land," he said decisively. "I'll work there, and you stay back here and put out any sparks that fall on the house." He took some wet sacks from the ground and strode swiftly to the plowed strip.

The smoke was so heavy now that it bit into his eyes. Lurid flames, showing duskily red through the smoke, swept upward and finally broke free in darting pinnacles that played weirdly against the sky. A faint humming sound deepened, the sound of a far-away strong wind, broken by sharp crackling. The heat was blistering. Then, as though the line of smoke were lifted by some signal, the fire broke into view, leaping toward the man with an unbelievable rapidity. The air was full of charred grass, smoke, and sparks. The heat seemed intolerable. Elias ran back and forth, slapping at small fires that started on all sides of him. The smoke burned his throat and bit into his eyes until he was forced to keep them closed most of the time. Then the fire was upon him. The steady roar had broken into a host of sharp sounds; there was a steady crackling on all sides, intensified whenever the flames caught at some dense patch of dead growth.

Slowly he was forced back. He fought savagely, his breath coming in great, rasping sobs that seared his lungs. When the smoke thickened, he choked, and retreating a few paces, placed the wet sack over his face.

He remembered Lizzie, and a wave of fear swept through him. If the fire was behind him, where she was, she would be helpless. He turned his back to the flames and stumbled toward the house. The air was so heavy with smoke that he did not see her at once. Then he caught a glimpse of a faded blue dress and found her on her knees, a few yards from the doorway.

He threw a wet sack over her head and, after commanding her hoarsely to keep her face near to the earth, went on with his fight against the fire. The flames had disappeared, but the smoke was so dense that he was forced to throw himself on the ground to avoid suffocation.

It seemed to the man that a great space of time had passed, but it could have been measured in minutes. After a while the smoke cleared away, and he saw the fire retreating in the south. In half an hour he had extinguished all smouldering clumps of grass. The buildings were untouched—miraculously, it seemed to him. He hurried back to the woman and found her sitting up. Her eyes stared redly from a black face.

"Well, it's over, Liz," he said, "and we're not burned out."

She did not stir. The red eyes seemed to stand out of her head, glassy and wide. He touched her. She cringed away, moaned, and fell soddenly back in a faint. He lifted her and carried her to the house.

All afternoon she remained in this semi-conscious state. The man sat beside the bed. Her face was clean now, for he had washed away the grime of the smoke. He looked at her dully; the cheeks, always thin, were sunken, and the cheekbones stood out prominently. Over the narrow forehead a few wisps of light yellow hair straggled.

A fear came to him as he sat there in the utter silence and studied the wasted face of his wife. Just a few months ago she had been *so* different; then she had expected romance and excitement; she had trusted him to lead her safely through life. Things had become black for her. His eyes drew away from the pale, immobile features of the woman and strayed to the small window.

The face of the prairie was changed. The long vista of brown had turned black, and a thin mist of smoke hung in the still, hot air. The sky was blue-white. Again the sense of the power of this country came to him: its emptiness, and the vague threat of disaster that seemed to hang over him. It was a world by itself; he and the wasted woman lying on the bed were man and wife living in an unpeopled region, alone, fighting defensively against an immeasurable strength. Curiously, the thought dispelled the gloomy mood. His face, still grimy, the face of an unkempt savage, grew hard.

The woman stayed in bed for two days. Then, when she was once more able to go about the house, she seemed to be in a trance, so that she forgot the details of her work. Her expression made him look at her often; her eyes had the far-away quality of one who is puzzled. She did not seem to know most of the time when he was in the same room with her.

The fall rains started one afternoon in early October. All morning the dun sheet of cloud had been edging up from the north and east. At four o'clock it began to rain, not with the violence characteristic of the summer storms, but slowly, tentatively. That night, as he lay awake, listening to the roar of the rain on the roof, he remembered the evening in the spring when it had rained on the canvas of their wagon, the evening before they had made the dangerous crossing at the ford. It seemed unreal now, a part of a youth that was far away. The summer had been years long, and now he was old. There was no rebellion in his thoughts, but neither was there ecstasy. He listened comfortably to the rain, breathed deeply of the cool, wet wind that wandered into the room, and lived in the moment.

Toward the time of Indian summer, a boy was born. The woman was transformed. Her face was alight, her eyes eager. Elias worked about the house and waited upon her. The rains came often now; the black had been washed from the earth, and there was a thin misting of green where new grass defied the frost. The air was invigorating; every thing was alive. Depth had come into the woman's eyes, and her face was soft and quiet; the baby caught at the man's thumb with sprawling hands; the father forgot the past and went about the house with the glint of humor in his eyes, as though something funny and very pleasant persisted in his mind.

XII

The wet weather lasted well into November. Then the wind forsook
the east, traveled by tentative stages into the northwest, and, after
a few days of clear, crisp sunshine, it went overnight to the south.
Now the air was mellow, and the soft haze of Indian summer took
away the starkness of the land and bathed it in mists that gave
delicate tints to distant, sunny ridges.

Elias went on day after day with the plowing. At night, when
he had unhitched, he always looked at the long lines of sod that
had been turned during the day. At such times, when the westering
sun glinted on the smooth, waxy surface of the black ground, he
felt a curious emotion swelling within him. It was fine, the way
things were going, he thought. There was work to do now; he
could see what lay before him.

Often, especially in the afternoons, he would leave his team at
the end of a furrow and hurry to the house. There he would take
the child in his arms for a few minutes, swinging it gently. One
afternoon he exclaimed, in a voice of discovery, "Why, he looks like
you, Liz—blue eyes and all!"

A quick, half wistful smile came into her thin face. "Oh," she
said, with the delight of a child in her voice, "do you really think
so?"

"Sure," he said heartily. "He's just going to be you over again."

She broke into a queer, soft little laugh, and he looked at her
quickly, pleased. He gave her the boy and returned to his work. As
he walked to the plowed land, the cathedral peace of the golden,
silent afternoon fell upon him. He remembered Lizzie's laugh.
She smiled sometimes, he reflected, but she hardly ever laughed,
and the memory of her pleasure gave him a gladness that added a

119

pleasant tinge to the afternoon. If only she would get over those far-away spells she had, when she acted sleepy and forgetful. He took up the long ropes which served as reins, called cheerfully to the horses, and in a moment heard the steady tearing of the stubborn sod as it curled over in an endless black ribbon.

Indian summer ended abruptly. The morning was unusually warm, but the haze thickened slowly until, at midafternoon, the sunlight shone palely yellow through a thin murk. The wind suddenly came up from the north, in cold, wet gusts. By the time the man had finished milking, snow was swirling down. Winter was upon the land at last. Next morning the snow was still flying in steady sheets of tiny hard flakes. As far as eye could reach the undulating expanse of prairie was white, until it merged, indistinctly, with the stormy, indefinite horizon.

Their days were passed in a new peace. There was not much work to do, and the man spent most of his time in the house. They did not talk often; the woman found her life in the life of the child, and the man frequently spent an hour in the afternoon looking out upon the snow-covered prairie, dreaming, and planning for the future.

The child did not thrive, and his face had a certain dry pallor. Whenever the woman left him for a moment, the boy cried fretfully, even though the father walked up and down the small room, singing lustily old tunes which came back to him from his own childhood. In desperation, he finally took upon himself the work of preparing the meals, as the child would not be pacified when his mother was not with him.

"Just wait till he grows up," the man announced, half vexed and half laughing. "I'll make a man of him. He'll be a real farmer!"

The woman did not reply, apparently having fallen into one of her lapses when she seemed oblivious of everything except the baby.

They lived in unnoticed hardship. The house, unprotected on all sides, did not keep out the cold when the weather was stormy. Their food was simple and lacked variety. Still, they lived in quietness and peace, and the time slipped away unobserved. One evening, after they had finished supper, the man took down the Bible from the shelf and read a chapter aloud. It was something that his father had always done, and Elias had been uneasily conscious of a feeling that it was heathenish to get up from a table without a reading of the Scriptures. The woman took this incuriously, and her husband, relieved that she made no remark, made this a custom.

March vacillated between winter and spring. In the latter part of April, the weather settled. The man was out with the sun and worked until nightfall. The small grain was put in, and then, in May, the corn was planted. When the man worked in the field, the woman spent much of her time in the garden, while the child lay on his back on an old blanket nearby.

In June the wild roses came out in bloom and made a marvel of the prairie. Great banks of flowers, delicate pink against the surrounding green, made glowing spots of color everywhere. Wandering winds gathered up their fragrance and bore it idly away. The weather grew warmer, but the rains came in season, and the grain, a thin, spindly growth at first, stooled out and became of a rich, dark color. Finally it headed out. The corn had been laid by after two cultivations, and was waist-high.

"Nothing can come along now very well to hurt us," Elias announced to his wife. "We're sure to get a crop, and a big one, too. I never saw things grow the way they do out here. This ground's rich enough to last forever. By the time we've got all the crops in, we'll make out mighty good for the year."

The woman looked at him quickly. "Why,—" she began hesitatingly.

He looked at her inquiringly.

"I wonder if Joey and I could go home some time for a visit? I'd like awful well to have the folks see the baby. You see, Mrs. Anderson was telling me last Sunday after church that there's a stage running from Junction City now, and it wouldn't be so hard to get us there, would it?"

He was silent for a moment. Then he said quietly, "We haven't the money now, Liz, you know. Do you care much waiting till next year? I've been buying barbed wire and posts for fencing, and then the cow I bought last spring—it all took up a lot of cash. After we sell the crops, I can fix it, I guess. Is that all right?"

She nodded, but he saw a weary disappointment in her face. For the rest of that day his expression was preoccupied.

The dry weather did not come until the small grain was ready for cutting. Again the sun burned down, and again the heated air wavered upward. The ground, however, was filled with moisture, and the prairie growth did not die down. There was much work to do, and the man had no one to help him in the field. The small patches of rye, oats, and wheat were cut with a scythe and then tied into bundles by twisting ropes of straw. It was hot work, but the man made no complaint.

One noon he came into the house and found the woman seated at the window with the baby on her lap. She looked at him in surprise.

"Why, I didn't know it was so near dinner-time," she sighed. "We've been sitting here trying to keep cool. It's so awful hot in here."

"Good corn weather," he remarked cheerfully. "Let it be hot and dry now! It almost seems that I can see that the corn's a little higher each morning."

"But it's so awful hot," she repeated, sighing. "It's roasting hot in the house, and when we go outside, there ain't any shade—it's hot there, too."

"Guess it's pretty bad, all right," he conceded. Then he added, "You stay right there, and I'll take care of dinner."

As he went about preparing the simple meal, the man looked often at the woman beside the window. For the first months after the baby was born, there had been a certain light in her face, something of the wistful girlishness that had appealed so much to him before they were married. With the coming of summer, it seemed that all eagerness of life left her. Her washed-out blue eyes had the look of contemplation that is without thought. It was as though she were going through an incomprehensible ritual, as though life had no meaning for her. Her love of the child did not seem entirely like that of other women for their children, women as he remembered them back home. They had caught up their children heartily, had crooned over them, had laughed at them and had scolded, half humorously. Lizzie never smiled at the small child. She held him close to her, intensely. She had become increasingly silent, often staring down at the little face that was so much like her own, with its blue eyes, light hair, and thin cheeks.

When the meal was on the table, the baby commenced crying fretfully as soon as the mother rose from her chair at the window.

Without saying anything, she resumed her former position, and the man ate the meal by himself. His thoughts remained in the same channel. It had been a long, hot morning, and now he felt tired. He kept thinking, impersonally, of the woman and the child. The fact that the child always drew back from him and cried for his mother now seemed to have a new significance to him. Maybe they weren't like him. They understood each other; they didn't seem to understand him. A queer sense of loneliness came over him, a loneliness that had lurked at the back of his mind often in the evenings of the last months. Everything was going along as well as could be: the crops were practically safe, and it was going to be a big year. Still, he felt that they did not care for this country as he did. His growing discomfort became too sharply conscious and he tried to throw it off. It would be all right; Lizzie and the baby could have a real visit back home next summer when the hot spell came on.

That afternoon, he suddenly began to feel giddy. He unhitched the horses, unharnessed them, and turned them loose. Then he went to the house.

"It's a touch of the sun, I guess," he said, trying to speak cheerfully.

"Oh, what can we do?" Lizzie asked helplessly. "There isn't a doctor anywhere around. We're all alone out here, and if you get sick—" Her voice trailed away, but there was a definite expression in her face now, an expression of dread.

"It's nothing," he answered quickly. "You mustn't get scared right away. I'll take things easy for a day, and then you'll see that I'll feel as good as ever."

His slight illness seemed to stimulate her. She wrung out cloths in water and placed them on his forehead in an effort to alleviate the headache. Every half hour she asked him how he felt, and invariably he declared that he felt a little better. After two days of this idleness, he was once more back in the field. There were oats lying loose on the ground, and he was in a fever lest rain should come before he had tied the grain into bundles and set them into shocks.

Summer waned into a long autumn; again the nights were chilly, and only at midday was the sun hot. The corn had long since attained its growth. Now it was ripe. Every day the man went to the ten-acre field and looked, half hypnotized, at the tall stalks with the heavy ears hanging down, with here and there a yellow tip of the grain showing out of the thick, fat husks. There was something opulent about the sight; more than any other grain, to him, well grown, thoroughly matured corn gave a sense of the richness of the land.

The pressure of the work remained the same. Long before, the woman had told him that another child was coming. Her strength seemed to be almost gone. He took care of the housework and, lest it interfere with the labor in the field, he rose earlier in the morning, long before dawn, and worked until dark. After the evening meal, he cleared away the dishes, and then they went to bed. He fell into sodden sleep as soon as he lay down.

After the first killing frost, the man stopped his work of plowing and started cutting and shocking the corn. The days were a marvel to him. The cool, quiet days seemed to feed a hunger that had been with him always. He did not examine his thoughts; he simply knew that, for him, life was full. Often he straightened from his back-breaking work, especially in the afternoon, and gazed out over the wide empty prairie country with wonder-filled eyes. His thoughts gathered character from this land.

The second child, a girl, was born in October. At once both the father and the mother saw that the daughter resembled the man. He was curiously moved by this; he had been lonelier than he had understood, and now that loneliness was gone. "She'll want to run around outside with me in a couple of years," he reflected happily. "I'll bet that she'll be me all over again. There'll be no keeping her in the house." Inwardly he pictured her as a hoydenish girl, a daughter who might have a touch of wildness in her, an untameable disposition, but who, at the same time, would go about the work with him and laugh at things in a comradely way. She was constantly in his mind.

It took a long time for the mother to gain enough strength to move about the house. Indian summer brooded over the prairie for two weeks, and then, by easier stages than the year before, gave way to early winter.

The man had worked half days trying to make the house more secure from the winter winds. It was of little avail. The weather settled down for a week of raw, damp cold. The baby took sick very suddenly. The woman held the child in her arms morning, noon, and night. The man stayed in the house, walking up and down the creaking floor. He could not leave them to go for assistance. If he could only get word to the Andersons, they would drive to Junction City for a doctor, but he didn't dare to leave the house for so long.

After four days of sickness, the child died. The man and the woman moved in a dazed silence. Now that it was all over, he had to leave his wife and boy, after all, to make arrangements for the funeral.

The baby was buried on a knoll near the stream. It was a cold day, with a thin, driving rain from the northeast. The Andersons and a few other people were there. They stayed until the service had been read, and then hurried away, as the weather threatened a snowstorm. The minister spoke to the Vaughns awkwardly, trying to give them comfort. The woman looked at him as though she did not understand what he was saying. Her husband, whose eyes had a strained, sick look, thanked him simply.

Life went on after that much as it had gone on before. There was always work for the man to do. It was following the death of his second-born, however, that silence became a habit with him. The stricken look remained in his eyes for a long time, and then, slowly turned to something inscrutable and quiet. The woman was as passive as she had been before. Her whole life seemed to be caught up in dumb love of the boy, Joey.

A week after the child had been buried, the farmer went out to the knoll and set a rude fence about the grave. It took him all day, for the frost was well down into the soil. He determined to set trees there in the following spring. It was getting dark when he finished. As he was about to leave, he saw Lizzie approaching, carrying Joey, who was bundled up until he resembled a woolly cylinder in her arms. The man waited for them to come up. She said nothing, but stared at the small mound of black earth.

The twilight of an early winter day hung in the air. In the west, the sunset was smoky red. A duskiness drew over it. The woman's face was held steadily toward the ground. The man's face was turned toward her, his shoulders bent forward. Seen against the dimming light in the west, he looked like one utterly tired.

It was almost dark, and a sharper chill came into the still air. "Come, Ma," the man said, reaching out awkwardly and taking her arm. "We better go back to the house now. It won't be good for you and Joey to be out in the cold so long."

She turned to him slowly. Her face was drawn and white in the semi-darkness. It was not blank now; instead, an intensity of expression was there that startled him. Suddenly she leaned against him and broke out into great, gasping sobs. He placed his arm about her. A queer tenderness for this woman came over him. He wanted to soothe her, talk to her as though she were a child, but the words would not come. Her grief was his grief, too, and the recollection of this girl-child who had looked like him strangled utterance in his throat.

"There, there," he said at last, huskily, "you mustn't cry like that, Lizzie. Don't cry." He patted her shoulder with his hand. "See, we must get over it. Next spring I'll set out some cottonwoods here, and we'll get wild roses to grow, and then it will be better." His words were without effect. The first violence of her sobbing had gone, but now she cried quiveringly, like a child that has sobbed itself to the verge of hysteria and is half exhausted. "Don't let it take you that way," he remonstrated. "It's just something we must get used to."

She drew away from him. "There," he said gently, "that's good. Now we'd better go to the house."

"I guess so," she answered dully. Then she turned to him and burst out, in a high, strained monotone "It's this country. Nothing can live here! It's always freezing cold or roasting hot, and there's nobody around to help. I wish—" Her words died out into labored crying again. In a half-strangled voice she repeated, "Nothing can live out here."

Finally he was able to persuade her to go with him to the house. He tried to carry the boy, but as soon as the child sensed that his mother was not carrying him, he commenced to wail, and Lizzie took him. It was dark now. Ahead of them the house stood dim and desolate.

Elias opened the door, lighted the lamp, and put fuel into the small stove.

"Just sit down and rest, Lizzie," he suggested. "I'll do up the chores as fast as I can and then I'll get supper ready."

"All right," she answered.

He left the house and went about the chores in the darkness. Everything was tranquil. The two cows were in a corner of the barn, tearing the ears of corn from an armful of stalks. In the one stall, the horses crunched the fragrant wild hay. It was strange, the man thought, that a sense of peace always came to him when he was here. But in the house there was a shadow. "I'll work and work," he resolved while he was milking. "We'll have things the way Lizzie wants them."

They ate their meal in the yellow light of the lamp. Now and then the woman gave the child bits of bread dipped in lukewarm coffee. Then they went to bed.

XIII

The news of bumper crops "out West" had traveled with that mysterious swiftness with which such news always travels; the handful of settlers had written letters to home folks, and for once the tone of the letters had not only been wistfully hopeful but also confident, sure. The information had gained ground. Left-at-home brothers had enlarged the golden prospects always inherent in a distant land, to cousins, and cousins had magnified the unparalleled crops of the romantic West to second cousins. Those in whom the blood stirred more than momentarily made plans. With the spring came prairie schooners, and in these canvas covered wagons were, for the most part, young married men and women whose eyes were aglow with half-formed dreams of the Adventure of Life in a new Land of Promise. Now, before them lay the Prairie, a land of soft, billowing green, touched, here and there, with the radiance of early flowers. There were few railroads in this country, few roads; the social contacts would not be those of the communities they had left; what crops were grown could not easily be marketed; in other years, there had been stories of drought, of grasshoppers. Nevertheless, they came; not because they saw the life that lay before them, but because this region satisfied that within them which longed for a new land, an undiscovered country. Even now, while the wagons creaked up long rises, they did not see the emptiness and the stillness that crowded them in upon themselves; their eager minds fashioned from the material of reality the age-old structure of human desire for freedom.

June had come with the promise of a fruitful year. Elias Vaughn, by dint of late plowing during the preceding fall, had added much to the cultivated part of his farm.

On a Sunday, when he worked at his chores in leisurely, after-breakfast fashion, he was brought to the door of the barn by the thudding sound of horses' hoofs. A team and buggy was approaching on the trail. Opposite the house, the team turned in sharply.

"It's the Andersons," Elias shouted to the woman, who had come out-of-doors. "Guess they'll be spending the day with us."

He could see her attitude change quickly. She turned and re-entered the house.

"Going to slick things up before they get here," Elias thought to himself. "That's the woman of it every time."

The horses came on the yard at a run, and Anderson drew them to a halt with a flourish, amid the audible, good-natured grumbling of his wife.

"He's just trying to show off," she cried, as Elias came up. "He's like a colt when he gets out on a trip."

The long, half lugubrious lines of her husband's weather-beaten face worked toward an expression of joviality.

"Ma ain't so skittish like she used to be," he volunteered, with an obvious wink at Elias. "If I'd kept the horses to a walk the way she wanted me to, we'd 'a' got here next week. A man can't listen too much to his wife if he wants to get anywhere." He jumped to the ground from one side of the buggy while Mrs. Anderson descended more carefully and with much deep breathing from the other.

Lizzie came from the house, leading Joey by the hand. Mrs. Anderson greeted her effusively. "You're looking real well," she said heartily. "You certainly have picked up this spring."

"I feel better," Lizzie replied simply. "I don't know how it is—last fall I thought that one more winter would be about all I could stand, but now I feel fine. You see, things are going better—people comin' in and so."

Mrs. Anderson leaned down and placed her hand on the boy's shoulder. "Ain't you goin' to shake hands with me?" she asked in a motherly, cajoling tone.

The boy did not answer, but drew away until he stood behind his mother.

"Scared, I guess," Lizzie said apologetically. "You see, nobody ever comes here."

"Sure, I know." Mrs. Anderson was all good nature. "He's lookin' better, too. His face ain't got that queer white it used to have."

"He ought to be better," the woman declared. "He's walking and digging around outdoors all day." Then she added, "But he never goes far from where I am."

When the men had unhitched the horses, they led them to the stream, and the women walked to the house.

"You saw the Meyers' place five miles back?" Elias asked, with a touch of eagerness in his voice.

"I saw where they're goin' to have their place," returned Anderson. "About all there's to see now is a lot of stuff scattered on the ground."

"They were over here for a while one morning last week," Elias volunteered. "Been married for ten-eleven years—both of 'em must be gain' on to thirty, although the woman looks quite a lot younger than the man. They didn't stay long. Didn't have the time, I guess. But we'll get to see them as much as we want when they get settled. I helped them out with some feed for the horses. They don't have much, but they're fine people. I'm mighty glad; it's been just like medicine for Lizzie. She just sort o' feels easy now that we've got neighbors."

"She had a hard time of it," Anderson remarked.

"Mighty hard," Elias agreed soberly. Then he added, "The Meyers say that new settlers are coming in almost every day, and that they're taking up land south of Hayes. Is that right?"

"Well—not every day," Anderson replied judicially. "But there's been quite a lot of 'em all right."

"I knew that this country was bound to fill up," Elias spoke complacently. "Just as soon as people back East hear how crops grow here, the place will be filling up fast. I can't say I'm anxious to have too many of them. Of course, it isn't going to be crowded in our neighborhood. This is pretty far from town, and there's that sandy strip just on the other side of the Meyers that nobody will want so long as they can get real black soil. Anyway, the country is filling up."

Anderson did not reply. Elias looked at him questioningly.

"Don't you think so?" he asked.

"Maybe they'll stay—and maybe not. Last year there was good crops, but the year before we were burned out, you know. Things look pretty fair for this year, but you can't tell how they'll turn out. Then, next year may be bad."

Elias grunted in cheerful disparagement. "You're one of the old settlers," he said, "and you always see the hard times that are past, and you can't see the good times that are coming."

The horses drank their fill at the stream and then were hobbled so that they might graze without straying.

"You sure are gettin' things into shape here," remarked the storekeeper. "You must've worked like a dog."

"Oh, I've always had to work, and I never liked it better than I do out here. Why, it makes it more exciting if there's always a chance that the crop may go big."

"Or burn up." Anderson smiled at his own perversity.

They looked silently up at the even green slope that ascended from the stream westward until it reached its greatest lift where the small house, its unpainted boards already appearing half dingy from the action of the weather, stood sharply cut against the soft, filmy blue of a mid-morning May sky. To the north of the house lay a large, irregular block of land in cultivation, more vividly green against the greenish-red color characteristic of the wild land even at its greatest verdancy. Nearer them, and northeast of the house, the small barn with its two rude additions stood a quarter way down the slope, the washed-out yellow of last year's straw thatch hanging down from the sides of the roof.

"I'll take you around after a while." Elias turned to his companion. "Maybe we'd better go see how the womenfolks are getting along."

"They'll be talkin'," observed his companion. "I ain't never known women to visit by keepin' still. It's all right, though. Dora will be more quiet on the way home. After I've been out for a day, I like to take it easy, and talkin' ain't my idea of loafin'."

Anderson had prophesied correctly. When they approached the house, they could hear his wife's voice.

"I'd like to show Carl around the farm, Lizzie. Is there anything I can do before we go?" Elias stood in the doorway and looked at the two women seated near each other in the straight-backed chairs, evidently engrossed in their conversation.

"No, no." Mrs. Anderson halted her conversation and waved her hand impatiently at him. "We don't want you men around. You clutter things up."

Elias smiled and returned to Anderson, who had taken out his knife and was cutting thin shavings from a piece of wood.

"You got the trees to growing, I see," he remarked, looking at the row of stripling cottonwoods, each with its bushy head of leaves.

"Got them started at last. You know, I put out trees that summer we got here, and they didn't take hold. Wrong time to put them in; I knew that at the time, but I thought there was a chance. I set these out last fall, and I guess they'll make it now they've a real start."

They walked slowly toward the barn. A few chickens had scratched hollows in the warm dust and were dozing in the warm sunlight. "I got them that last time I was in town for a load of stuff, you remember," he said, "and it was queer how mighty glad it made Lizzie. That same night I put them in the barn and the next morning when we were having breakfast, the rooster crowed. The funniest look came in Lizzie's face, just like she was on the edge o' crying. It made her think of the old farm back home, she said. It never struck me how quiet it was out here till we got the chickens. They liven things up a lot, and I believe that Lizzie just feels good whenever she hears them cackling. And then, we get a few eggs every day, and that helps out with us."

The barn was deserted. Anderson peered into the dimness of the interior, filled with the musty smell of the rotting straw thatch.

"You've got all the stock turned out, I see. No trouble to keep the stock in feed this spring."

"I picked up two head of cattle last fall," the farmer volunteered. "They were cheap, and I could just make it. I'll tell you, Carl, stock-raising is the thing for this country, and I'm going into it just as fast as I can. It takes money, but it's going to pay. Last year we had a good crop, and when I got to figuring how hard it would be to haul the grain after a year or so, it didn't take me long to see that feeding stock was the only idea."

Anderson nodded. "It's a gamble, but it's as good as any other out here."

Talk of crops and other farm matters occupied them while they walked around the fields of corn, oats, wheat, and rye. Then, by slow degrees, they turned back toward the house.

They had dinner upon their return. As they sat down, it came to Elias that the little room, which had always seemed to be dominated by the steady ticking of the clock on the shelf, took on a really festive appearance. The black building paper which was tacked in strips against the wall even seemed to add to this feeling of comfortable festivity.

While they ate, they talked. Anderson was still in a railing mood.

"You folks gone over all the news already?" he asked, directing the question to his wife.

"Guess we talked as much sense as you folks did," she returned.

"We men-folks always get the worst of it, don't we, Joey?" Anderson turned to smile at the small boy who, seated between his father and mother, was eating in furtive silence. The child's face filled with fear, and he stopped eating.

"There, there," Mrs. Anderson said, in that motherly tone that Elias liked to hear. "You're making the poor boy afraid."

Elias placed his hand lightly on his son's head. "A few more years and you and me'll both be farmers, won't we, Joey?"

The child still maintained his stricken attitude, and the talk went on to other matters until the meal was finished.

The Andersons left early in the afternoon. As the team trotted away, Elias turned toward his wife. She was gazing to the west, watching the team and buggy as it turned into the trail and swung south.

"Have a good day of it, Lizzie?" he asked.

She turned. There was a hint of color in her cheeks, and her eyes had an excited brightness. A wisp of hair had fallen down her forehead, and she brushed it back.

"It just seemed like old times," she answered. "I just enjoyed every single minute."

"I told you it would get nicer and nicer all the time, didn't I?" He placed an arm about her shoulder and smiled at her with a certain kindly superiority.

"Yes," she assented, drawing slightly closer to him, "it's getting to be nice now." Then she added wistfully, "But it was pretty bad, too."

He remembered sharply the baby girl who had died. "Yes," his tone was low, "it was bad enough."

The poignancy of their mood faded into quietness. They stayed outside for the rest of the afternoon, not talking a great deal. The light remained in her eyes, he noticed, and there was a suggestion of a smile about the thin, drawn-in lips.

The genial sun dipped farther and farther into the west, out of a field of blue into fields of green, yellow, rose, and red. Imperceptibly, the peace of night gathered over the land.

A few weeks after this, just as the small grain was coming into the milk stage, a dry wind blew steadily for three days. It came from the southwest. The nights were calm, but with the coming of daylight, a slow breeze freshened in half an hour into a steady roar of wind. The deep green of the small grain became withered and dusty. The long, broad leaves of the corn curled. After the third day, the weather became settled, but rain held off until a week later.

"It struck us at a bad time," Elias sighed, as he rose from his chair one morning after breakfast. "The crop's going to be light."

The woman was gathering the plates. She did not reply.

He got up, moved toward the door, and then hesitated. "You remember, Lizzie," he began, in a casual tone, "I told you last year that I thought we could fix it so's you and Joey could go back home for a visit. Well, I don't really see how you can go. I haven't got the money."

She straightened up. "You bought some cattle, didn't you?" she asked, in the same mild tone she always used, "and you bought fencing, and other things."

He turned his hat about in his hands. Her voice was quiet enough, but her cheeks were red.

"Sure, I bought some stuff, but it was for the farm—for all of us. I've got to buy things if this place is to grow." He spoke placatingly. "I thought that you might think it was all right to wait another year. Then Joey will be bigger, too, and both of you can have a better time."

She stood beside the table without seeming to hear what he said. Her eyes took on a vacant expression. Then she answered, at last, "All right."

"There's people moving in this year and I thought maybe you'd just as lief be around now that there's more excitement."

The color had gone out of her cheeks, and her eyes met his. "All right," she repeated. "It's pretty nice this year, and we can wait till next year. You'll let us go then, sure?"

"You'll have your visit next year," he promised. "If there are any crops at all, you folks can have your trip back home."

It was a summer of hard work for the man and woman—for she sometimes helped with the field work during haying time and harvest. Every second Sunday they drove to town to attend services at the church. The congregation was larger now, and the new settlers gave to these Sundays a feeling of buoyant optimism.

Toward noon on an August morning a prairie schooner appeared on the rise to the south. Elias hurriedly unhitched his team and placed them in the stable. Then he went to the house.

"Strangers coming, Ma," he announced. "New settlers. I guess they'll be staying for dinner."

They all went out-of-doors and watched the slow progress of the canvas-covered wagon. It turned in from the trail and advanced toward the house.

Elias saw that the team which was approaching was jaded. The animals held their heads low. Lizzie went into the house to prepare dinner, and she was followed at once by the boy.

Finally the wagon came to a halt where Elias was standing. A tall, grizzled man, with touches of gray in his hair, looked speculatively at Elias.

"Think you can put us up for dinner and give the horses some hay? We've had a long morning of it."

"Sure," Elias replied cordially. "We'll be glad to have you. Strangers don't come every day, and we like company."

A tall, lean woman, whose hair also was gray, came from the interior of the wagon and climbed down by the hub of the wheel.

"You go right on to the house," Elias directed. "You'll find my wife there."

The man led the horses to the barn and filled the manger with hay. Elias cleared the grain boxes and gave each animal a liberal measure of ear corn.

"Oh, they don't need that," the stranger expostulated. "They're used to gettin' along on grass, with a little wild hay now and then."

"Well, they'll eat it, I guess," Elias remarked. "Horses need corn when they're putting in full days."

The men walked through the hot, dry yard to the house. The woman was in the kitchen with Lizzie. Elias noticed that they were not talking. He saw that the woman sat back in her chair in an attitude of sagging weariness.

While they waited for dinner, the man gave their story in disconnected sentences. They had tried pioneering in other places. Failure had dogged them. Flood and drought had come, and every time they had moved on.

"We've had a bad time of it," the man said, in his low, husky voice, "but this country looks pretty good to me. We'll strike out a little farther west and north, and then we'll make a try at it again."

There was little talk at the meal. Both the man and the woman were silent. When they had finished, the woman offered listlessly to help with the dishes, but Lizzie refused this help.

"Guess we'd better be gettin' along then," said the man. He fumbled in his coat and drew out a leather purse from which he took a half dollar. He handed it to Lizzie.

"This'll be about right?" he asked. "We had a mighty good dinner here, and the horses did, too."

Lizzie was about to accept the coin when Elias said sharply, "We don't want pay for that. Out in this country a stranger's more than welcome. We're only too glad to have folks come."

Lizzie looked queerly at her husband. The strangers stood near the door in awkward silence. Then the man stretched out his hand to Elias.

"Then we want to shake hands with you folks," he said. "You've been mighty good, and I guess we need help." There was a curious quaver in his voice. Elias felt a certain pity and embarrassment as he looked at these two weather-worn and life-worn old people.

As they left, they once more expressed their thanks. Then the wagon moved creakingly toward the trail.

Before Elias went to the barn to hitch up the team for the afternoon's work, he turned suddenly to his wife. "We're never taking money from people for giving them meals and rest, Lizzie," he said quietly.

"Why," she answered, "we need money, don't we? And there was nothing wrong about it."

"If we didn't have a cent in the world," his voice was as quiet as before, but emphatic now, "still we wouldn't take money for something like that."

She did not see that he was angry. Her expression was somewhat bewildered. Without saying more, he turned and walked to the barn.

XIV

The burning heat of August noon beat in at the open door. At the small table, set without a cloth, the woman sat hunched forward in her chair, steadily regarding the man opposite her. He kept his face averted and drummed listlessly with his fingers on the table.

"But you promised two times that we could go," she said, with a dull plaintiveness. "Last year you put it off, and now you put it off again."

He turned quickly toward her. Her thin, brown face did not express anything, but there were tears in her eyes. He withdrew his gaze once more to the window, which looked out upon a white sky in the west. Half consciously, he was aware of the dizzying heat of the room. Again his finger tips tapped on the boards of the table.

"It's just goin' to be that way always, it looks," she resumed in a monotonously strained voice. "You'll keep on putting it off and putting it off, and Joey and me will never get to go back home."

"Is that all you can think of?" he burst out suddenly, bending forward toward her. The black, unkempt growth on his face and the wide gray eyes, filled with the sick expression that always came with these fits of temper, gave him a startling appearance. His voice became deeper, more deliberate. "That's all you've been thinking of since you came out here—to go away!"

She had drawn back at first at his display of anger, but again she hunched forward. A thin color showed through the tan of her cheeks. "That's about all I've been thinking of, I guess," she said bitterly. "And it's no wonder. I've been afraid ever since we came here. In winter we're about froze to death, and in summer you never can tell when a bad storm will come up, and if the storm doesn't come, there ain't any rain. Nothing grows here anyway, except rattlesnakes. This ain't a place for people to live!"

"It's good enough for me," he answered sharply. "What do you want? I'm not going back East to beg for work. We made up our minds to come here,—and we're here. I've always liked this country. There's nothing wrong with it, except the way you look at the whole thing."

She was crying now, soundlessly, her face drawing up into wrinkles about her eyes. He stared at her stolidly. The anger slowly drew out of his face, but the eyes remained wide, and filled with puzzled weariness. The small boy had finished his meal and had left the table to go outside, without saying a word.

"I know it sounds like I don't mean it, Ma," he said at last, quietly, "but I'll do everything I can to let you folks have your trip next summer. You know why I haven't the money. When Joey came down with the lung fever last spring, it took every cent we had. If it hadn't been for that, you could have gone. I didn't know last year when I promised that you might visit back home that the sickness was coming. Such things happen, and we've just got to take them as they come."

Her emotion had exhausted itself. He got up from his chair and stood quietly beside her, stroking her hair with an awkward hand. "It's all right now, Liz?" he asked, and there was something of the tenderness of a boy in his tone.

She raised her head slowly. "Oh, I guess so," she replied dully. She stood up and listlessly began to clear the table.

He took the broad-brimmed straw hat from the chair and went outside. At the barn, he halted. A bitterness came over him as he looked out over the yellow stubble field to the north. The summer had been hot and dry, and the crops were light. The straw had been too short in some places to make the grain worth cutting. The sun blazed down through the motionless air upon him. The long days of backbreaking work he had put into this land were recalled sharply. He had done all he could do, and always something came along to blast his hopes.

The mood stayed upon him, and he worked through the long afternoon in a spirit of dull revolt. Then, toward evening, the air cooled, and a steady wind flowed out of the southwest. The sky was dim. As always, the magic of this open country quieted him. He remembered what he had said when he first came, that the land had to be tamed first. Pioneers always had to face hardships. Things were bound to turn out well, at last. The crops were going to be light this year, but next year maybe there'd be big yields. If the weather was right, this rich black soil could produce as much as any land on earth. While he went leisurely about the few chores, his mind was aglow with hope for the future. After he had finished work, he sat for some time in the doorway of the barn, looking out to the fading sunset sky.

By imperceptible degrees, the days became cooler as August drifted into September, but the back of summer was not broken until, after a night of rolling thunder and roaring rain, morning came with a steady cold wind from the northwest and a deep sky of spotless blue. In a day the new grass was throwing a tinge of green over the brown desolation of the prairie, a sweet new grass that lured the stock from the bottom land along the stream to the upland country. One morning, when the clear sky had the depth of color that comes when sunrise is imminent, Vaughn suddenly caught sight of one of the horses as the animal stood stock-still on the crest of a distant rise of land. It stood there, black and motionless against the brilliance of the northern horizon, and to the man there was something wonderfully wild and free in the sight, and there swept through him again that longing of his earlier years, a queer, incomprehensible longing for great spaces. For some minutes he watched the horse, with the light of glamour in his face.

So summer merged into autumn, and autumn sharpened until the nights brought heavy frosts. Thin spicules of ice fringed the bank of the stream at early dawn and disappeared at the first touch of the sun. Now and then, at night, especially when the air was heavy, from the murky void of sky came the hub-bub of migrating ducks and the steady, haunting music of wild geese trumpeting their way through a sad darkness toward a new land. Once, when there was this uneasiness in the wind the man left his accustomed place at the table and walked from the dim flare of lamplight into the soft blackness outside. An elation seized him. He lifted his face; he sniffed eagerly of the cool, wet wind. The far-away honking of the geese played over him with the thrill of a dreamed melody. For him, there was ecstasy; and still, poignantly woven into the phantasy of his delight, was a sense that he was not one with this wild, lawless spirit. He could not go away—and he did not want to go away. But he wished that he could say what this gladness was. He turned from his thoughts and gave himself over to the elusive spell.

After an hour he returned to the house and found the woman bent over some piece of knitting, her eyes sharp with the necessity of working in the dim, wavering light.

"You look all excited," she observed, as she glanced up.

He wondered why he could not tell her what he felt. But already the exaltation was ebbing. "It's fine outside," he said.

"It's goin' on to rain, ain't it?" she asked, without great show of interest. He had said earlier in the evening that the sky was thick-ening.

"We'll have rain before morning, by the way it looks," he replied absently.

Indian summer came late. During this interval of mellow weather, they were again attacked by a prairie fire. A threatening red in the sky long after sunset kept them up. This time, however, they were well protected and, when the leaping flames swept up to the broad strip of plowed land, they disappeared suddenly into blackness while, around to the southwest, the wall of fire retreated into the night. In the darkness the flames played awfully in the writhing, swirling pall of smoke.

It was these things that gave measure to their lives: after the prairie fire, the first snowstorm; after the snowstorm, Christmas and the New Year; and after the New Year, the brief illusion of the January thaw working through the long white days of February and the lethargy of March into the reality of spring when April and May mounted into their ascendancies.

On a Sunday in May, the man came in from the barn with a pail of milk, which he strained into pans and placed in the cave just to the north of the house. Then, when he had returned to the house once more, he seized the woman's shoulders and forced her into an awkward dancing step. She drew away, surprised.

"You must be feelin' good this morning," she said, looking up at him in mild curiosity.

"I'm feeling fine!" he exclaimed. "This morning can't be beat. After breakfast you're going to let your work take care of itself, and we're all going for a trip around our farm. It's too nice to stick around inside, anyway. We'll let Joey be the leader." He stooped and caught the small boy in his great red hands and swung him up until his head touched the low ceiling. The child broke out into shrill, excited laughter.

After breakfast they set out. The boy held his mother's hand on one side, and his father's on the other. All three were dressed in everyday garb. Many washings had almost blurred away the small white figures in the faded gray gingham dress the woman wore. Her light hair was pulled back in a careless knot, and wisps escaped to hang over her forehead. Beside the taller, well-knit man, she seemed frail. He was heavier now than he had been when he came to the prairie; the face seemed more square, and the gray eyes, shadowed by the bushy eyebrows and a heavy mop of dark hair, gave a certain strong reserve to the features, burned to a dusky red by the sun and wind. Tiny wrinkles radiated from the corners of his eyes. Between the father and mother, the son, too tall and too lean for a boy of his age, moved along with the careless insecurity of a child.

They walked into the wind, which blew from the west with a smooth, steady current, freshening now and then into a gust that combed the grass flat.

As they went along, striking the trail and then swinging to the north and east, the man stopped often. A meadow lark sat facing them on tall dead weed.

"See him, Joey?" the father spoke eagerly, stopping them. The bird broke out into irrepressible melody, a song and a whistle, a clear "Gee, Gee, Whittaker."

Later, where the ground was higher and more windswept, there was a space that was mistily lavender with tiny grassflowers. The boy caught the eagerness from the man and broke away from them, running in advance to herald new discoveries. The parents walked more leisurely.

They heard Joey shouting to them. He was standing near a bank on the slope where an irregular splash of pink stood out against the dark green background.

"Come here, Joey!" the woman cried sharply.

"Why?" the husband asked. "Let him run around and have a good time. It looks like he's found half an acre of wild roses. Don't they show up fine from here?"

The woman did not hear what he said. Her hands twisted over one another nervously.

"Those places always make me think of snakes," she said, keeping her eyes anxiously on the boy.

"Oh, what's the use of being afraid?" Elias expostulated. "I've seen only three or four since we came out here, and they were always in a hurry to get out of my way. No use being scared." Then he added, "I like to see Joey get around by himself a little more than he used to; it isn't right for a boy always to stay close to his folks."

They once more approached the house, from the north. Between them and the farmyard lay a broad belt of grain, already so high that it undulated in long green waves before the wind. Beyond, to the east, were the straggling corn rows.

"Oh, just so nothing happens to the crops this year!" The woman looked out over the fields with wide eyes.

The expression on the man's face quieted. "If they turn out good, you and Joey will get to visit with your folks," he said. After an interval of silence, he added, "We haven't any money now, but if I have crops to sell, I can borrow what we need from Anderson."

After that, as they walked to the house, he was in a contemplative mood and said nothing. Joey again walked between them; at the last, he cried for his mother to carry him.

Hot days in May were occasional; in June they became more frequent. By the early part of July the midsummer sun once more blazed down on the wide prairie. All the color of the spring burned out quickly; at noon, when the man returned from his work in the field, the country seemed a world of unreality, bathed in a shimmer of hot, white light that rebounded back from the hard soil in weaving currents of air. He looked at this as at a spectacle. Hot weather came each summer.

"Rain seems to be holding off just on purpose," the woman said fretfully. "Just because we need it so bad."

His habit of silence had come back with the hot weather, and he merely shrugged his shoulders. Besides, the long days of heavy work left his mind almost blank; he was in a state of awareness that was so dulled by weariness that his thoughts and emotions were blurred.

During the harvest, there were several sharp storms. One afternoon, after a heavy downpour, the man remarked, "This is going to be fine for the corn. The wheat and oats didn't amount to much, but corn can stand the hot weather as long as there's some water in the ground."

Lizzie looked at him eagerly. "If the corn turns out good, everything will be all right?"

"Yes," he answered slowly, looking to the northeast, where the tall corn stood stiffly unmoved by the pelting rain. "You'll get your trip if nothing happens to the corn." Then he looked at her with so strange an expression in his face that she turned away uneasily.

The rain lasted but a quarter of an hour. Before the late twilight, the surface of the ground was dry.

In the next two weeks there was but a single shower, and this did not soak into the ground, but steamed away. Every morning now the man saw that the corn looked dustier. In the hot, quiet air of day, the long sword-like leaves curled into cylinders that hung limply from the stalks. The leaves nearest the ground were becoming yellow.

"It's got to rain!" the man said to himself, over and over. But day succeeded day; hot, breathless night followed hot, breathless night.

On a morning in August they started out in the one-box wagon for Hayes. It was the Sunday when services were to be held at the church, and they always attended church now that there were many new settlers in the congregation. At this early hour the air was almost cool, and the horses broke into an awkward trot now and then. By the time the church steeple came into sight on a distant rise, heat devils were dancing again, and the horses plodded along with heads low.

They spent the hour before services at the Andersons, sitting out on the tiny porch, too hot to talk. Then they walked slowly down the two-rutted road to the church. When they entered, the minister was announcing the first hymn.

Elias relaxed his body as best he could against the hard back of the wooden bench. Although the windows were open, the air in the church was stagnant and heavy. Remotely, he heard the heavy tones of the preacher, but the words carried no meaning. He was aware that the severe black of the long coat which the preacher wore distressed him.

The services ended, and they were outside once more in the blinding white light of noon. Here the air felt cleaner, but the heat was more direct. Around them, the other people milled in aimless, futile efforts to find some relief.

They had their dinner with the Andersons. After the meal they returned to the front porch. The women talked in desultory fashion, but the men found nothing to say. Joey sat on the edge of the porch, his thin little body sagging against the side of the house.

"Better stay and go to church this afternoon," Anderson suggested finally, turning toward Elias. "Reverend Miner sort o' hinted that he was gain' to make it pretty strong for rain. Can't say I believe an awful lot in that—dry weather's something that comes pretty often to this country—but there might be something in it."

Lizzie had overheard this. Elias saw that she wanted to stay.

"It'll make us pretty late before we get home," he said slowly. "But the traveling will be easier on the horses later in the afternoon."

When they once more approached the church, they found that the people had divided into groups. Here and there, women were walking patiently in the hot sun, trying to soothe irritable children. The men were off by themselves. The two women and Joey joined a ragged circle of women who sat on the thin grass under a small cottonwood tree, the only one on the churchyard. Elias and Anderson continued toward the group of men.

"We'll git what's comin' to us," a heavy-faced, weather-beaten old settler was saying as they came up, "and I don't see much in this business o' preachin' and prayin' for rain. It's a minister's business to preach the Scriptures, and it ain't his business to be takin' up his time with weather."

This was followed by a silence.

"There was a fellow once," began a younger man reminiscently, "who came around with a funny proposition. That was when we was living in Kansas. It was getting to be pretty dry, and the wheat was having a bad time of it. He told us that he could make it rain if we'd pay him. We didn't take much stock in it at first, but he got us excited at last and we paid him quite a lot to show us. He shot a cannon a few times—said it would make the clouds come—and that was all there was to it. He got away with the money, though."

"And you didn't get the rain," finished another man, with pessimistic conviction.

"Not a drop."

The talk droned along. Elias stood at the edge of the group, and often his eyes shifted to the thin purple haze on the horizon. The sky was just as it had been for the past week, cloudless and far away. If only a heavy bank would grow out of the west!

The bell started to ring, its clamor seeming to linger on the hot, dead air. Anderson and Elias joined their wives and the small boy, and filed slowly into the church, taking a bench toward the rear.

Again the farmer fell into an uncomfortable, half awake state of mind. During the singing he was vaguely conscious of the strident, metallic voice of a woman who was in the bench in front of him. Then there was silence once more. The heavy voice of the minister came to his ears without meaning. Suddenly his mind caught on something familiar the man was saying. It came to him in an odd pattern. "… when the sound of the grinding is low … and the grasshoppers shall be a burden, and desire shall fail; for man goeth to his long home and the mourners go about the streets … or ever the silver cord be loosed or the golden bowl be broken … 'Vanity of vanities' saith the Preacher, 'All is vanity.'" The minister's voice was deep-toned and deliberate. To Elias this which he was hearing, the last chapter in the Book of Ecclesiastes, which he remembered as one his father had often read, brought forth a strange mood. In his fancy he saw a desolate land of rocky hills and sandy valleys thinly traced with green. Over all this desolation was poured a hot white light. It was a land of silence, a strange land where life had been and from whence life had gone, mysteriously, drifting from doom, from the plagues of grasshoppers, slipping away silently before a sense of immanent Evil, … finally caught in oblivion.

The vague spell of an unknown Orient fell upon this hot and breathless place in which he now was. There was something spectral in the drooping postures of the dark-clad people in the pews ahead of him, dully dominated by the deep voice of the lean, black-coated man at the front of the church. Where the tall, narrow windows were opened, squares of blue-white sky seemed insipid beside the deeper blue of the tinted glass, upon which were brown images of sacred figures that had known being in dim, remote ages when men walked the earth, it seemed, in God-like strength.

The man shifted his position slightly. Joey, who had fallen into a sleep and was resting against his father's arm, protested against this movement fretfully. Elias, looked at the damp, thin face of the child, and then he placed his arm about the boy so that he might sleep more comfortably. Lizzie was the third occupant of the bench, and he saw that her eyes were vacant.

The mood he had been in died away. Now he gave his attention to the preacher. The speaker paused often to wipe his face with his handkerchief. It was hard to understand at first what he was saying. After a time, Elias sensed that the man was trying to express the need of the people before him, a need for rain, for the bare chance to live decently. He talked on and on; his long, lean face became touched with weariness, but in his eyes was the expression of one in combat. At last he stopped. There was the rising and falling volume of voices raised in the final hymn and then, after the benediction, the people straggled out of church.

There was no talk now. The men hitched the teams to the wagons while women clustered their children about them and waited until they were summoned. Elias and Anderson hurried on to the house. By the time the two women and the boy came up, the wagon was waiting.

For an hour there was no sound save the rumbling of the wheels on the hard ruts of the trail and the thudding of the horses' hoofs.

Toward dusk a warm breeze sprang up. To the man it seemed infinitely refreshing, like a flow of cool water about his naked body. He changed his position on the spring seat.

"Well, it's been a queer day, hasn't it, Liz?" he remarked, in a conversational tone.

"Yes," she agreed. "I can't say that it was much fun." After a short silence, she added, "And it doesn't look like the sermon is going to bring rain either."

"No," he admitted quietly. "Not just now. But if rain comes in a day or so, the corn will make it all right. Corn can stand a mighty lot of hot weather."

She looked away from him, out toward the west where the green of twilight was driving the afterglow of sunset from the sky. "It's got to rain soon!" she said. "We've had more than our share of hard times. It's just got to rain!"

The rest of the trip was finished in silence. When they came to the last rise, they saw the farmhouse a half-mile ahead of them, made curiously unreal and lonely in the first light of a full moon in the east.

During the next two days, the heat did not abate. The man worked doggedly, cutting with a scythe the rank grass that grew near the creek. He had to stop often to seek the shade of some willow bushes. Then as soon as the throbbing heat in his blood had spent itself, he returned to his work. He rarely glanced up the slope to the west, where the house stood in the burning sunlight. At noon and at evening he dreaded to go to the house. There was an expression in Lizzie's eyes that he didn't like—as if he were somehow to blame for this.

The fourth day of the week was hotter, if that were possible, than any of the days preceding. Not only was the air stagnant, but it seemed to be a weight pressing down suffocatingly. At noon, when Elias returned to his work, the purple mist in the west was deeper than otherwise. The sky at the zenith was almost white.

He worked steadily. Perspiration rolled down his forehead and into his eyes, so that he blinked with the stinging pain of it. Nevertheless, he kept on working. There had to be some feed for the stock during the coming winter.

Suddenly he became aware of a low sound, a heavy vibration that he seemed to have been hearing for some time without knowing it. He straightened quickly. The low sound, scarcely more than a murmur at first, deepened into a faraway rumble. It was thunder!

The sharp rise of ground cut off his view of the western horizon, from whence the thunder sounded. He placed the scythe, blade up, in a willow clump, and walked rapidly up-hill. When he reached the crest, he stopped.

The west was an inky black, not of the blackness that comes in a fragment of cloud, but of the unbroken darkness of a heavy bank of storm, that slowly spread farther both to the north and to the south.

Almost at a run, the man made for the house. "Lizzie!" he shouted, when he was still some distance away. As he came up, the woman appeared in the doorway. Her face was filled with eagerness.

"Joey and me have been watching it from the window. It looks like a big rain, doesn't it?"

"It looks mighty good," he said. "Come, let's stand away from the house so we can see it better."

They stood in the dusty farmyard, without saying a word, staring away to the west. At first the blackness seemed to grow slowly; then it advanced more rapidly The rumble of thunder became deeper, more constant. Black, turbulent pinnacles reached out to the zenith, jagged, and constantly changing in outline. Behind this vanguard was the solid mass of the storm, stretching back to the horizon, thin wisps of scud whipping in shreds over the blue-black cloud.

The wind came suddenly, in a strong breeze, cool, and filled with the smell of the coming rain. The sun was blotted out. Chain lightning zigzagged continuously. Thunder crashed down the sky and rumbled heavily until its fainter note was lost in another crash. A spatter of large drops fell.

"We'd better go to the house," Elias suggested. "We can watch just as well from there. It looks like a big rain is coming." He caught the boy into his arms and, laughing, called to Lizzie that he'd race her to the house. The woman accepted the challenge, and the three entered the living room almost at the same time, their faces flushed, their eyes filled with laughter. They took up their station in the doorway.

A moment later the sky seemed to open its flood-gates, for the rain fell in sheets, blotting out everything. They were bathed in a mist; they drew in great breaths of the wet air, filled with the grateful odor of mingled rain and dust.

The roar of the rain on the roof added itself to the roar of the thunder that echoed in long, rolling crashes. Lightning cut through the mist and rain in jagged, piercing lines of flame, orange and yellow, giving them startled glimpses of a tawny and turgid sky. Huddled together, they stared at the wall of rain with faces half-hypnotized.

For a long time the downpour continued. When it lightened enough for the spattering mist to lift, they saw a world new-born. Water lay in pools about the farmyard.

Elias turned to his wife. "We got the rain, didn't we?" he said, more as a statement than a question.

She nodded. The girlish look that came to her when she was pleased was in her face now.

"This will see the corn through all right," he prophesied. "It can get along now."

The rain had lost its force, coming down in little more than a drizzle. To the east the receding storm still made the sky black. Through the window, on the opposite side of the room, they could see a brightness in the west. The woman stood by the window.

Joey was out in the yard, and the man watched him wading in the mud puddles. He set his feet down gingerly, so that the soft ooze squirmed out between his toes.

Lizzie left the window and touched her husband's arm.

"Come over here," she said, pointing to the window. "The sky looks queer."

He looked out to the west and saw a greenish light growing, rising out of the horizon and working rapidly upward, a pure, misty color of transparent green that was fairy-like. He became aware of a distant hum. As he listened, the sound deepened.

The body of the man at the window was crouched, tense. He turned suddenly and called to Joey that he should come into the house. The boy obeyed and had hardly entered the room when the hum gathered sudden volume. A sharp rattle sounded on the roof of the house, and hailstones bounced upon the grass outside. In a moment the ground was white; hailstones danced about like little live demons of destruction. The roar of their fall filled the air.

For a long time Elias stared out of the window. Finally he turned around. Lizzie was looking out at the cornfield, and she seemed to be in a trance, emotionless.

The boy, who stood beside his mother, tugged at her sleeve. "Look, Ma!" he cried in shrill, happy excitement, "see that big one out there? It's 'bout as big as an egg!"

She did not answer at once. Then, as if the voice of the child had recalled her, she looked down at him. Her face was white and dry.

The man stepped toward her but stopped as her eyes met his.

"Well, what do you think of it now?" she asked, and there was in her tone a new quality, a mockery he had never heard from her before.

He was silent. His hands rubbed over one another slowly.

Red spots grew on her high cheek bones and her eyes were hard and bright with enmity. "That's what you get for all your believing that things will always turn out all right! You're just like your father—" She raised her clenched hands to her side. "I say it ain't right!" she cried, in a half strangled voice, "to give us rain first—only to make the hail come to kill the corn!" She raved on, her words becoming unintelligible. Joey shrank away from her. The woman saw this, and recognition came into her eyes. She sat down on a chair and broke into heavy crying. Wrinkled with the effort of her grief, her face was grotesque.

The man stood motionless. The dry palm of one hand rubbed raspingly over the other, ceaselessly.

Lizzie stopped crying. "Can't you say anything!" she cried bitterly.

He looked at her, and there was hopelessness in his face. "There's nothing to say," he replied heavily.

It had stopped hailing and light streamed over the world from the west. The farmer picked up his straw hat from the floor and went outside, to the barn. He looked for a moment toward the cornfield, where each stalk stood stripped of its leaves, and its life. Then he turned his face away.

In the barn was the familiar musty smell of the straw thatch. Vaughn threw himself on a small pile of new hay in the alleyway near the mangers. It seemed to him that there was something heavy in his head which kept him from thinking. He looked out through the open doorway.

A widening rift of blue grew in the northwest, making it a rarely beautiful evening. The sun held his course far in the west, where the dusk of the land was ruddy and slumbrous.

XV

That night after the hailstorm Elias Vaughn did not sleep until late. He arose before dawn and went out to do the chores. The air was crystal clear and of a velvety coolness. Above him, the sky was an even gray-blue. He finished the chores in a short time and then carried the pail of milk to the house. Lizzie had started a fire in the small cookstove and was listlessly preparing breakfast. She did not speak in reply to his brief greeting. He looked at her curiously for a moment. After pouring the milk into two pans that stood ready on the table he left the house.

The man walked rapidly down the slope toward the creek. When he approached the stream, he turned to the left and walked in the rank, wet growth that grew in the narrow bottoms. He had passed the sharp curve where the stream turned to the east and came upon the horses, hitherto hidden by the dense growth of bush willow that lined the water's edge.

"Come, boys," he cried, "come along here!"

The animals had learned to know that this summons was in some way a precursor of a long day of work, and they edged away, their heads held high in alert distrust. The early morning sun glinted on their clean, dark bodies. The man circled cautiously until he was behind them, and again urged them forward. For a moment they seemed to contemplate making a break for freedom. Then, docilely, they plodded ahead of him, up the slope toward the gray little stable. At the barn, the man filled the mangers with the pungent wild hay and, while the animals crunched their feed, harnessed them.

The man and woman ate their breakfast without saying a word. It was unusually early, and the boy was still asleep. When he had finished his last piece of cornbread, Elias looked up at his wife.

"I've got to go to town today," he announced. "Do you mind staying home?"

She looked up quickly. Again he saw the look of enmity in her eyes. "Why?" she asked.

"Oh, I'm not staying long," he answered evasively. "You and Joey could stay and look after things here."

"Not much to look after," she remarked. Her tone, although the words were mocking, was as flat and colorless as ever.

"I have a little business to take care of," he said rapidly. "Some other time we'll all go together." He did not wait for her to reply, but went to the wall, took an old coat from the nail and threw it over his arm. Picking up his straw hat from the floor, he left the house.

The team was hitched to the wagon. After the last tug had been hooked to the chain on the doubletree, the farmer gathered up the ropes that served as reins, and climbed up on the spring seat. He looked almost furtively toward the house. The woman was not in sight.

"Giddap, boys," he commanded sharply. The wagon moved creakingly from the yard.

When the horses drew up before the store at Hayes some hours later, Anderson had just finished his morning sweeping. He stood in the doorway of the store, broom in hand, an expression of surprise on his face.

"You're sure gettin' around early," he cried. "Nothing wrong at home, is there?"

"No, we're all right," Vaughn replied.

The men engaged in desultory conversation for a short time. "Fine rain we had yesterday, wasn't it?" Anderson remarked, seating himself on an empty space on the long wooden counter. "Guess it will pull things through in good shape now."

"The hail got us," the farmer said briefly.

"Bad?"

"As bad as it could be. It just cut the corn to pieces. There won't be a dozen good ears of corn in the whole field. It'll start rotting after a few days of hot weather."

They were silent.

"It's hard luck," Anderson said at last, drumming his finger tips contemplatively on the counter.

"It's hard luck for Lizzie and Joey," Elias burst out. "You know, they were going to have a trip back home if the corn turned out all right."

The storekeeper nodded. "She told Dora about it a couple o' times." Again he drummed on the counter.

"Well," Elias began, clearing his throat, "there's no use beating about the bush. I haven't the money to send them home on. Will you help me out? I'll need fifty dollars."

Anderson looked toward the dusty window at the front of the store, apparently lost in abstraction.

"I'll sign a note," the farmer added, desperately, "And I'll pay it up just as soon as I can pick up something. You see, I haven't anything to sell just now—not a thing."

The other man remained silent.

The expression in Vaughn's face changed. The deep gray eyes grew wide and his lips closed grimly.

"Well," he said sharply, "I guess I'd better be getting along."

"Here," Anderson placed his hand on the other's arm, "don't get on a high horse right away."

"I'm not begging. If you think I won't pay you, why, I guess we can go without the money."

"Now see here, Elias," the storekeeper expostulated, "that isn't the way to talk. You know mighty well that I'd trust you to the limit. But—" He hesitated.

"What?"

"That's the way it goes with all of the people here. You're goin' broke. Every year you think next year's goin' to be good, but it will always stay the same—you'll never quite get even up with things."

Vaughn did not reply. Then he repeated, "Well, I guess I'd better be going."

"I'll make out a note, and you can sign it." Anderson spoke as though he had not heard what Vaughn had said. He went to the rear of the store where there was a small desk set in the midst of a confusion of merchandise. In a short time he returned to the front of the store.

"Here you are," he said. "While you sign this I'll get the money out of the safe."

After Elias had carefully folded the bills and placed them in an old pocketbook, he turned to the storekeeper. His lips were working strangely.

"I wouldn't have asked for this if it was for myself, Carl," he said huskily. "But Lizzie's been thinking about this trip so long that I just had to let her go. It's mighty good of you. I guess you haven't money to throw away, either. But you can depend on it, I'll fix it up with you—every cent." He reached out and gripped Anderson's hand.

"Sure," the storekeeper seemed to be uncomfortable. "That's all right, Elias. Glad to help you out. You folks come in and see us before Lizzie and Joey go."

It was not more than an hour after he had tied the team to the hitching post that Elias set out for home. The sun was high; the horses, after their long trip earlier in the day, plodded along slowly, lines of white lather showing where the harness chafed their bodies. The man sat back on the high spring seat, shoulders drawn together, head down.

The horses broke into a feeble run down the last slope, in sight of the house. The driver raised his head. Without a pull at the reins, the animals turned from the trail and followed the grass-grown ruts to the house.

No one came out to greet him as the wagon drew up near the barn. Vaughn unhitched the horses, unharnessed them, and turned them loose. The animals shook themselves in relief. Kneeling on their forelegs, they lay down and rolled from one side to another in the gray, hot dust of the barnyard. More decorously, they struggled to their feet and walked sedately down the hill to the stream.

Lizzie and Joey were in the house. The table was set.

"Why," the farmer exclaimed, "did you wait dinner for me?"

The woman nodded. "Yes," she said, almost diffidently, "I just kind o' thought you'd be back as soon as you could, and Joey and me thought we'd wait to keep you company. Guess you're pretty hungry after your long trip?"

He looked at her. There was no enmity in her face now, and her voice was placating, as though she were afraid of him. She met his glance and looked away.

"I guess I said things yesterday I didn't mean," she spoke in a low, hurried tone, meanwhile drawing chairs up to the table. "You know, I got all nervous about that storm, and when it began to hail, I didn't know what I was saying. Did you go away to town this morning alone because you were mad at me, 'lias?"

She asked this with the naïve questioning of a hurt child.

"Why no, Ma," he said heartily. "It was something else. It's a surprise. I'll tell you after dinner."

Her face became wistfully eager, and the blue, misty eyes lighted up.

"Tell me now," she begged. "Is it nice?"

"It's pretty nice, all right. I'll tell you after while." Then he added, with an access of pleasantry, "If you're good."

She seemed to catch the good humor from him and smiled patiently.

After they had begun the meal, the man turned to the boy. "How'd you like a little trip, Joey?"

The boy observed his father seriously. The woman said quickly, "A trip? Where to?"

"Well, let's see," he replied, as though recounting possibilities, "there's California, and South America, and—" his words trailed away as he saw that tears were in her eyes. "… and back home," he concluded quietly.

She had not touched her food. "I don't just quite make out what you mean, 'lias," she said. "Is there a chance yet to go?"

"A pretty big chance, I'd say." He resumed his jovial tone. "You see, it struck me that you and Joey might like to take a while off and go for a visit with the folks back East. Of course, it's just up to you. I don't want to force you to go …" Again his voice trailed away as he saw the strained expression on her face. "It's this way, Liz," he continued soberly. "I went to town this morning to see if I could borrow a little, and I wanted to go alone so that if I couldn't get anything, you wouldn't know about it. Anderson helped me out."

She stood up. Her fingers twined in and out, nervously, and her lips were pressed together tightly.

He rose and stepped quickly to the other side of the table. "Why, Lizzie, you mustn't cry," he said, and then, because she very promptly disobeyed this injunction, he placed his arm about her and looked down at the blurred, distorted face with an uncertain smile. Slowly she quieted.

"When do you want to go?" he asked. "You see, I turned the horses loose so that, if you can get ready right away, they'll be rested enough to make the trip tomorrow. The stage starts out at one o'clock, so we wouldn't have to start out from here so awful early. Would you like to go tomorrow?"

"I guess so," she replied slowly. "You see, I've been thinking about this so long, and I just kept things half ready all the time."

"All right; then you go tomorrow," he decided. "Now you just rustle around and get everything together, and I'll go and do a little work outside."

She nodded happily.

He spent the afternoon near the stream, cutting the heavy wild grass for hay. He stopped when the sun was still high in the sky, did the milking, and then went to the house.

"It ain't supper-time yet, is it?" the woman asked, looking up in surprise. "I just finished washing out some of Joey's waists, and I didn't look at the time."

"It's early," he reassured her. "You go on with that, and I'll fix supper."

That evening they talked more than they had on any other evening since they had come. While the woman packed the things in a small, canvas-covered box, stopping to examine each article of dress to see if something were missing, he gave her directions as to the way she should take.

"When you get off the stage at Junction City, you ask the driver where you take the stage to Eldon. You just do like he tells you. That won't be hard, but you got to be careful when you get to Sioux City—that's a bigger place. Just ask people you see how to get to the depot, and find out as soon as you get there when your train goes. And be sure," he cautioned, "not to take the wrong train. Just keep on asking people until you're sure."

She nodded in agreement. "I'll get along," she declared. "I ain't ever been on a train, but I know how it goes. Don't you worry, 'lias; it'll be easy enough."

As they were preparing to go to bed, he remarked casually, "Be sure to write as soon as you get home—and after that, too."

"Oh yes, sure; I'll write real often," she promised quickly.

They started out early the next morning. Vaughn drove the horses to the house and waited for Lizzie and the boy. They appeared in a short time, the boy in advance, walking stiffly in the unaccustomed glory of a newly made white waist. Following him came the woman, walking almost as stiffly as the boy. She wore a long dress of blue gingham with a pattern of broken white lines.

Elias jumped from the wagon. "Say, you folks look nice!" he exclaimed. "Let me help you up to the seat, so you won't get your dress dusty."

She flushed with pleasure. "Do you really think we look nice?" she asked anxiously. "You know, I want the people back home to think that we can dress as good as them."

"You folks are dressed mighty fine; it couldn't be finer!"

The woman talked a great deal as they rode slowly down the trail to the south. The boy sat between them on the seat, silent for the most part, evidently heedless of their conversation, now and then exclaiming to himself as some jack rabbit jumped up from a clump of prairie grass. The sun was some distance from the zenith when the church steeple at Hayes came into view.

"We'll be plenty early," observed Elias. "Guess we'd better stop at the Andersons; they'll want us to stay for dinner, and then you folks can get rested a little before the stage comes."

As was her custom, Mrs. Anderson came out of the house to greet them when the wagon pulled up on the yard near the house.

"So you're goin' today!" she exclaimed, her face wrinkled into its vast, expansive smile. "I'm glad of it! I was tellin' Carl yesterday evening that it would do you a world o' good." She turned to the man, who was unhitching the team. "You ought to be goin' too, Elias."

"Somebody's got to stay home and keep an eye on things," he said, smiling. He saw Lizzie look at him quickly, and flush. As he led the horses to the barn, it occurred to him that his wife had never mentioned his going.

The noon meal was prepared hurriedly, as the stage left at one o'clock from the store. As they scraped back their chairs from the table, Anderson remarked, "Guess this will be a big surprise for your folks, Lizzie, when you two come steppin' in on them. They don't know you're coming, do they?"

She shook her head. "You see, we don't write letters hardly ever," she explained. "Pa and Ma can't do it very easy, and I don't do it either, somehow. I guess they'll be surprised, all right."

"Say good-bye to us right now," Mrs. Anderson ordered. "You'll want to be by yourselves until it's time to go. Anyway, Carl ought to be gettin' back to the store, and I'll be washing things up."

They shook hands with a degree of formality. "Have a good time!" Anderson said, in farewell. Mrs. Anderson folded the younger and slighter woman to her capacious bosom, kissed her moistly on one cheek, and repeated her husband's injunction to "have a good time." Joey took their hands mechanically, with the expression of distrust he always wore when he was among people outside of his family.

They were finally left alone on the porch, where they could see the stage when it drew up before the store. The man and woman were seated on straight-backed chairs, and the boy sat on the edge of the porch. They were silent.

Elias went into the house. He looked at the clock. It was a quarter to one. "Funny," he said, as he returned, "I guess I'm sort o' restless. I thought it was 'way after time for the stage to be here."

She turned to him. "I guess I'll be seeing your pa," she said hesitatingly. "Do you want me to say anything to him for you?"

The farmer did not reply at once. The muscles of his face set into grim lines. Then he answered, speaking carefully, "You can talk to him, of course, if you happen to see him,—and I guess you will. Just let him do most of the talking, though. Don't make out that everything isn't fine with us out here. If he wants to be nice, all right. If he says anything about our coming back, don't give him to think we'll do that. Tell him we like this country."

They looked into each other's eyes. She was the first to glance away. "I'll tell him," she said, submissively.

"Only if he asks about it," he repeated.

She nodded acquiescence.

"I guess maybe he'll want to see Joey," Elias reflected aloud, looking at the silent, stiffly dressed little figure swinging his feet against the side of the porch. The man's face lightened. "And Joey's quite a boy to show him, too!" There was pride in his voice.

They spoke in brief snatches, broken by long silences.

"It seems awful long for that stage to get ready!" Lizzie stirred uneasily. "I feel kind o' queer, in a way."

Elias once more repeated the directions which he had given her the night before. She listened gravely.

A team of horses drawing a light spring wagon came into view down the road.

"There's the stage!" exclaimed the woman, starting up excitedly.

"We've got plenty of time," her husband replied. "They got to pick up a few things before they start out." He drew her to one side of the porch, where they were somewhat hidden from view of the store. "We'll say our goodbyes here," he said.

She clung to him for a moment, as though she were frightened. He kissed her twice, and then let his hand rest on her shoulder reassuringly. "You just have a mighty good time, Lizzie," he said.

"I wish you were going along," she whispered.

He did not make an answer to this.

"You won't forget all about me?" he asked, with a half humorous inflection in his tone, although his eyes became serious. "You and Joey'll come back to me, won't you?"

His meaning seemed to come to her after a pause. Then tears came into her eyes. "Why, 'lias," she said, her voice quivering. "Sure—" She closed her lips tightly and looked up at him pitifully.

"There, there," he soothed her, "I just wanted to be sure. We just belong all together." He hesitated, and then he added, "I guess, when you come back, things will start going our way more, and everything will be just fine out here."

They walked across the road and up to Anderson's store. The driver sat alone on the front seat. Elias helped the woman to the second, and only other seat, which was set up high from the box, on springs. Then he lifted the boy from the ground, kissed him heartily, and swung him in beside his mother. "Bye, Joey," he cried gaily. "Be a good boy and don't forget your pa."

The thin face of the child grew longer. As the strangeness of this adventure seemed to dawn upon him, he began to cry. The woman drew the boy to her. The farmer's face was set into a fixed smile. The driver gathered up the reins, called to the horses, and the stage rattled away down the gray road to the southeast.

Elias watched until the stage was out of sight. Then he went to the barn where the horses were tied, and again hitched them to the wagon. After stopping at the store to make a few purchases, he started out for home.

The afternoon had come with a thin film of whiteness in the sky. The air, not hot, was warm and sticky, presaging rain. Through the murk that lay low in the east, piled thunderclouds showed dimly. The earth seemed sunny, and yet, shadowed. The horses' hoofs pounded heavily in the stillness of the afternoon. Elias sat immovable in the seat, his eyes unchanged in their expression of staring abstraction. He held the reins loosely in his one hand. The other arm lay along the back of the seat. Up and down the winding trail the wagon rolled, while the sun, dipping farther and farther into the west, a sharply defined yellow disk, shone through the haze. The nebulous thundercaps had become a mountain range of grotesque peaks and abysses along the entire eastern horizon. Vaughn lifted his head in a movement of attention. Just audible above the whining of the wheels came the faint murmur of thunder.

At last the animals halted before the barn. The man descended from the wagon, stretched his arms stiffly, unhitched and unharnessed the horses, and started the few chores. That night he ate his supper alone. Now and then he looked through the open doorway to the east, where broad lightning played in the gathering dusk. It looked as if it might storm, he reflected. Well, anyway, Lizzie and Joey would be in Junction City long before it started to rain.

He washed the few dishes at the wooden sink. After sitting for half an hour at the table, he went to bed. During the night, a crash of thunder woke him. Dazed, his mind seemed to be trying to establish something. In an instant he remembered: Lizzie and Joey were gone. He lay back. Lightning came in blinding flares, and thunder rolled through the darkness. But there was only a spatter of rain. He drew the blanket loosely about him, and fell asleep.

XVI

The crops had been light, but this meant little diminution of labor to Elias Vaughn. True to his prophecy, the corn had rotted on its stalks, and there was not much of feed value left for the stock to winter upon. The two small stacks of wild hay set in the low land near the stream could not be enough, so, while he started once more on the long round of plowing, the man studied how he might work out his affairs on the farm. At last he decided that two head of cattle would have to be sold, and this would, in turn, allow him to sell more of the small grain. Anderson, in addition to his business at the store, occasionally bought livestock. In this way the debt of fifty dollars might be cleared.

It was somewhat more than a week after the woman and boy had gone on their visit that Elias made the trip to town. Anderson was waiting upon a farmer and as there were two other men awaiting their turns, Elias decided to step into the cooler air outside. Before he went, Anderson looked up.

"Wait a minute, 'lias; there's a letter from your wife."

Anderson left his customer, walked behind a desk near the front of the store, and drew out a letter.

Elias looked at the small, cramped handwriting. "It's from Lizzie, all right," he said. "I'll be back after while, Carl, when you're not so busy."

He walked outside and opened the letter hastily. There was one pencil-written sheet. Lizzie and Joey had made the trip safely and were now at the home of her parents. The woman ended with the wish, expressed in stilted, almost formal words, that he was getting along well. That was all. The man read the letter again; then he folded it carefully, replaced the sheet in the envelope, and slipped it into his inside coat pocket.

After looking through the window of the store and seeing that Anderson was still serving the same customer, Vaughn sat down on the narrow ledge near the door. Then, restlessly, he started walking down the path that led along the side of the store to the west, in the direction of the church.

For a time he lay in the shade of the cottonwood tree on the churchyard. He was aroused by a familiar voice.

"Taking a rest, Mr. Vaughn?"

Elias sat up quickly and rose to his feet as he saw the minister approaching. He extended his hand.

"I'm tired, too. Let's sit down," suggested the older man, suiting action to the word. Elias returned to his former position, meanwhile eyeing the man near him rather casually. The latter, whose long black hair escaped untidily from under the shapeless felt hat he wore, gave Elias a quick sense of irritation. The tightly fitting black coat, in a way the badge of his calling, was soiled at the sleeves and had evidently been pulled hurriedly over a blue work shirt which was open at the throat. The narrow face had something defeated in its expression, not hidden by the forced smile that drew the thin lips back over the teeth.

"I hear that your wife and boy have gone home?" the minister remarked, with a rising inflection of voice.

"Just a short visit," Elias replied briefly.

"Well, I suppose they deserve it," the minister observed, speaking with a certain precise thoughtfulness. "This isn't exactly the best place in the world for women and children."

The farmer plucked a stem of grass and began cutting it into small pieces between his finger nails. "Oh, it isn't bad," he said slowly. "I believe I'd have liked it here when I was a boy."

The other man shook his head doubtfully. "It's a hard life," he averred, solemnly. His voice became deeper, as it did sometimes when he was preaching. "After all, this prairie country takes everything and doesn't give much in return. I shouldn't be surprised if your wife may want to stay back East, and that you'd follow her in a short time. Probably it would be as wise."

Elias sat up. "She'll come back," he said quietly. "She and Joey'll be back in about a month or two."

The minister smiled tolerantly. The eyes of the young farmer deepened.

"Anyway," he continued, somewhat sharply, "I'm staying here— right here."

"Not if your wife and your boy stayed away."

"Yes."

There was a silence. Elias felt that he had not given this man the truth; he had sounded harsh, and he had meant no harshness toward Lizzie and Joey. Again there came over him an eagerness to tell someone what he found in this country.

"Don't think that I could get along without my wife and boy," he said, speaking carefully. "They'll come back, I know. And as to leaving here, I'll not go away. There have been bad years since we came here—our baby died, our crops have been burned up and hailed out, we haven't gone ahead very fast,—but all that doesn't matter in a way. We have our own farm, a big enough farm to make a man feel respectable. There's elbow-room, lots of open country. It's hard to tell what I mean. Why, anyone seeing this country in the spring would think it was a kind o' paradise." His voice had become more earnest, and he spoke eloquently.

"Oh, you're like the old-timers," the minister declared with a discounting smile. "You're always seeing what's coming next year." After a silence, he added abruptly, "I received a call just a few days ago from a church in the East. It's all I have been thinking of since Tuesday."

"You're not going to leave, are you?"

"I've spent wakeful nights, seeking guidance toward a decision," the other spoke in a solemn, ponderous tone, "and I think it's the Lord's will that I accept the call."

"But will there be anyone to take this church?"

The minister hesitated. "No," he replied at last, "I'm afraid not. You see, living conditions here are pretty bad and the salary is small. A preacher is human; he has to get along, as well as other men."

Vaughn said nothing.

"You don't understand, I'm afraid," the minister remarked finally. "It isn't for my own sake at all. I believe it is God's will that I accept the call that has come to me."

Elias continued to regard the ground at his feet. "I used to wonder how some people seemed to know just what God wanted. It's a pretty handy knack to have." He got up slowly, and the minister followed his example. The men shook hands formally. The minister walked quickly in the direction of the small house that stood just on the other side of the church. The farmer returned to the store and walked to the rear of the building, where Anderson was working.

The latter looked up as Vaughn approached. "Well, did Lizzie and the boy have a good trip?" he asked.

"Yes, they got along fine," Elias answered abstractedly. Then he asked, "Buying any livestock now, Carl?"

"We-el, not much. You see, this summer's been pretty good for most of the settlers out here, and nobody's selling."

The farmer cleared his throat. "You see," he began, "I'd like to clear up that note soon; it'll fall due in a short time. I thought maybe you'd be buying."

Anderson considered this for a moment. "I'll tell you what I can do," he suggested. "You bring in your stock—it's a couple o' head o' cattle, I guess?"

"Yes."

"That's what I figured. You ain't got enough feed to winter 'em, the way I worked it out. Well, you bring 'em in; I can sell again to people right out here. Some of the farmers got more feed than they can use, and they'll take the cows off my hands. And anyway," he concluded, "don't worry a lot about that note. You're good pay."

Vaughn purchased a few groceries and then started back home. It was long after nightfall when he arrived there.

Day after day the plowing went on. The long strip of black in the stubble became a rectangle, and then a square. In the morning, when the farmer walked to the bottoms for the milk cows, the heavy dew, ice-cold, soaked into his shoes. The sky took on the steady, tranquil blue of autumn. The fine green of new grass blurred into the fading brown of dead prairie growth.

After the one brief letter, Elias received no further news from his wife and boy for a month. In the meanwhile, he had made two trips to town. Each time when he had asked for mail, trying to hide his eagerness, Anderson had shaken his head in the negative. The second time, the storekeeper had said, "Guess they're having the time of their lives back home."

"I guess so," the farmer replied.

Then, when her next letter came, it was not much longer than the first. Everything was going well, and she thought that as long as they were there anyway, they might as well stay out the winter, if it was all right to him. Elias stood with his back to the few people who were in the store at the time, folding and refolding the letter absently, his eyes fixed unseeingly on the dirty square of window before him. At last he borrowed paper and pencil from Anderson and wrote, briefly, that they should extend their stay as long as they wished. He could get along through the winter, and they would have a fine vacation.

The customers had left the store. Anderson looked at Vaughn questioningly.

"They're going to stay out the winter," the farmer said, in an offhand manner.

The storekeeper's eyes shifted aside uneasily. "This is a doggone country, anyway," he said gloomily. "This ain't no place for women and children to live."

"They're coming back in the spring," the farmer added.

Anderson scraped the sole of one shoe along the floor in meditative silence. "If I was you, I'd make tracks for the East if I could get the money together. Try to sell out what you got, now that people here can buy a little, and go back. Your woman doesn't like it here. She doesn't want to come back."

Vaughn shook his head. The gray eyes looked inscrutably from the heavy, dark face. "We're staying here," he said with finality. "A little trouble isn't going to make me throw up the game. And don't you forget it, my wife and boy will be here in the spring!" He strode out of the store.

After that, he stayed at home.

Most of the plowing was finished by the latter part of October. Down by the creek, the red branches of the willow stood leafless. The golden-pearl smoke of Indian summer slept over the land.

On a Sunday afternoon in November, he walked out to the little knoll where the grave of the baby was. Within the enclosure of rusty barbed wire the wild tangle of coarse prairie growth had all but obliterated any trace of the grave. The small, round stone which he had found in the creek bottom and had placed at the head of the mound as a mark, had sunk somewhat into the soil, and it was entirely hidden by the tangle of bunch grass that had grown on all sides. The man worked for an hour on hands and knees, pulling out the larger plants and tearing away the sod from the stone. Then he went down the slope to the nearby stream and found other stones, and with these he marked the boundary of the grave.

As he worked, his thoughts revolved, half-numbly, about the memory of the little girl who had lived only long enough for him to know that she looked like him. He forgot his work and dreamed what the child might have been had she lived. His mood grew easier. She would have gone with him to the work in the field, her hand in his; she would have laughed often at little things he said— not funny, but just kind o' happy. Joey almost never laughed. The farmer's thoughts swerved sharply.

He pulled some grass from a nearby clump and rolled it between his palms and fingers to clean away the dirt. Then he stood up and looked about him with the air of one who has been oblivious to his surroundings and finds suddenly that they have changed. The yellow, misty light of early afternoon had changed to grayness. The sun, well down the western slope of sky, shone thinly from a red murk. The light, aimless wind, that had held from the southwest for days, had

died away, and the sudden crow of a rooster from the farmyard at the
head of the slope came with an eerie, muffled sound.

"Change of weather," thought Elias instinctively, and he started
toward the house. Then he thought of the empty evening ahead of
him, and a sharp distaste made him turn abruptly and walk out on
the prairie to the south. He strode along, feeling a queer response
to the sense of uneasiness, of bated breath, of fear, that seemed
to make all of the familiar scene wear an aspect of unreality. The
long, winding black line of low-growing willows that marked the
course of the stream lost itself prematurely in the indefinite, closing
horizon. The usual contours of the land, swell after swell, were
distorted; far-away ridges melted indistinctly into obscure levels.
He walked on and on, without changing his course, striking out
diagonally toward the trail.

The sun was lost to sight. Grayness drew up from all sides,
heavy, stifling. A wild, yellow light permeated the thick sky; on the
ground, twilight was almost darkness. Vaughn swung more directly
to the west. He kept his face up, as though watching the process
of this strange transformation. A breeze eddied past him, with a
thin shrilling as it moved through the stiff grass clumps. It died
away again. After a short interval, it came once more, from the
northeast, in a sharp gust that moaned through the darkness.

More by a sense that his footing had changed than by actual
sight, Elias knew that he had struck the trail. Before turning north,
and toward the house, he halted, his face raised to the sky in an
attitude of listening. From the region of darkness above him, where
the sky had melted into universal gloom, came a faint whining
sound. As the gusts swept past his feet in growing violence, he lost
the high, sustained note for a moment, but it returned again, like
the vibration of some celestial steel string at the tentative touch of

the master of storm. The earlier uneasiness was gone. The wind
came steadily now from the northeast, cold, wet; and filled with
exhilaration. The man drew in deep breaths of this air. Within him,
he felt that curious tumult in his blood that he had known often
before. Curiously, he felt that he wanted to sing. He could not,
and then a queer, soundless laughter seemed to well up through his
body. He was all alive. A touch of wet on his cheek brought him
back to a sharper sense of his position. He saw, indistinctly, large
snowflakes clinging to his shirt. At once he started toward the north.

Before the man came to the place where he had to turn to the
house, a great wind roared about him. The first large snowflakes,
wet and heavy, had changed to small, gritty pellets that stung his
face. The wind was bitter cold, but the exertion of pushing himself
through this wall of wind made the blood pulse warmly through
him. Head down, he walked into the storm, without thought, only
dimly aware of a savage, exultant delight within him.

Again, more by habit than by sight, he struck the slight ruts
that led to the house. A dusky whiteness spread itself into the
darkness, where the wind-blown snow caught in the matted grass
and could not be dislodged. Constantly, keeping to one steady,
deep note, the blizzard thundered through the night. The snow
streamed against him, not from above, but in lines parallel to the
earth.

When he was in the house, at last, a pleasant, wakeful languor
possessed him. He filled the stove with wood, prepared and ate his
simple supper, and then moved the chair near the west window.
In the room, yellow with lamplight, the steady roar of the storm
was dominant. Yet, it seemed to bring out the silence of the house.
And there were overtones and undertones not noticed when he
had been out in the wind. Against the deep, heaving tone of the

blizzard were smaller sounds. Thin shrieks sounded now and then; the sharp rattling of dry snow against the window suddenly became a volley. And, distinct from the mighty sound of the wind was the comfortable crackling of the wood burning in the stove. The man sat by the window, motionless, arms resting on the red tablecloth, his eyes quiet and contemplative. At last, when the small clock on the shelf pointed to nine o'clock, he went to bed.

The next morning, the face of the prairie had changed. The earth was white, the sky a stormy blue-black; the small barn, indistinct through the flying snow, had changed from a weatherbeaten gray to a dark blot in the universal whiteness.

The woman and the boy returned in the latter part of February. After they had alighted from the stage, Elias led them into the store, where they warmed themselves at the stove before starting out on the trip home. Anderson joined them and asked Lizzie innumerable questions about things "back East." Elias stood somewhat back of them, holding the small boy in his arms, his eyes fixed on the woman. There was something different about her, he thought in a puzzled way, but he couldn't tell just what it was. She was talking with more animation than was usual in her, and her eyes shifted about quickly.

"She's tired and nervous," the farmer decided. He asked her if she was ready to start, as it was early afternoon and time to leave if they wished to reach the farm before night.

"Sure," she said, "I'm ready to go. I'm always ready."

Vaughn looked at her again, in surprise. She met his eyes, and hers turned away.

It was a sharp, clear day. Elias helped the woman and the child into the sleigh, where he had placed some blankets on a layer of straw. Then he took up the reins, and they started out, the horses keeping up an awkward half-gallop. For the first hour she talked a great deal, telling him scraps of gossip about people they had always known.

"I was sort of surprised to get your letter saying that you folks were coming back," Elias remarked, after a short pause. "I thought you'd stay till warm weather set in."

She did not reply for a moment. When she did speak, her tone had become colorless. "It wasn't very handy for us to stay any longer," she said dully. "You know, pa never had very good luck farmin', and the owner, Old Man Loucks, told him he couldn't have the farm another year. Pa tried to rent another place, but he couldn't seem to get anything. They had to get off the farm by the first of March, and so they rented a little place in town. They ain't very well fixed, you know,—so Joey and I came back."

They said very little after that for the rest of the trip. The steady drive of cold wind penetrated all of the coverings, and they sat motionless in the box of the sleigh, in numb discomfort. On all sides, the snow-covered prairie rolled away, a broad, empty expanse, without a sign of life. The man, sitting toward the front of the sleigh, dully watched the trail as it flowed noiselessly under them.

They arrived at the farmyard when red was gathering in the west. Elias threw blankets over the horses and then led the way to the house, carrying the roll of scarfs and coverings that contained Joey. Inside, it was warm. After he had put fuel on the fire, he went out-of-doors to unhitch and unharness the horses.

After supper, he dried the dishes for her.

"Seem pretty good to be home again, Liz?" he asked.

"Yes," she said slowly, her eyes avoiding his, "I guess I won't care to go away any more."

Later, after she had put the boy to bed, she again joined the man. He sat resting his elbows on the table, waiting for her.

Suddenly he said, as casually as he could, "I guess you saw my father while you was home?"

She looked up sharply, and there was hate in her eyes.

"I saw him," she said, "but he wouldn't even look at us. Joey was with me, too. We was in town with the folks one Saturday afternoon. I saw him and thought I'd say something to him, but he walked away. He saw us coming all right." Her voice had become strident.

Vaughn's face hardened as she told about this meeting. "Just as well you didn't say anything to him," he spoke heavily. "He'll go his way, and we'll go ours."

The woman's lips were moving nervously. "I thought he'd want to fix things up when he saw Joey," she confessed, "but he ain't got any use for me, or for my folks, or for Joey. My folks are just common—we rent our farm, and then we can't hold it!" Her eyes were bright and hard.

Elias stood up, threw the chair aside, and strode up and down the room.

"Didn't I tell you all along?" he cried. "Now after this I don't want you ever to bring up his name again."

"I guess not!" she promised bitterly.

He returned to his former place at the table. There was a long silence.

"I guess I better go to bed," she said, rising with a sigh. "I'm dead tired."

He nodded sympathetically, without speaking. Some time later, when he went into the adjoining room, she was asleep. In the mingled glow of snow and moonlight that came in at the small window, her face seemed to him to be almost terribly thin now. She stirred restlessly, and groaned in her sleep.

XVII

It was an early autumn morning, some years later. The farmer had finished his second cup of coffee and pushed back his chair from the table so that he might cross his legs comfortably. He fumbled in the pocket of his coat and brought out a pipe and a pouch of tobacco. He pressed the tobacco into the black bowl with his little finger, scraped a match on the chair, and drew at his pipe for a few moments, looking out of the window reflectively.

In this attitude of comfort, the marks of the past years were more evident. His body was heavier, more set, and without that suggestion of litheness it had when he came to the prairie. His face had a greater repose; the chin, slightly jutting, added emphasis to the quiet certainty in the deep-set gray eyes.

"Country's growing up all right," he announced suddenly. "There's a school starting up in the neighborhood this fall—next week Monday."

The woman, opposite him, who sat forward on her chair, her arms resting on the table, turned to look quickly at him. One of the sleeves of her dress was torn near the shoulder. Wisps of uncombed yellow hair fell over one eye.

"Lots o' use to have a school when there ain't nobody to teach!" she observed.

"Well, the school won't be exactly in the neighborhood," he amended. "You know that settlement west and north of Hayes— we went through there last year when I picked up the two heifers. Remember? Well, there's a woman who has a piece of land out to the north of the settlement and she's going to have school right in her house. Mighty good idea, I think. You know, we got to see to it that Joey gets to learn something."

"Joey!" his wife exclaimed sharply.

"You want to get along, don't you, boy!" Vaughn turned to look at the lean, inquiring face of the lad. Joey looked from his father to his mother, and the doubt in his face deepened.

"It will be quite a drive to make twice a day," the father continued. "It's eight miles southwest of here, but I'll have a horse you can use, and you can make it on horseback."

Joey sat back on his chair, his face filled with indeterminate wistfulness. He was tall for a boy of his years, and his narrow shoulders seemed to draw together.

"It's too far for him to go," Lizzie remonstrated sharply. "Anyway, he don't need it; he can get along without goin' to school." She pushed back the wisps of hair from her face with a quick, impatient movement. Her cheeks, running in straight lines from the cheek bones to the narrow chin, were flushed. She turned to the boy. "You don't want to be away from Ma, do you, Joey?"

The boy shook his head. "I don't want to go," he repeated.

"See!" she exclaimed. "He'd just as soon stay at home."

The expression on the man's face, serious and quiet as before, was unchanged. He uncrossed his legs, pulled the chair nearer the table, and leaned toward her.

"Want to or not," he said in a heavy, even voice, "he's going."

"Even if I don't want him to go, and he doesn't want to, either?" the woman cried.

"He doesn't know what he wants," the farmer continued. "I want him to go to school—it's the place for a boy. He should have started before this; he's eight years old now. I don't want Joey to grow up to be just common."

"I guess you're thinking that I didn't have much schooling?" Her voice kept to its high, artificial pitch.

"I wasn't thinking of you," he said calmly. "I want Joey to have more schooling than either of us had. And then, he's got to get around with other boys. He'll learn a lot that way." The man rose from his chair. "I'll take him to school for the first day or two and get him in the evenings, until he gets used to it."

He went outside and finished the chores. Then he returned to the house. The woman still sat beside the table. The boy had gone outside.

"What do you say, Ma—let's work out in the yard today?" he suggested breezily. "I thought I'd take a day off from the plowing and work around the house."

She did not answer at once. He waited silently for an answer.

"Yes," she replied at last, as though arousing herself, "that will be fine."

"I want you to know just why Joey ought to go to school, Lizzie," he said abruptly. "It isn't that I like to hurt you. We've got to do it. Joey'll be one of the big men here when this country's settled up. I've been planning to send him to school; then, after he's through, we'll square out the farm, fence in the yard and have a lot of green things around the house, and all that. Why, we're going to have a place here that can't be beat!" The man's eyes glowed.

Her expression was somewhat reassured. He took her arm. "Let the dishes go, Ma," he ordered cheerfully, "and come along outside and be the boss while I work." He smiled down at her and then, as her face grew lighter, broke into a queer laugh, both serious and gay.

"Come, Lizzie girl, and make the old man step lively!"

She smiled uncertainly, half abashed, and walked outdoors with him. Except for the brief interval at noon, when he helped her prepare dinner, they stayed outside all day. In the morning, she smiled more and more at his sallies, but as the long, quiet afternoon drew on toward twilight, her face grew sombre again. The boy had helped with the work, now and then, but had grown tired and lay on his back in the grass, looking silently upward into the dimming sky. The woman left the man and sat down beside the boy. She reached for one of his hands and held it between hers. The man gathered together the tools with which he had been working and carried them to the barn.

In the days that followed, the farmer saw that his wife kept the boy constantly in sight. When he left the house, she stepped to the door to see where he was going. To the man, she said nothing.

On the Sunday night before school was to commence, the farmer and his wife sat in their customary attitudes at the table. The dishes had been cleared away, and the yellow light of the small oil lamp on the red tablecloth filled the room with duskiness. The boy had gone to bed. In the feeble light, Elias pored over a chapter in the large Bible which he regularly took down from the shelf each evening. The woman rested her folded hands on the tablecloth and stared at the uneven flame of the lamp.

He found it a hard chapter to understand; he felt the grimness of the denunciations Isaiah hurled against the people of Israel, but he comprehended the meaning of the words only dimly, or not at all. As his eyes retraced the lines, he heard a whispering sound that made him look up at the woman. She was talking to herself in a curious, breathing voice, counting, it seemed, for the index finger of one hand went from one finger to another of the hand that rested, outspread, on the table. "One—two—three—four—" He could see her lips form the words. She stopped, as though trying to continue with the enumeration.

"What are you saying, Liz?" he asked uneasily. "Are you figuring something out?"

She looked up at him slowly, a frightened expression in her eyes.

"Tell me what you were thinking about," he urged quietly. "I've seen you talking like that before. Is there something you're counting?"

The frightened expression died away. "You know," she said hesitatingly in her faded voice, "such queer things come to me nowadays. It's funny—folks are always leaving; first we went away from our folks, then the baby died, then all the people went away from here—just like they didn't want to be near us—and now Joey is sort o' going away too."

She had enumerated these points on her fingers. Now she smiled.

Elias stood up and placed the Bible on the shelf. For a moment he remained beside the window, looking out into the darkness.

"Liz," he said, turning toward her, "don't say such things." He spoke in a halting voice of the happiness they might have.

"I guess Joey's goin' to school tomorrow morning?" she asked, after a short silence.

"Yes," he replied shortly. Then he added, in a more gentle tone, "I'll hitch the horses to the wagon, and we'll all go. What do you say, Lizzie?"'

"I guess I better stay home."

"It isn't like he's going to be gone all the time," the man said reassuringly. "He'll be home Saturdays and Sundays, and the school only lasts seven months. You'll get used to it in a little while."

The clock on the narrow wooden shelf behind her struck eight times, sharply. She rose from her chair and, after setting out pans for the next morning's milk, went into the other room.

The man and the boy left early the next morning. Leaving the team standing near the barn, Elias went to the house.

"Time to go, Joey!" he cried. "Got his dinner fixed up, Ma?"

She was on her knees, buttoning the boy's coat. "No," she said, guiltily, "I forgot about that."

"I can spread some bread for him," Elias offered. "It won't take more than a minute."

"No," she exclaimed quickly, "I want to fix his dinner." She turned to the dazed boy. "You want Ma to get your dinner for you, don't you, Joey?" The boy nodded his head mechanically.

A few minutes later the wagon rumbled from the yard. Elias, looking back, saw the woman standing in the yard, staring at them, her hands wrapped in her dress. He waved his hand. She made no response.

"Turn around and wave your hand good-bye to Ma, Joey," the man ordered. In docile obedience the boy raised his arm and fluttered his hand. Elias saw his wife's attitude change instantly. She straightened and her hand answered this farewell eagerly, almost frantically.

The horses seemed to feel the buoyancy of the cool autumn morning, and it was not long before they drew up before a small shack.

Leading Joey by the hand, Vaughn walked to the door and knocked. A woman, short, rather plump, and pleasant of face stood in the doorway.

In a short time the farmer had explained his mission and Joey had been assigned to a chair in the room.

"Make him learn," Elias admonished the woman seriously. "That's what he's here for."

"I know he'll learn," the teacher responded optimistically. "You see, I've taught children for years."

"Fine!" Elias turned to the boy. "Now be good, Joey!" he said. "I'll be back to get you this afternoon."

The boy whimpered, and Elias stopped for a moment at the door. "It won't be long," he spoke soothingly, "and after while there'll be other boys and girls coming."

Once outside, he halted irresolutely. Then, quietly, he walked to the house, stepped to the one window, and peered within. The woman was busily talking to Joey, who looked up at her with wide, wondering eyes. He had stopped crying. Noiselessly the farmer returned to the wagon and took up the reins.

"Giddap, boys!" he called cheerily. "Time to get back to work."

Arrived once more at the farm, Elias stopped in the house before hitching the horses to the plow.

"He's going to like it," he told Lizzie, "I believe that woman—her name's Mrs. Lange—is a good teacher. She acts sensible."

Lizzie looked out of the window, her eyes troubled. She did not reply.

XVIII

In the next few years, the earth was good to the farmers in this prairie region. Rain came in due season, and the frosts held off until the corn crops were safe. All went well. Slowly the country was being settled. The Great Northern Railway had started a spur line that would come as far as Junction City. People who had been to the latter place on visits or matters of business spoke vaguely of land booms that were "in the air." The region south of Hayes was comparatively well settled. To the northwest of the little town, settlement had also been rapid. To the north, however, because of the wide strip of light land that lay between Hayes and the Vaughn farm, there had been few new land holdings, so that the Vaughns still remained in comparative isolation.

One evening, toward dusk of a day in December, Joey entered the house with a great stamping of feet and swinging of arms. His mother, who had been ironing clothes on the table, quickly placed the iron on the stove and helped the boy take off his long knitted scarf and heavy coat. She placed a chair at the stove, opened the oven door, and the child settled back to warm his feet without a word.

Elias came in with two pails of milk. He also stamped about noisily as he set the milk on the table in the small kitchen.

"Mighty cold," he said, returning to the room where the woman and boy were. "Feels real Christmasy outside."

"Oh, that makes me think of something," Joey observed. "We're goin' to have a program over to school next week Friday. It's a Christmas program, and I got to speak a piece."

Both the man and the woman looked at the boy with immediate interest.

"That's mighty fine!" Elias said heartily. "Makes me think of the times I had to give recitations in our school. Remember, Lizzie?"

She nodded, the happiness of reminiscence in her face. Then her expression became anxious.

"He hasn't got anything to wear for a program," she declared. "And I want him to look just as good as the rest of the children."

"Don't you worry," Elias promised. "We'll get you an outfit, Joey. You'll show them that you can look just as neat as any of them, and you're going to speak that piece a lot better. Let me see it. Have you got it with you?"

Joey fished about in the high pocket of his blue waist and brought to light a much-folded and rather grimy piece of paper. Elias took it over to the table, where the light was stronger.

"Three verses. That won't be hard to remember. Now you get right down to learning it—start this evening. Then you can recite it to us and we can tell you how it goes." Elias returned the paper to the boy, who carefully placed it in his pocket.

While they were eating their supper of freshly baked cornbread, covered with hot fat and syrup, fried pork, and coffee, Elias seemed to be preoccupied. Suddenly he exclaimed, "Let's make a big Christmas of it! A real old-timer!"

She looked at him half doubtfully. The boy was too engrossed with his meal to do more than look eagerly at his father.

"We'll go to town soon and buy presents for each other and hide them till Christmas morning. Joey can get something to wear at the program, and you can buy yourself a new dress, Lizzie— something that'll make you look dressed up. We'll celebrate in high old style!" He sat with chair tilted back, his deep gray eyes smiling at them, watching their faces.

"That'll be fine!" Lizzie said, a return of liveliness almost obscuring the vague expression that now lay on her face almost habitually.

"It's goin' to be a real old program," Joey remarked, with an air of some importance. "There's goin' to be a lot of speaking and singing."

A few days after this, they drove to town in the sleigh. After Elias had climbed over the side and had tied the horses to the one hitching-post in front of Anderson's store, he walked to the rear of the sleigh and helped the woman out.

"Now you get just what you want, Lizzie," he said, putting a folded bill in her hand. "Get a dress—something nice. I'll see that Joey gets some spending money, too."

The interior of the store had taken on a different aspect within the last year or two. There were more shelves along the sides, and a farmer girl had been hired as a clerk. Lizzie and the boy, whose head came to her shoulder now, went to the long counter on the left side, where the dry-goods section was, while Elias walked toward the rear of the store. Here he found Anderson standing with his back to the stove. The two men exchanged greetings, and then they fell into the usual channel of talk—farm topics.

The farmer's eyes were upon his wife, who wandered up and down before the counter. The clerk drew down bolts of cloth from the shelves, one after the other. Elias noticed that there was a certain cool disdain in the girl's eyes.

"How do you like this color, Joey?" he heard Lizzie ask the boy.

Joey nodded vague approval. The woman, however, seemed dissatisfied. "Maybe you got something nicer?" she asked. The girl, sighing audibly, pulled out more bolts of cloth.

Elias turned toward Anderson. "Going to the Christmas program over to the schoolhouse next week, Carl?"

"Sure, we're going. You don't catch my woman stayin' away from any excitement," Anderson replied dryly. Then he added, "I guess about everybody will be there. And that'll be quite a crowd. You know, that section's beginning to look like real farm country now; it's real settled-looking."

Elias rubbed the palms of his hands together comfortably. "It was sure to come," he said. "Don't you remember my saying that wild country sort o' tamed down when people came in and started stirring up the sod and planting trees? Ten years from now this will all be farming country, just like it is back East, and the ground will be richer. There isn't better land in the whole country than there is here."

"Things are getting going now, all right," Anderson agreed.

A woman had come into the store and stood leaning against the counter, watching Lizzie, who was still deciding what cloth she would have. Just as Elias glanced up, he saw the clerk look from the corner of her eyes at the newcomer, place her finger on her forehead significantly, and smile impudently at the woman before her who was running her hands over a piece of bright red cloth. For a moment, the blood mounted to his head so that he was dizzy with anger. The veins stood out on his forehead. He quickly walked up to his wife. The clerk, who saw that he had noticed her action, looked fearfully at him and became cringingly civil.

It took them an hour to make the purchases. Then, while Lizzie and Joey were making a last inspection in search of a present for him, Elias left the store and went over to the Anderson house.

"Come in," Mrs. Anderson invited, as she opened the door in answer to his knock.

"Just a minute," the farmer said. "I want to get Lizzie something for Christmas, and I wish you'd pick something out that you know she'd like. When you folks come out to the program Friday night, I can put it in our sleigh so she won't see it."

"We don't have anything so awful stylish in the store," Mrs. Anderson reflected, "but I'll tell you what I'm going to do. My sister back East lives in a big place, and I'll have her send something real up-to-date."

They talked this over for a few minutes, and then Elias returned to the store, where he found his wife and boy awaiting him.

It was a long ride home. Lizzie and Joey were almost lost in the wrappings of coats and scarfs and looked much like two bundles set on the spring seat. Elias, who stood at the front, keeping tight rein on the horses, looked back at them often.

The sun was just in that space of the west where it makes of the sky a brilliant green, when the horses topped the last rise.

"We're almost home," the driver announced. His eyes looked out toward the place to the northeast where the little house, painted white now, with green trimmings, stood snugly within the line of halfgrown cottonwoods. To the east was the stable, its sharply slanting roof covered with snow. There was not a sign of life on the place; there was about it that queer sense of mystery and isolation that a winter landscape gives to dark objects. A warmth seemed to go through the body of the man. It was fine to get back home again, even after being gone for just a few hours. Everything was quiet and peaceful; things were getting along so mighty easy. For a moment his mind caught upon the incident of the afternoon, when the girl at the store had placed her finger on her forehead in derision of his wife. The little fool! She didn't know what Lizzie had gone through! Then his mood lightened again and, before the team came to a halt, his mind was busy with anticipation of an early and leisurely supper.

In the evenings during the next week, Joey recited the three stanzas of his "piece" until he could give them without effort of memory.

"Don't say it like a parrot!" Elias commanded impatiently. "Say it just like you was talking without thinking of making a speech. Take your hands out of your pockets!"

This made the boy sullen, and the woman came to his defense.

"Oh, I'm not trying to make Joey mad," the man declared, "but I just want him to make a good job of it."

On Friday afternoon, chores were finished early. Elias ate his supper alone, for Joey was beginning to feel the imminence of his appearance before the public, and his mother was busy putting him into his new clothes. This finished, the woman directed the boy to sit on a chair, and then she disappeared into the bedroom. Elias continued to eat in unhurried enjoyment, looking often at the rather unhappy boy seated on the edge of a chair. Joey's thin neck rose rather abruptly out of the formlessness of his dark new suit and white waist. The peering eyes, giving him a certain nearsighted appearance, were worried. Above his narrow face, the light hair had been brushed with the aid of water until it was pasted close to his head.

The door of the adjoining room opened, and Lizzie entered. For a moment Elias blinked. The dress she wore was of a violent red that seemed to eclipse and make a blur of her face. In the interval of shock, Elias drained his coffee cup.

Lizzie stood near the door, looking at him. There was something shy, half afraid in her face. "Do you like it?" she asked.

"Fine!" he exclaimed. "You look mighty nice in that, Lizzie. It just makes you look young."

A girlish smile lighted up her face.

It took him but a short time to dress. Then, as it was almost six o'clock, Elias went outside and hitched the team to the sleigh. He drove to the house. "All aboard for the program!" he shouted.

The light in the window went out, and the door of the house opened. The farmer placed the spring seat on the hay that he had thrown into the box and, when they were seated, drew the blankets closely about them. Gathering up the reins, he shouted cheerfully at the horses, and they started out. Instead of turning south when they reached the trail, the horses' heads were held to the west.

"No road out here," the driver observed, "but I guess there won't be any bad bumps."

The horses had been in their stall for some days and now, facing the sharp wind, wanted to break into a run. Elias stood in the front of the sleigh, keeping a firm hold on the reins. When the way led uphill, he placed the reins over one shoulder and under the other arm, and thrashed his arms about his body. In a moment the warm blood tingled in his fingertips. Then, as the sleigh reached another low crest, he was forced once more to take the reins in his hands, both to restrain the horses and to guide them.

When they arrived at the farmhouse which also served as a school, they found that there were others before them. Most of the teams had been unhitched and tied to the sleighs. Vaughn allowed his team free rein when they approached and drew them up with something of a flourish. He turned around to the silent figures on the spring seat. "What do you think of our race horses?" he asked, with a laugh.

"Jump out, Joey," he commanded gaily. Then, to the woman, he said, "Come to the back, Lizzie, and I'll help you down."

She stood up slowly and came toward him. "Lift me down," she asked.

"Cold?" he questioned, as he swung her to the ground.

"I just seem to get cold as soon as I get outdoors," she said, the words coming jerkily from her. He could feel her entire body shivering.

"Here," he said, with gruff kindness, "I'll give you a lift." He placed his arm about her and half carried her to the house. He opened the door. He had a confused impression of a number of people crowded into a small room. "You'll be all right now," he declared. He turned to the boy. "You stay with Ma," he directed. Joey had followed them to the house and now stood looking fearfully at the strange people inside. Elias went back to the horses, unhitched them, and tied them to the box of the sleigh.

Everything was quiet when he entered the room again. The school teacher was standing in a small cleared space at the front of the room, and was saying something which he couldn't understand. He saw Lizzie on the other side of the room, where the brilliant red of her dress stood in vivid contrast to the more sober garb of those about her. As he came up, he saw that she was with Mrs. Anderson and that there wasn't a vacant chair anywhere, so he joined the line of men who stood at the rear of the room.

The teacher had evidently been announcing the program for, just as soon as he had taken up his position, two small children were pushed forward to the cleared space. One began to speak in a high, unintelligible treble. A burst of applause, mixed with much laughter, followed. The other child became frightened and began to cry. The teacher went up and soothed her. After much prompting, the speech was given. Then the two children raced madly back to their seats.

The men about Elias were talking in a steady undertone, but he scarcely heard them. He had caught a glimpse of Joey's face, well ahead of him, and the dumb fright he saw there almost brought panic to the man. Joey had to go through with his recitation! These people who had laughed at the stage fright of two children would laugh the harder if Joey broke down. One after the ether, the pupils marched before the people and recited "pieces" in strained, unnatural voices. Elias did not hear what they said. When, finally, Joey's name was called, a hot wave passed over the father. His body was tense; his eyes were fixed, undeviating, on the boy who was walking stiffly to the front of the room.

When he faced the audience, Joey's face was drawn with misery. His arms hung down at his sides, limply. However, he spoke his lines without hesitation, clearly, giving words the accent and emphasis that his father had taught him. While he spoke there was an attentive silence. Then, when he had finished, there was a quick burst of applause, followed by a murmur of approbation. To Elias, who now felt weak with relief, the appreciation of the people about him, expressed by their attitudes, was a delight. He felt his face beaming, and consciously took on an expression of remoteness.

"Your boy, wasn't he?" asked the man next to him.

"Yes," Elias replied dryly.

"He was the best one of the whole lot," the man declared. "He's got real stuff in him."

In spite of himself, a broad smile came to Vaughn's face. To conceal his pride, he said jokingly, laughingly, "Sure, he's the best boy in the country—my boy!"

He tried to recall the name of the man who had said this. Finally he remembered. It was Henderson—a fellow who had taken up land near Hayes about a year ago. A fine fellow!

Joey's speech concluded the program. After that, small bags of candy and nuts were given to the children, and the parents were served with coffee and meat sandwiches.

The small room was in a hubbub. The women had collected on one side of the room and the men on the other. Towards the front, the older school children, freed from the feeling of strangeness incident to starched clothes and an unusual occasion, were in a state of riot. The door to another room opened and some women came in to serve refreshments. Elias, who saw them approaching, looked around eagerly to see if Lizzie were helping. She wasn't, and he felt a slight disappointment.

"Here, let me fill your cup." A woman, whom Elias knew to be Mrs. Helmer, wife of a square-shouldered barrel of a man not far from him, urged Henderson.

"No, thanks," Henderson replied. "I guess I've had enough for tonight."

"Then you better have another piece of cake. You better, because I baked it, and I'll feel hurt if you don't."

"Well, if you baked it—" Henderson said, in awkward gallantry, "sure, I'll take the biggest piece I can find."

"Now, then, let me fill your cup so you won't have to eat it dry," she urged again.

He hesitated. From across the room came a loud voice. "Go ahead and pour out his coffee, Mrs. Helmer. He's just trying to be polite."

Henderson capitulated. "I guess Ma gave me away all right," he confessed, "I just thought it wouldn't look well to take three cups o' coffee in company."

The men had been interested listeners. "Ol' Herm Henderson is aimin' to get into society," affirmed one, "and he's practicing up with us. See, he's sportin' a collar and tie. Pretty slick bucko, I say."

There was a general laugh, and Henderson, passing a finger between his collar and his neck, joined the laughter nervously, meanwhile spilling a part of the coffee on his knee, whereupon calmness came with pain.

The dishes were gathered, and most of the women went into the adjoining room to help wash them. After half an hour they returned. The school teacher walked to the front of the room and rapped sharply on her desk with a ruler. There was instant silence.

"One reason why we had this program," she began, "was because I wanted to get you all together and have you choose a director. It looks like I've been teacher, director, and everything else, and it's about time we got things in order. Now, then, we'll vote for a director who will serve the rest of this year and all of next year. Call out your nominations."

"Jake Helmer!" a voice shouted from the rear of the room.

The barrel-like man arose. "No," he addressed the teacher earnestly, "don't put down my name. That's just a joke. I ain't had any schooling to speak of. But," he continued, "I got somebody to nominate who's just the man. Elias Vaughn out there's got us all skinned when it comes to knowin' things in books. I heard him talk in Sunday school a year or two back, and I tell you he made the minister act pretty careful. So I say, let's vote for Vaughn."

A queer warmth came over Elias. He felt that eyes were upon him, and the muscles of his face grew rigid and his eyes were filled with a studiously serious expression.

"Well, I guess that's a motion," the teacher decided. "Is there any second to the motion."

"I second the motion," Henderson said heavily.

"Why, when it comes down to that," came the voice of the man who had nominated Helmer, "so will I."

The teacher joined in the laugh that followed this, and then frowned. "I'm not just sure what comes now," she said hesitatingly. "But first—are there any more nominations?"

There was a silence. Then the wit responded, "If you're asking me, I say 'no.'"

"It has been moved and seconded," the teacher chanted solemnly, "that Mr. Vaughn be chosen director of this school for the rest of this year and all of next year. All in favor signify the same by saying 'Ay.'"

There was a chorus of ayes.

"Those opposed say 'No.'"

None was opposed.

"Mr. Vaughn is elected," announced the teacher.

There was a hearty burst of applause, and several men who sat near Elias slapped him on the back. He smiled seriously. Glancing quickly toward the other side of the room, he singled out Lizzie at once by the flaming contrast of her dress to those about her. She was clapping her hands vigorously. The glow of elation cooled at this. He wished that she wouldn't do that.

"Speech!" cried someone, "We got to have a speech!"

Elias stood up and was about to speak when he was interrupted. "No, no; go to the front, behind the desk."

While he walked forward, a sensation of weakness seemed to weigh him down and, after he had turned to his audience, he dreaded to lift his eyes. Then the fright passed. A curious sense of power possessed him.

"It was mighty good of you to elect me," he said carefully, "and I'll do the best I can to make this school work smoothly. Of course, the teacher is really the important part of the school, and since we have a good teacher, I won't have heavy work, I guess. But if anything ever comes up that you want, you let me know and I'll do all I can for you." His eyes traveled slowly over the mass of faces before him. Then he returned to his seat. Long-drawn-out applause followed.

Without formality of a motion for adjournment, the people began to make preparations to leave when a child cried fretfully and the mother called across the room to her husband that it was "high time to get home."

Out in the schoolyard, while he was getting things ready, men whom he knew only slightly came up and shook his hand, expressing their pleasure at his election. A strange mood had come to Elias after his speech, and it remained with him. A sense of triumph was mingled with the feeling of dominance, and the sense of the cordial good will of these people brought a queer yearning to him. "Best people on earth!" he said to himself.

Mrs. Anderson appeared suddenly with a parcel, which she hurriedly pushed into the man's hands. "Here's that present you wanted me to pick out for Lizzie," she said. "It's a dress."

"Thanks for the trouble." Elias took the package and placed it toward the front of the sleigh, where he covered it carefully with straw. It wouldn't do to let Lizzie see the bundle.

When he had finished hiding the gift, he turned around and found that Mrs. Anderson had not gone.

"I don't like to say this," she began awkwardly, "but if I was you, 'lias, I'd keep an eye on Lizzie. She says such queer things. And then, that dress she wore tonight—"

"Yes, I know," Elias spoke slowly. "Lizzie isn't very strong in her mind, I guess." Then he added quickly, "It's been a mighty hard row for her to hoe—this living out here. She's all right, but it's kind o' hard for her to think the way other people do. And she's so wound up in Joey that she's got to be like a child, too."

Mrs. Anderson nodded. "Goodnight," she said abruptly and left.

A few minutes before this, the man's mind had been all aglow; now, in the reaction to what Mrs. Anderson had just told him, it seemed that all of the brightness ebbed from his thoughts, leaving only an empty dejection. He threw the reins into the box of the sleigh and strode to the door.

"Ready to go!" he shouted, looking with a new awareness at the woman in the red dress. "Here, Joey, let me help you with your coat." He buttoned the boy into the long, tight-fitting overcoat with impatient hands. "You ought to be doing such things for yourself," he said.

Once out in the open air again, looking back now and then at the woman and the child who were huddled together in the sleigh, silent as always, the depression lifted somewhat from the man's mind. His thoughts would not turn aside, however. It was true enough: Lizzie was queer in her ways, and getting worse all the time. Although he didn't know much about women's clothes, he knew that his wife should not have worn that brightly colored dress. That wasn't so bad, after all. But more and more often she would fall into a dead stare, her eyes vacant of expression, her hands idly folded in her lap. Most often she was this way in the evening. A certain helplessness was growing upon her, he saw now; life seemed to be getting sleepier for her all the time. Every few days he would come into the house and find that there was no preparation for a meal. Then, as he appeared in the doorway, a startled expression would drive away the vague dreaminess from her face and, in sudden hurry, she seemed to be so distraught that she did not know what to do. Always, at such times, he had done most of the work himself. Strange, he thought to himself now, that he hadn't seen this clearly all along; anyone could have seen that things were not at all right with Lizzie. But he had gone on from day to day, hardly noticing. Maybe he hadn't wanted to notice. The sleigh came upon uneven ground, and Elias gave all of his attention to the team. Then, when the driving was smoother again, he turned around.

"You folks all right?"

"Uh-huh," the woman replied, in a muffled tone.

"You're not getting cold?"

"Huh-unh."

"That's good," he said cheerfully. "We'll be getting home soon."

His thoughts returned to his problem, but at a new angle. What had brought this upon his wife—this drawing away of her mind, this helplessness? She wasn't really sick. He remembered her when he married her. She had been all alive then. His mind held wistfully to that picture of her. But even at that time she had had something of this remote quality. And then, the thought came with a certain heaviness, Lizzie and he were getting older. He was probably a lot different too. People changed with the years. He'd do all he could for her, make things easy, and he'd talk and joke more. She had been awfully lonesome for a while—so lonesome that she had had to take that trip East. That hadn't been much pleasure for her either, it seemed. After that, she had begun to have these queer spells, he discovered now. Oh, well, well. A queer business, this living. Everything was getting better and better on the farm—it had been paid for years ago; there was more land under the plow than he could handle—and still that final satisfaction toward which he had been working did not come. There was always a little something to add a bitter aftertaste to the sweetness of accomplishment. Like it had been tonight: Joey had spoken better than any of the children on the program; he himself had been elevated among his neighbors as a man who had brains, and a new sense of dominance and power had come when he made his little speech before his neighbors. And now—all that seemed unreal, a mockery, before the fact that Lizzie was not holding on to life as he was. Again he sighed softly, "Oh, well, well."

The mood began to dissipate itself. The driver thumped his feet together. It surely was a cold night! You could tell by the sharp screeching of the runners on the snow that it must be 'way below zero. High time for them to be home! A wry smile came to his dark face. Years ago, such a ride would have been nothing at all, just some more excitement; now, he was in a hurry to get home. Getting older, all right! The wistfulness of the smile stayed in his eyes, although he drew his mind impatiently away from the train of thought that had held him most of the way. He turned around again.

"You folks all right?"

"Uh-huh."

"That's good. We're almost home now."

The horses knew the ground and held to the smoothest places. They were tired, too, and he did not have to hold them in check. His eyes roamed about. It surely was a fine night. Overhead, out of the pale blue duskiness of sky, the stars shone like white metal. Just like they were sown there, he reflected; some places there were just a few, and some places they were thick, and they lay in curves, too, as if they had been scattered by hand. The northern sky was lighter than the rest; the southern horizon was lost in heavy gloom. Out in the east, almost quartering the sky, stood a large, blazing-red star. The man's eyes dwelt on it. It was unlike all of the other stars; its red color seemed to have life and depth. A star in the east, he mused. His mind caught a significance that came from memories of his youth. "Wonder if it's the same star that brought the Wise Men from the East?" he speculated, half seriously. "It's so different, so alive. Maybe it's the sign of something. And his memory added, "Peace on earth, good will toward men." Tomorrow would be Christmas. He'd make a day of it—stay in the house with Lizzie and Joey. They'd have a good time.

They were almost home. Out of the dim whiteness that lay to the east, came a blur of darkness, standing out more and more sharply against the pallor of snowy prairie as they approached. Now he could begin to see the outlines of the house through the dark line of cottonwoods. The horses freshened their gait. The sleigh was drawn into the old trail, and the riding was like moving on a smooth carpet. At a restrained gallop, the team entered the yard and came to a halt at the gate.

"Well, here we are again!" Elias sprang over the side of the sleigh and walked to the rear. "You jump out, Joey, and kick your legs around a little," the man commanded heartily. "You'll be warm in no time." Then, as the woman seemed to have difficulty in getting to her feet in the midst of the blankets that had been thrown about them in the box, he said, "You're awful cold again, Lizzie?"

"Oh, so terrible cold!" Her words came disjointedly. "I thought we'd never get home."

He carried her to the house, making a joke of it all. Then he added fuel to the fire smouldering in the kitchen stove, opened the oven, and placed her chair before it. After that he returned to his team, unhitched and unharnessed them, and before securing the swinging doors for the night, refilled the manger with hay.

The kitchen was warm when he re-entered the house. Joey had drawn up a chair beside his mother and had placed his feet on the oven door. On the little table set against the wall, the standing lamp threw a dim, comfortable light into the room. The crackling of the fire, the warmth, and the occasional flicker of firelight that came from the open draft, seemed most inviting to Elias. He brought up a chair and joined the other two at the stove. Leaning back, his hands locked behind his head, he relaxed into a feeling of easy comfort.

"You gave your recitation just fine, Joey," he remarked. "Henderson said you spoke best of all on the program."

"I won't speak another piece," Joey replied quickly.

"Why not?"

"I was scared, and there ain't any fun in speaking recitations anyway."

"That's the way to get along," Elias spoke with some emphasis. "You'll get to like it after a while. And then, it's your business to do some things you don't like to do."

"Well, I'm not going to." The boy spoke sulkily and turned toward his mother, as though seeking agreement.

Her face had become anxious. "I guess you don't have to speak if you don't want to, Joey," she said, placing a comforting hand over his. "Just don't even think about it."

The man said no more for a time. "Well," he yawned, stretching his arms above his head, "I'm sleepy and I'm going to bed. Tomorrow's Christmas, and we'll all sleep until we're slept out, for once." He carried the lamp into the adjoining room and the woman and child followed him. While his wife was helping the boy take off his new clothes, he filled the stove to the lids and closed all of the drafts, so that there might be a fire in the morning. When he came back, Joey had climbed into bed.

Lying awake, Elias once more went over the events of the evening. Again he felt the glow of pride when he remembered Henderson's praise of his boy. Joey hadn't liked his experience of speaking before people, but then, all boys were like that; he'd soon get over it. Once Joey got it into his head to be the best in everything he did, why there'd be no stopping him. Elias probed into the future with a sudden faith. "He'll have this farm, and when I get ready to take things easier, it ought to be a pretty good place, if I do say so myself," he planned. "He'll be one of the big farmers, and people will expect a lot of him." This brought to the mind of the man lying there in the darkness of the small room, the triumph he himself had enjoyed. "Never thought in all the world that they were going to elect me for director," he mused. "I guess it's up to me to think a little about things off the farm— about the community." He looked down the way the years would lead and he saw himself taking on the role of patriarch, of kindly dictator, whose advice would be sought by all of the people in the countryside. "I've got to think things out," he decided, "and know this school business now that I'm an officer for the district." Then, at last, came the memory of what Mrs. Anderson had said. Not that he hadn't known for a long time that Lizzie was queer. But his mind and body were too healthily tired for depression now. "She'll be all right," he assured himself drowsily. "It's just a little spell, and she will be feeling better soon."

XIX

Next morning, the farmer dressed quietly so that he might not waken the woman. Shoes in hand, he went into the living room, where he slipped them on. After shaking down the fire and adding fuel from the box beside the stove, he pulled on his sheepskin coat and went out to do the chores.

The air was keen, with the bitter touch of cold that comes at winter sunrise. Elias hurried to the barn with the milkpail, hung it on a hook, and then gave the horses their oats and hay. He filled a half bushel measure with ear corn from the bin and carried it out to the small, straw-roofed shed set against the north side of the barn. When the ears rattled down to the frozen ground, the hogs rushed from the shed into the pen, grunting and squealing in their eagerness for the food.

Back in the stable once more, Elias tied the milk cows to the two-by-fours which served as stanchions, gave each animal a small forkful of hay, and started to milk. As he pulled the milkstool from the corner of the stall, a large black and white cat crawled from a hole in the bottom of the horses' manger and sleepily approached him.

"Merry Christmas!" the farmer called in greeting.

He seated himself and soon the sound of the milk striking the side of the metal pail mingled with the sound of the horses and cattle grinding their hay. The cat sat beside the milkstool, lazily watching the man's hands. As if in anticipation, she washed herself daintily with her paws.

"You're looking for something extra because it's Christmas, are you?" the farmer addressed the cat humorously. "Well, don't be too sure."

When he finished the milking the cat suddenly became frantic, purring excitedly and rubbing her body against his leg. Elias took down a small tin pan from a nail in the wall and filled it. "Now you ought to be satisfied," he declared, and watched the cat fall to her breakfast. She was all daintiness now that she was assured that her meal was before her, and the red tongue lapped the milk in leisurely enjoyment.

He first turned the milk cows out of the barn into the yard, where they joined the rest of the herd on the south side of the strawstack. As they saw him climb up the small mountain of cornstalks that were piled against the west side of the yard, they left this comfortable retreat and came up to the fence, their eyes watching him with quiet melancholy. It was cold work digging out the stalks which were frozen together and covered with a thin coating of ice and snow. At last he had thrown enough down into the yard. He stood there a moment longer, swinging his arms about his body to bring the blood back into the stiffened fingers. He looked down at the cattle below with proprietary interest. Ten head now—beginning of a big herd. What with cattle and hogs, a few head more each year, it wouldn't be long before he could turn off quite a few annually for market. Prices were getting better the last few years, and the freight rates to Kansas City and Omaha would not eat up all the profit.

The sharp, appetizing smell of boiling coffee came to him before he had opened the door.

"Merry Christmas!" he shouted, even before he had turned the knob.

Lizzie was near the stove. "Merry Christmas!" she returned the greeting with a half surprised smile, as though wondering at his animation.

"I beat you!" he said, laughing. "Remember how we used to try to be first to give everybody a 'Merry Christmas' back East?"

She nodded, her face hidden as she bent over the pan of frying pork.

"Where's Joey?" he asked in a muffled tone, while rubbing his face vigorously with the towel after washing himself in the icy water from the pail at the sink.

"He's sleeping."

The farmer tiptoed to the door of the room where the boy slept. Opening it a crack, he boomed out, "Merry Christmas, Joey!"

"Ah, I beat you too!" the father boasted. "I guess I'm the early bird in this family all right." Then, more quietly, "Better get up, Joey Boy; Ma's got breakfast about ready to put on the table."

The boy nodded.

At the morning meal, Elias kept up his high spirits. Lizzie and Joey smiled at his sallies, but said little in reply. When they had finished their breakfast, the farmer became solemn. He stood up, reached for the large family Bible that was on the shelf above his head, and thumbed the pages slowly. "We've not got up to the Gospels, like I hoped," he said, as though addressing strangers, "and I don't believe in skipping around every time we read the Bible, but today's a special day. Listen close, Joey!" In a heavy, reverent tone, he read from the second chapter of Luke. As he read, his mind was filled with the sense of beauty that always came with these words. Again he felt the magic and enchantment that he had felt in his boyhood at the Christmas season. His voice became more gentle as he reached the part of his reading that seemed to him to have most of the spirit of Christmas: "And there were shepherds in the same country, abiding in the field, and keeping watch over their flock by night. And an angel of the Lord stood by them, and the glory of the Lord shone round about them: and they were sore afraid. And the angel said unto them, 'Be not afraid; for behold, I bring you good tidings of great joy which shall be to all the people: for there is born to you this day in the city of David a Saviour, who is Christ the Lord. And this is the sign unto you: Ye shall find a babe wrapped in swaddling clothes, and lying in a manger.' And suddenly there was with the angel a multitude of the heavenly host praising God, and saying, 'Glory to God in the highest, and on earth peace, good will toward men.'"

The man closed the Bible carefully and then finished the morning's devotions with a prayer, a simple statement of thanksgiving and hope.

"Well, no work for me today." Elias took his pipe from the pocket of his sheepskin coat and filled it with long-cut tobacco from a leather pouch in another pocket. He tipped back his chair against the wall and sighed comfortably.

"You haven't said anything about me being elected school director, Ma," he observed casually.

"It's pretty nice, I think," she said timidly. "All the people clapped their hands so after you talked to them. I guess you can do it better'n anybody around here."

The farmer's head rested back against the wall. He blew out great puffs of blue smoke that eddied slowly toward the stove. He sighed again, more comfortably.

"Oh, I don't know," he replied after an interval. "There's lots of good men in this country."

"Yes, they're good enough; but they don't know books so well, just like the man said last night when he put your name up for director." She hesitated. "You're kind o' strict, too," she added. "If you make up your mind to a thing, you get it every time: just sort o' set in your ways."

Elias smoked in meditative silence. The kitchen was filled with slanting sunlight from the east window. There was a rattle of dishes as Lizzie washed them. Joey had a towel and dried the plates, maintaining a far-away silence, as was his wont. It surely was a fine morning, Elias reflected,—as fine as any he could remember. Why, Lizzie was feeling all right again; there was nothing wrong with her.

"I was thinking that Joey and I would go down to the crick for some things—twigs and leaves, you know—to fix up the house to show that we're celebrating. Then we'll come back and give our presents. What do you folks say to that?"

"Oh, I'm so anxious to get my present!" She turned a flushed face to him. "I hope it's something I like."

"I guess it is," he replied. "What about it, Joey—will you go along with the Old Man for decorations?"

"It's awful cold outside for him," the woman objected, and the boy looked at her gratefully.

"Cold!" sniffed Elias, "It's just a fine day for a boy to get some life into him. Sure, he's going with me. You're finished with the dishes, anyway, and Joey has to work up an appetite for a big dinner."

The woman forsook her work at the stove to bundle the boy into his coat and wrapped a long woollen scarf about his neck and face. The father watched this with a slight touch of humor in his eyes.

"Be careful to give him enough room to breathe," he observed. "He'll need his breath to keep up with me."

"Now don't you go too fast for him!" warned Lizzie, patting the boy's head in farewell.

The sun stood well up in a spotlessly pure blue sky. Elias stamped exuberantly into the snow, the boy floundering along at his heels. At the rise of ground that fell sharply before them to the bottom lands of the creek, the man halted, and stared out over the winter prairie land, turning slowly to enjoy the entire sweep of country that lay before him. All was radiance and sparkle. Mile after mile of rolling prairie shone a dazzling white under the intense blue of the sky. There was not a stir of wind; so great a stillness was upon the earth that he could hear the ringing in his own ears. To the west was the house, looking utterly homelike there, cuddled into its refuge of well-grown cottonwoods, and with a slow curl of woodsmoke weaving itself out of the chimney and thinning imperceptibly against the blue of the west. In the north and south, the light of the snow was caught up into the horizon, and it seemed to the man as though there were hidden suns sending up a crystal radiance from below the far rim of a winter world. To the east, there was more change. Below them, at the foot of the slope, the tortuously winding line of willows followed the creek. The light against them, with the snow beyond, gave them a tawny-red color. All the world was breathless with Christmas, the man felt, new-born, blue and white. He drew in great breaths of the mellow, cold air. "Can't you just taste the snow in your mouth!" he exclaimed, more to himself than to the boy.

Along the edge of the willows near the stream were great clumps of prairie grasses which the wind had not found and beaten down in the early winter storms. The man gathered them carefully and filled both his own arms and those of the boy.

"Cold, Joey?" he asked, as they were returning.

"Pretty cold," the boy quavered.

"Breathe deep and kick your legs. It's just that you stay inside too much. You want to be out more with me and then you'll never even know that it's cold. You're going to be a husky farmer some time, and you might as well get into trim for it right away."

Back in the house, Elias did most of the decorating of the living room. Lizzie helped a little, but had not time to spare from her cooking. Over doors and shelves, in deep pitchers on the table, the foliage was arranged, until the room was made warm by massed browns and tans and reds.

"Pretty nice, I say." Elias stepped back into the doorway of the kitchen and surveyed his work with pleased eyes. Then he suggested, "Now for our Christmas presents!"

The man went to the barn to get the packages he had hidden in the hay, and when he got back, he saw his wife placing other packages on the table.

"Shall I hand them out?" he asked.

The woman nodded assent.

"This is to Joey, with Merry Christmas from his ma," he said, as though reading this on the package he took up from the table. He waited until the boy had unwrapped the parcel and brought out a pair of black knitted mittens, held together by a long red string of yarn; after that, there were two little waists, of blue with broad gray stripes and, last, a pair of knitted stockings.

"Say, isn't all that just fine!" exclaimed the man. The boy nodded mutely, his face filled with happiness. Elias looked up and saw his wife's eyes fixed with devouring eagerness and tenderness upon the child.

"Next is a present from Mr. Vaughn to his wife, Lizzie," the man continued with an air of humorous gallantry.

"Thanks," she whispered shyly, and began to open the package with nervous fingers. When the dress unrolled under her fingers, she held it against her and stood before them. Her eyes shone.

"It's just beautiful!" she said. "So fine and soft, and such a pretty gray."

There were other presents, and Elias took a great deal of time in presenting them. Joey, by his father's purchase, gave his mother a bottle of cologne. Elias made this the occasion to remark, "You'll sure have an outfit like a lady now. And that's the way it ought to be. We're making out well, and it's time for us to be mixing around with other folks; they kind o' look up to us, you know, and I want you to look well."

Joey received a book, *Robinson Crusoe*, from his father, and a knife. The man opened his own parcels last of all: a stiffly-starched pleated shirt from Lizzie and a warm cap, with a fur lining that he could pull down over his ears, from Joey.

"Thanks," he said to both, feeling a queer embarrassment. "You folks got me mighty fine presents."

Later, he announced, "We'll all dress up for Christmas dinner! Joey'll put on his new waist and stockings; Ma will wear her new dress and put some cologne on it; and I'll wear the new shirt." He sniffed appreciatively of the odors that came from the kitchen. "Um, that smells good," he declared. "Is dinner going to be ready soon, Ma? Joey and his dad are getting hungry."

"In half an hour," she promised. "You go and dress, and help Joey put on his things and then, while you keep an eye on the stove, I'll change my clothes."

The dinner was another feature of this day to be long remembered, Elias decided somewhat later. He sat at the table rather stiffly, feeling the unaccustomed glory of a new shirt with a stiff bosom. Opposite, Lizzie sat, with the coffee pot resting on a saucer beside her plate. She had never looked so fine, in his judgment. The dress was of a soft gray woollen material, with the collar and cuffs of a dull blue. Somehow, it made her look slim and girlish and added to that wistful expression he liked to see in her eyes.

"You look ten years younger, Lizzie," he declared, while passing his cup to her to be filled for the second time.

Joey confined all of his attention to the meal, with the presents he could not wear placed about him on the table. The spirit within Elias expanded. He rubbed his newlyshaven chin with his hand and looked about him with growing satisfaction. The platter of chicken, fried a golden brown in butter, showed little effects from the first inroads made upon it; the blue bread-plate was stacked high; a dish of cranberry sauce glowed festively in the center of the table, flanked by a dish of potatoes and the bowl of gravy. And all this, food in rich array partially hidden by brown and red clusters of foliage gathered that morning, was set upon a tablecloth of red and white squares. In the red squares was a white figure, a king's royal crown, and this became a red crown in the white squares.

As they pushed back their chairs at last, Elias cleared his throat and remarked, "I like your dress more and more, Liz. Come to think of it, I believe it looks a lot better on you than your red one. Tell you what, you keep this one for going out and for company, and wear the red one on special days at home, like the Sundays when we don't go to church."

"All right," she agreed, in a satisfied way.

After the dishes had been washed, Lizzie came into the living room, where Elias was smoking his pipe, his legs crossed, his eyes fixed ruminatively on nothing.

"I'm kind o' tired," she sighed. "All this excitement and all—"

"It's been too much for you?" he asked quietly. "You better go and sleep awhile."

She took up the tablecloth from the table, folded it carefully, and placed it in the top drawer of the brown cupboard which stood in the corner. Then, as though she had just decided to act upon his suggestion, she assented, "Guess I'll lay down a little while. There's nothing much for me to do, I guess."

"Joey and I will keep quiet as mice," he promised.

She went into the other room. The boy sat on the chair near one of the west windows, his presents spread out on the table, taking up each one and giving it a long careful scrutiny. The man stood up, knocked out his pipe into the wood-box, and crossed over to where the boy sat. He picked up the book which he had given Joey, a book with a brown binding, the outside cover of which had stamped into it, in black and red lines, the picture of an uncouth man wearing a cone of thatch on his head and carrying a formidable gun over one shoulder. Elias thumbed the pages casually.

"Ought to be real interesting," he observed, and soon he found himself starting to read. He looked up. "Better start reading this now, Joey," he said. "That will be a good way of putting in the afternoon."

"Oh, I don't care to just now," the boy replied.

"I'll read the first for you," the father offered. "Just as soon as you get the hang of the story, you'll want to hear all of it, and then you can read it for yourself." He resumed his chair, and with a voice heavy and artificial in the effort to read with some expression, he read several pages. The story was worth getting into, it seemed, and as he forgot himself in the tale, he read more easily. Suddenly he glanced up and saw that the boy's head had fallen forward, and that he was fast asleep. The man sighed. Joey ought to care a little more about books.

He picked up the book again. Page after page was turned. The heavy, red face was full of absorption. The deep-set gray eyes, steady and concentrated, now and then took on an intensity of excitement, and again lightened into their former absorption.

The mind of the man was far from this little room of a prairie farmhouse. He moved in strange countries, was at odds with his parents, ran off to sea, and had, one after the other, high adventures, braving adversity of wind and wave. All caught up in the story, still there was at the back of his mind a knowledge of his delight. He became Robinson Crusoe, an adventurous man, wayward of fancy, but at heart moral and righteous. He suffered captivity among the Moors, escaped, was a planter in Brazil, and finally set off on a voyage for slaves. It seemed almost right to go for slaves. That wild land needed a lot of cheap labor for clearing.

The boy awoke from his sleep and went about his affairs. The woman came from the adjoining room, looked curiously at the man, but made no remark. He seemed not to know that they were there. The clock on the shelf ticked loudly in the room. The panes of the west windows began to show rose color in the sky. The woman cleared her throat, looked at the man, and said nothing. The rose in the sky deepened to red. Lizzie put her hand on the man's shoulder. He looked up, as though awakening from a dream.

"About time for the chores, ain't it?" she asked, in her thin, colorless voice.

He looked out of the window and then at the clock. He jumped to his feet as though he had suddenly realized what she meant.

"I should say it is time for the chores!" He quickly pulled on his coat and cap and went outdoors, with the milk pail swinging in the crook of his arm.

In spite of the cold air and his activity, he could not throw off the spell of the story which he had been reading. As the milk streamed soapily into the froth of the pail, his mind was off on a rocky, mysterious island in a far-away sea. He could see it all, and his mind pondered over the dangers to be met in this strange place. He stood up, threw the milk stool into the cornet, took the lighted lantern from the nail in the wall, and left the barn, closing the door behind him carefully.

During the evening meal he said scarcely a word. As soon as they had finished eating, he filled his pipe, drew down the hanging lamp until the long cut glass pendants hanging from the rim of the white shade were on a level with his eyes and brought the flame to him in violet, red, and yellow, and then leaned back in his chair once more, book in hand.

Almost at once the spell came back upon him. When he issued forth with his gun and shot a goat, he exulted; when he took that first extended trip into his domain and discovered vines loaded down with grapes, he was filled with thanksgiving, and the rich flavor of the fruit was in his mouth. He'd dry these grapes, too, and eat raisins. His wheat crop, grown from hidden kernels in discarded chaff, was on his mind. Then, finally, there was the horror of a human footprint on the yellow sand of the beach, and his scalp crawled. On and on he read, until at last all was over. Half hypnotized, he came to the end. For some time he sat there motionless, staring up toward the lamp. Again, without awareness, his eyes noted the violet and orange flashes that came from the sharp edges of the glass pendants.

The fog began to draw out of his brain. It seemed to him that he had been gone on a long trip, that he had been to the very ends of the earth, amid danger and enchantment, that he had known a delight of physical struggle which now was over. A queer, happy weariness was upon him. Slowly he became aware of the loud ticking of the clock. It was long after midnight! Startled, he stood up. Lizzie and Joey must have gone to bed hours ago. He shook his head as though to dispel the illusion in which he had lived for most of the day. "What a book!" he exclaimed to himself, aloud, in a pondering, wondering tone. "What a book!"

The mood would not leave him entirely, and he felt almost foreign in this room, which he now fully recognized. He opened the door and stood outside for a few minutes, breathing deeply. Reality seemed to draw into him now. He looked at the sky. The stars were shining with unusual brilliance out of a soft, velvety darkness. The air, too, had lost its sharpness and had a mellow touch.

"Change of weather coming all right," he prophesied to himself. "Maybe snow."

As he undressed in the dark room, he looked back over the day. It had been full and overflowing, a happy day.

Next morning he saw his prophecy fulfilled. The sky was gray and lowering, with a sullen wind blowing in from the northeast. Toward the latter part of the afternoon it began to snow.

That Christmas was doubly memorable to Elias Vaughn because it seemed to mark the end of his wife's strength. With the bitter cold of that winter, a slow, creeping sickness came upon her so that she was scarcely able to leave her bed until warm weather returned. Now, with the boy gone to school five days a week, Elias took upon himself the entire burden of the housework. He said nothing about it: an hour earlier in getting up in the morning and an hour later in finishing the chores at night did not bother him. Sometimes, however, especially in the days of early spring, when sky and earth were in dour mood, he pondered over things. Lizzie never was really well anymore; her mind seemed to be in a fog, far away. Of course, Joey had to keep on with his schooling, and so he couldn't help much. But the work on the farm had been growing steadily; there was more stock every year, a few more head of cattle, a few more hogs. All of the farm was working now, Vaughn reflected with a touch of satisfaction, and there wasn't an acre that had not been plowed down or placed in pasture. And they were getting on.

Under the constant weight of heavy work, his habit of silence was strengthened. His movements became more deliberate, and there was a curious change in his face. The fine lines in his cheeks and around his eyes, seemingly drawn by the buffeting weather, became deeper and took on the significance of advancing years. The bushy mass of hair was mixed with gray. The alertness of youth had long gone from him, and the gray eyes looked out about him in quiet, steady speculation. The man's body, as powerful as ever, was more stooped now, and the shoulders were drawn together. As though to counteract this, the head was held forward, the mouth was set more grimly.

That which as change was painful to him—Lizzie's sickness and the constant overwork—was soon accepted as a normal part of life, inevitable. That winter of decline was not unhappy, and the slow succession of seasons, winter and spring and summer and fall, saw the sowing and the harvesting. Theirs was a full measure of the peace that is in quietness.

There was more stir in their lives when Joey finally finished "country school" and his father decided that he should go to the school at Hayes. The boy made no objection; the woman did not seem to comprehend the change much, even though Joey came home now only on Friday evenings and had to leave again before dawn on Monday mornings, making the fifteen miles on horseback. At Hayes he lived with the Andersons. He still maintained the remote, impersonal expression he had had ever since he was a child, but sometimes he talked, especially on the first evening of his return home. He spoke infrequently of his school work, but most of the time he brought news of settlers coming in and the prices that were being paid for land. At such times the man listened eagerly. Then, one evening, the boy informed them that people were coming into their own section. An Iowa man, John Schneider, had bought the half-section running up to their south line, and he and his family were coming in the spring.

The farmer smoked silently for some time over this piece of news. Then, as he knocked the ashes from his pipe into the stove, he remarked, "Guess maybe we'd better try to buy the eighty on our north line before land gets too high. Even if we can't work it right away, it'll save money for us if we buy now. It won't be long before you're out of school, and then we can tackle it together."

The boy did not reply.

It was the time of Indian summer and of corn-husking. Next morning, long before daylight, they were about the chores, and the sun was just above the horizon when the wagons pulled into the field. At mid-morning they halted their work to eat their lunch, large slices of bread thickly spread with butter, which the man had prepared just after breakfast. As the father unfolded the newspaper into which the food had been wrapped, he asked, "What do you think of our getting that piece of land I was talking about last night, Joe?"

The boy ate hungrily, without replying. At last he said briefly, "I don't know. It'll mean a lot more work."

"Oh, the work won't hurt us," the man said, with a touch of displeasure in his voice. "When you get out of school, there'll be two of us." As the boy did not say anything further, the man stood up, and soon there sounded again the regular thud-thud as the ears of corn were thrown up against the backboards of the wagon.

Early Monday morning, as they rose from the breakfast table, the farmer drew the boy aside. "Ask Anderson to let the land office at Junction City know that I'm in the market for a piece of land," he instructed.

"Don't have to send to Junction City any more for that," Joey informed him. "There's a railroad land man over to Hayes now. He's been there two or three weeks. I seen him lots o' times." There was a touch of importance in his tones. "I'll tell him myself."

"Just tell him that your dad might buy if the price was right. And tell him, too, that if he's coming up, he might as well come some time the last of this week."

The farmer turned to the woman, who still sat at the table. He thought that he detected a certain curiosity in her face.

"We're going to be big farmers, Ma," he said jokingly. "It won't be long before there'll be a farm for each of us."

She smiled and stood up to get the boy's coat and cap. Joey accepted her help without remark.

The land salesman came on Thursday of that week. Elias heard the rattle of buggy wheels while he was at cornhusking. When he saw the team headed in toward the farmyard, he climbed into his wagon and drove to the house.

The agent met him as the wagon creaked from the soft, spongy earth of the cornfield to the harder sod in the yard. The men exchanged abrupt greetings. The newcomer helped Vaughn to unhitch his team.

"I'm Farring, land agent for the Great Northern," he introduced himself, as they led the horses to the water trough. "Your boy told me that you were in the market for a piece of land."

"Maybe," the farmer replied noncommittally. "That depends on a lot of things." He looked up and saw the agent, a tall young fellow whose face was a deep, even brown, smile good-naturedly. Elias decided that he could deal openly with this man; he gave an impression of utter honesty.

Leaving Farring outside for a few moments, Elias went into the house.

"We'll have company for dinner, Ma," he explained.

The woman was working at the table. "I know," she replied, without turning.

The two men walked over the line of the half section to the north of the farm. Their talk was desultory, about the weather and the crops. Each knew that the other had already decided the conditions attending his part of the transaction, and that this inspection of the land was merely out of respect to immemorial custom.

They came out at the southeast corner.

"Not a bad half section," commented Farring.

"We can't handle more than an eighty," countered Elias.

They walked diagonally toward the barn. Both men were chewing reflectively on timothy stems.

"Well," the agent said at last, "the Company will want twenty-seven and a half an acre for the half section, and thirty for the quarter."

"I'll give twenty-five on the south eighty, on terms."

The younger man shook his head firmly. They said no more about it. The farmer led the way to the house.

When he entered, Elias saw that Lizzie's cheeks were flushed, her eyes bright. She smiled at Farring. The agent nodded to her and then followed the farmer to the sink, where the men splashed water over their faces until, refreshed and half blinded, they groped for the roller towel.

Following the custom of the country, the men did not talk during the early part of the meal, but devoted all of their attention to the food.

"You've got a pretty nice place here," Farring remarked to Elias as his coffee cup was being filled. The farmer, whose face had been bent over his plate, looked up and nodded briefly.

"We're gettin' to be big farmers, all right," the woman said, in her soft, shy voice. "Joey's goin' to town school, and Pa's director of the school out there. They all voted for him, so he just had to take it."

Elias lifted his face to stare at her. There was a momentary alarm in his eyes, and then the features became as steady and unemotional as always.

"Oh, it isn't much of a job," he declared, a slow smile widening his mouth. "Somebody's got to be director."

"Well, they made him super'ntendent of the Sunday school at Hayes, too," the woman continued eagerly, "and just a little while back there was some talk that they wanted 'lias to have a real big job over to the county seat."

The farmer had stopped eating. "Oh," he expostulated pleasantly, "it was just that the east part of the county has always elected its own men to the county office jobs, and some fellows around here got together and decided that I ought to run for the County Treasurer's office. That doesn't mean that I would've been elected—not by a long shot! And anyway, you wouldn't catch me leaving this farm for a white collar job in town! I've put in too much work here, and it won't be long now till my boy can help me out."

The woman did not again return to the subject. For some reason, which Elias felt that he understood, she talked a great deal during the meal, and always to the stranger. The farmer sat back in his chair, his heavy face in repose. Now and then his eyes lifted slowly to glance at the woman. Her thin face, usually white and listless, now had wisps of red at the cheek bones. Her expression was almost animated, the weak eyes as lively as they had been for a long time.

"He's company," the farmer thought, "and Lizzie always did like to have people around." He stood up, and took the pail of tobacco from the nail in the wall.

"Better light up, Farring," he advised. "Ma isn't very strong nowadays, and I'm giving her a little lift with the chores in the house. By the time you got a big pipeful smoked out, I'll be ready."

The woman had pushed her chair to its place at the window. As he cleared the dishes from the table, Elias glanced at her often.

The animation had gone from her face now, and the old wistful weariness was there again. The sunlight from the window brought out the lines in her cheeks. The hair, neatly combed for this occasion, was of that lifeless color between yellow and gray.

The farmer took the dishcloth down from the hook behind the stove and began to make the water soapy. Farring, who had tilted his chair back against the wall in silent enjoyment of his pipe, stood up.

"Where's a towel?" he asked.

"No, you don't have to help," Vaughn replied. "Fill your pipe."

"It isn't every day I get such a good dinner," Farring observed, turning toward the woman, "and I'd like to give a lift, too."

The farmer saw that his wife had not heard this. He decided that he'd tell her about it in the evening; she'd like to know what the stranger had said. He gave Farring a towel, and the men went about their work with that awkwardness and concentration peculiar to men who are used to heavier toil.

When they were once more out-of-doors, sitting on the green carpet of grass under one of the cottonwoods, they maintained the silence that had come upon them in the house. Through the windless air the waxy, yellow leaves of the cottonwood fluttered lazily to the ground. All about them was the mellow haze of autumn, deepening into purple shadow where the sky met the earth far to the east of them.

"So you can't pay more than twenty-five an acre for the south eighty?" Farring turned his lean, brown face to the farmer.

"No, I guess not," Elias replied. "Not just yet. Of course, if I wait, it may go up, but I can't let myself in debt for too much. You see, we just finished paying off on this farm a little while back." After a pause, he told the agent the story of their coming to this prairie region and of their struggle to stay. He talked in abrupt sentences, minimizing the difficulties, trying again to express what this new land meant to him. The young fellow lay back on the grass, his eyelids narrowed to slits.

When Elias had finished, he got up. "Time to be going," he declared. "I want to get back to town before dark."

They led the horses from the barn and hitched them to the buggy. Farring gathered up the reins.

"Just how much could you pay down on the eighty, Mr. Vaughn?" he asked suddenly.

The farmer stared at him in surprise. "Why, I could scrape about four or five hundred together," he stated. Then he asked quickly, "Are you thinking of letting me have it at my price?"

"The Company lets me go my own way pretty much in selling the land." Farring stepped into the buggy. He added, with a quiet friendliness in his tone, "The land's a bargain at that price, but I'm going to let you have it, and I'll tell you why. For one thing, you're an old settler, and you stuck it out here. You have the best farm anywhere this side of Hayes, and you're good advertising for us. All we have to do is to point to what you've done to show people that this is real farming country. And then," he finished slowly, "I've had dinner with you people, and I guess I know you pretty well. You're the kind that this country needs—solid and dependable." He held out his hand. The farmer gripped it. A queer look, almost of exaltation, was in his face.

"I'll come around with the contract next week," Farring promised, as he drove off. "Tell Mrs. Vaughn that I'm coming around for another of her good dinners."

The farmer went into the house and spent half an hour telling about the land deal. Lizzie showed passive interest. Then, when he

told her how Farring had enjoyed his dinner and would come again
in a week, her eyes brightened.

"He liked it, didn't he!" she exclaimed. "He's so nice!"

"You bet he is!" the man agreed fervently.

Later, he left the house and spent the rest of the afternoon on
the piece of land that would soon be his. Seated on the brown
prairie grass at the head of a swell of ground, his eyes traveled
dreamily over the rising and falling expanse of land before him.
Now, with the yellow light of late autumn afternoon softening
its contours, it seemed a magic land. In his mind he was already
working this addition to his farm. Out there on the west side
would be pasture land, and on the east he would put in wheat and
corn.

And so he dreamed, while the day went on toward evening.
There was not a cloud in the sky. The sun idled down toward the
western horizon, bathing the distances in a clear yellow light. Not a
sound broke the spell of silence that lay upon far-spread prairie.

XXI

The worst blizzard in years came in the January of Joe's last year in the Hayes High School. He still made the trip on horseback, starting out early on Monday mornings and returning home on Friday evenings. The weather for the two days preceding had been unusually mild, a "January thaw." By ten o'clock of the first day, under the influence of the warm Chinook wind, the glassy surface of the snow had become sodden and dull with concentrating dirt. At night the temperature went below freezing, and in the morning the eaves of the house and the barn showed long rows of ribbed icicles. The sun came out warm again and, before mid-morning, the air was full of Spring. The water seeping down the roofs loosened the icicles and they fell to the earth in a steady succession of tiny crashes. At noon, the thin sound of running water was everywhere. On the slopes were wavering, converging lines where runlets had formed, eating narrow canyons through the dirty, pallid snow. Here and there, on southern exposures, patches of washed-out brown grass appeared. And there was the smell of Spring out-of-doors, that indescribable, exhilarating smell of soggy earth that comes on the first days of thaw.

In the morning, Vaughn drove down to the small haystack built on the bottom land east of the house, as the hay in the small loft of the barn was almost gone. He had made the wagon-rack years before from odd pieces of board which had now become so rotten that nails would no longer hold them together, and even the use of wire at the corners of the rack did not prevent the boards from slapping loosely as the horses, full of spirits after a month of rest, galloped down the rough wagon trail as fast as the restraining reins would allow them. The man pulled the team to a halt beside the stack and fell to work, first pitching the wet hay at the top to the ground and then filling the wagon. Several times he jumped into the rack, tramping the hay down before piling in more. At such intervals, before taking up his work with the pitchfork again, he stood, leaning on the fork handle, breathing deeply of the warm air. His eyes were filled with the glow that comes when the blood is running free; but there was in the eyes, too, a quietness. As strong now as it was when he was a boy, this sense of the mystery of the earth and sky and air was upon him. Then it had been exuberance; now it was life to him. All this went over him as high emotion that only dimly worked toward thought.

By the time that the hay had been pitched into the loft, the wagon driven away, and the horses unhitched, the farmer saw that there was no shadow on the west side of the barn, and he made his way to the house, his heavy shoes sinking into the soft mud of the yard. Before he came to the trees near the house, he stopped for a moment and looked about him, almost aimlessly.

The sky was blue, but the color had thinned out. The sun stood at the zenith, sharply cut against the sky, a yellow ball that was touched with faint red along the rim. The wind was not as strong as it had been in the morning. Mists had drawn in, and the horizon was pale gray. The man turned and continued on his way to the house.

"It's been a fine morning, Ma," he observed cheerfully, as he helped the woman with preparations for the meal.

"Yes," she assented, smiling.

It struck him that she was in a more tranquil mood than she had been in the earlier years. There was an ease in her face like that of a child.

"It's Friday," he remarked. "Joey will be coming home tonight."

Her face lighted up. "Why," she said confusedly, "I guess it is, all right. I don't seem to keep track of days very well."

"But you're not forgetting Joey, I guess."

She shook her head in the negative. "He's always gone so long!" she sighed, "and I just keep thinking of him all the time. I just feel sort o' good when he's around."

"Well, just a few more months," he said cheerfully, "and Joe will be through school, and then he'll be with us again."

Their conversation kept on while they ate their dinner. Afterwards, he cleared the table and washed the dishes.

"You better lay down for a while on bed," he suggested. "It's a kind o' lazy day, and when I get through here, I believe I'll settle down by the stove and get a little sleep, too."

She got up from her chair and went docilely into the bedroom. The man placed the dishes on the shelves of the tall brown cupboard in the kitchen. Then he took down his fur coat from the hook and spread it before the woodburner in the dining room. His fingers fumbled for a long time at the wet knots of his shoestrings, but finally he pulled his shoes off and set them beside the stove to dry. With a deep breath of relaxation he lay back on the overcoat and almost instantly fell into a deep sleep.

He awoke slowly, his mind hanging pleasantly in that region where he was dreaming and was aware that he was dreaming. Then, suddenly, a sense of something impending brought him to full consciousness. He rose to his feet.

The room was dim. In her chair by the window the woman sat, her elbow resting on the table, looking out with wide, unseeing eyes into the murk that had come over the world.

"I must 'a' slept all afternoon!" the man exclaimed. "It's high time I was getting at the chores." He stepped closer to the south wall where the long clock ticked slowly in its brown case. "Why, it's only half past four!" he said in astonishment. He quickly stepped to the window where she was. "I wish Joey was home!" His tone was touched with anxiety.

"I'll see him when he comes up the road," the woman said. "He'll be coming in a little while. It's going on to five; he most always gets home by five."

"Well, I'm going to do the chores," the farmer said. He filled the stove with fuel, lighted the hanging lamp, and then went out-of-doors.

In the interval of time since noon, the face of the prairie had become unutterably dingy; a lifeless, low-hanging sky brooded over an indistinct, murky earth. The wind had gone down, and the sodden air pressed down like a dead weight, so that it seemed to the man that it was hard to breathe.

Usually all of the stock except the milk cows were allowed to remain in the cornfield during the night. Now, however, after he had hung the milk pails on their hooks in the barn, the farmer walked out to the field and rounded up all of the animals, both cattle and horses. He drove them into the small yard near the barn and fastened carefully the horizontal poles which served as gates. Every now and then he looked to the west, where the trail led to the farm yard, but there was no sign of life.

He finished the milking hurriedly, gave the horses their hay and each of the cows a bundle of cornstalks. When he left the barn, he closed the door and then, because the latch was insecure, placed a piece of timber slanting against it.

"I'm going out to meet Joey, Ma," he said, when he entered the house. "The weather looks kind o' bad. Just take it easy till we get back. We can take care o' supper all right. Maybe I'll be gone a while, but you mustn't worry."

"No," she promised. He saw that she did not know that anything was wrong. He looked at the clock again. It was twenty minutes after five.

Vaughn quickly placed the bridle on the oldest horse and, riding bareback, rode through the black screen of the cottonwoods into the open prairie. He kept his head down, his mind filled with speculation about the boy. Subconsciously, he noted all the signs that pointed out the gathering storm: the darkness all about him made uncanny by a strange, pallid light that stayed in the sky, the boding silence, the uneasy gait of his horse. He had gone several miles before the first puff of wind from the northwest struck him. It was dark now, with a blackness deeper than night. With the arrival of the fitful wind, a strange rising and falling moan, like the sigh of a great host, rose from the earth. The air had grown sharp. Suddenly the snow came down; large, wet flakes swirled about him. His horse stopped.

Vaughn looked up. In a moment he saw that the horse had halted at the fork where the trail to the district school branched off to the west. The rider sat there for some minutes, undecided. He remembered that the boy sometimes came home the longer way, especially this last year when one of his former schoolmates had started going to the high school at Hayes. Well, it had to be one way or the other; Joey surely might have seen that the weather looked bad, and in that case, he would have taken the direct road straight north out of town.

In sudden decision, Vaughn pressed his knees against the sides of the horse, and the animal started obediently down the better traveled trail.

To the man it seemed that they rode for an hour. The wind, although it came from his back, had become a wild, raging thing now. The darkness was less intense as the snow deepened underfoot, lending a little reassurance. The man had the wide collar of the sheepskin coat turned up about his neck and ears. The swirling wind drove hard pellets of fine snow into his face, so that he pulled his cap down as far as he could. No use trying to see, anyway; the horse would keep to the road.

Just then it seemed that the storm had abated. All about him there was a great tumult, but the wind had apparently gone off into the upper regions of the air. The horse stopped. The man struck the animal lightly with his foot. The horse did not move.

The farmer looked up in perplexity. Could the beast have heard something? Maybe he heard Joey coming down the trail. Then Vaughn caught a quick glimmer of light. In a moment he had slipped from the horse and stepped a few paces forward. His outstretched hand came into contact with a board. No wonder that it had seemed to him a short while before that the wind had changed its direction! The horse had turned on the trail and had gone back home. The light he had seen was from the house. The man opened the door of the barn and drove the animal inside, without removing the bridle. Then he strode to the house, stopping twice to make sure of the light. There had been stories of men lost in blizzards, frozen to death within a few rods of their dwellings.

The farmer turned the knob slowly. Surely Joey would be home now! He must have come back by the other trail, after all, and so they had missed each other on the way. A sweep of wind tore the knob from his hand and the door crashed open. At the same moment the flame of the hanging lamp flared wildly and went out.

Violently the man caught the door and pushed it shut, pressing against it with his foot until the latch clicked shut. Then feeling in his pocket, he found a match and lighted it on the hot surface of the stove. Before he applied the flame to the wick of the lamp, he looked quickly about the room. The woman was there, standing in the middle of the room, but there was no one else. The wick took the flame quickly, and the room filled with yellow lamplight.

"Where's Joey?"

At the sharp intensity of his wife's voice, the farmer turned quickly. The woman stood before him. He stepped back before the wild light in her eyes. Her hands were drawn to her sides, clasping and unclasping nervously.

"Where's Joey?" she repeated.

"Why," he stammered, "I don't know. I thought maybe he'd be home."

"He's out alone!" Her voice gathered power and rose into a cry.

"Now, now, Ma—"

She had turned toward the door, but he intercepted her and placed his back against it.

"Let me go! I can find him!" Her voice, wild and beseeching, was as he had never heard it. Almost roughly he pushed her back.

She stood stock-still, facing him, her face partially shaded from the light. The room resounded with the roar of the storm. The woman's hands worked ceaselessly. Her face, framed by an unkempt mass of hair that had come down about it, was filled with an expression of malign violence.

"You—you!" Her words grated from her throat in a harsh whisper that came to him clearly. She came closer to him, with a stealthy movement.

"Now, Ma," the man expostulated again, "I'm goin' right out again. I'll meet Joey sure this time."

She didn't seem to hear. "You took him away," she said, in a strange, high monotone. "He wanted to stay here with me, but you made him go away! And now he's gone!" Her features became convulsed.

The farmer took one stride forward, caught her swiftly in his arms, and held her powerless.

"We've had enough of that! Now be quiet!"

She struggled futilely.

"Be quiet!" he shouted into her face.

He felt her body relax in his arms. Lifting her, he carried her to a chair. Then he stood before her.

"You stay there, d'you hear!" he commanded. "Now I'm going out to find Joey, and you're going to stay right on that chair till we get back."

His heavy, red face, covered with a ragged growth of beard, glowered over her. She became submissive.

Before he opened the door to leave the house, he ordered again, "Stay right there till we get back." Then he slammed the door behind him, and in a moment was caught into the bitter tumult of the blizzard. More by guidance of habit than by sight, he made his way to the barn, pulled the unwilling horse out, and again rode out of the yard.

Before he had gone far, his horse neighed. The man raised his head sharply. There was no sound except the thunder of the wind. The horse neighed again.

"Ho—Joey!" the man shouted with all the strength of his lungs. "Ho-o, Joe!"

He could hear no reply.

Then the horse stopped dead in his tracks. The straining eyes of the farmer caught a deeper blot of darkness ahead. This came up and took on the vague outline of horse and rider.

"All right, Joey?" The man's voice, curiously bluff and hearty now, roared into the storm.

"Half froze!" he heard, as though from far away, pitched in a high key.

The farmer kicked the boy's horse and then, as the animal started forward, followed behind.

When they reached the barn, Vaughn slipped the bridle from his horse and turned him into the stall. Then he turned and lifted the boy from the saddle and set him down. Joey swayed and crumpled to the ground. Swiftly the father took the bridle off the horse, drove it into the barn, and closed the door again. He lifted the boy in his arms and strode through the darkness toward the house. Twice, as he walked into unexpected drifts, he stumbled. The lighted window loomed up before them. In a moment they were inside.

Elias looked quickly toward the corner of the room. The woman still sat there, where he had told her to stay. She started up. When she saw the boy, she began to cry, soundlessly as always, but her face was alive with joy. The father placed Joey on a chair near the fire. The woman bent over the child, her hands fondling his cheeks, reaching down for his hands. He pulled away.

"I'm cold!" he said irritably. "Can't I warm up by myself?"

Vaughn had stepped outside and now came back with a panful of snow. He stooped, pulled off the boy's shoes and stockings, and began rubbing snow over the feet.

"Let me do it!" the woman asked eagerly, and the farmer silently gave her his place.

When the blood began to circulate once more, the boy began to groan out in pain. Elias, who had started to prepare the supper, said almost sharply, "Come now, you can stand it all right. That will go over in a little while. Your Ma's doing all she can."

The boy relapsed into silence. The woman continued to rub snow over his feet, her face now and then lifting to look up at the boy in wistful reassurance.

"That ought to be enough," Joey said, after a short time. "That snow's cold." He turned in his chair to look at the table. "Ain't we ever goin' to get anything to eat?" he demanded.

The farmer's eyes gleamed.

"I'll go and help Pa," Lizzie said quickly. She rose, leaned her hand lightly on the boy's shoulder for a moment, and then helped to set the table.

All through the night and all through the next day the storm continued with unabated violence. On the second evening, as the man scratched the thick frost from the window, he saw a rift of sunset flaring sullenly low in the west.

"Going to be clear tomorrow," he predicted.

XXII

The farmer and his boy were cultivating the corn for the third and last time of the season. This spring the field lay to the east of the house where, on the preceding year, there had been wheat.

Vaughn pulled up the shovels of his cultivator as the horses came to the end of the row and walked out upon the meadow that bordered the cornfield on the south. "Whoa, boys," he called cheerfully. The horses, apparently knowing that they would get a rest, put their heads down to crop the thick mat of grass at their feet. The boy's team pulled alongside.

"Where'd you put the lunch, Joe?" the man asked.

"I'll get it," the boy replied briefly. He walked a short distance to the corner of the field and stooped down for the parcel which he had left there when they had come early in the morning. He unwrapped the newspaper that had been folded about two large dried beef sandwiches. One he handed to his father and the other one he kept.

They sat cross-legged on the soft carpet of grass and ate the food with the heartiness of outdoor appetites. Then, when they had finished eating, the boy lay back and blinked lazily up at the sky. The man started to read something in the paper that had caught his eye, but it did not hold his attention. He leaned back against the cultivator and gazed about him in relaxed enjoyment.

It was a warm, cloudless day, with a soft wind blowing from the south. Overhead, the blue of the sky seemed curiously remote and transparent, while at the horizon was a soft duskiness of color—like the color of wine, the farmer thought. In the genial heat of the morning sun, rising silently to its meridian, the whole world seemed to be pleasantly a-drowse. All around him in the meadow multitudes of crickets were chirping and singing in rhythm, a mighty pulsation of delicate sound that emphasized, curiously, the silence in the air. A bumble-bee droned drunkenly by and alighted on a bending spike of purple flowers, like small pea blossoms. Suddenly, above all this ebb and flow of earthy sounds, came a ringing burst of melody. The man looked up alertly and saw the singer, a prairie meadow lark, perched on a fence-post at the pasture's edge. The song came in a sustained, joyous call that drenched the drowsy air with music. Then the bird flew away, and again the sleepy silence asserted itself.

For these moments the man had been lost in a kind of ecstasy. Without consciously thinking about it, he knew that he was unlike other men: he was closer to the glory that is in the earth. In turbulent storm, in the white quietness of winter days or the golden glamour of Indian summer, on blue days or gray—it was always the same—the mood of earth and sky was his mood.

He was roused by the boy, who, yawning, pulled himself to a sitting position. The farmer looked at his son.

"Been sleeping, Joe?"

"No."

"About time we were getting into the corn again. We'll have to finish the field by Saturday night. I'd like to get started with haying on Monday." The man stood up.

The boy cleared his throat. "When I was in town last Sunday," he began, speaking with difficulty, "I was talkin' to Hollins—he's surveyor for the railroad, you know—and he said he could find me a job in Junction City this fall."

The man straightened. His face was impassive, his eyes quiet.

"But you don't want a job in Junction City," he said, after an interval. "You've got a job right here."

The boy's expression became sullen. "I don't care much for the farm," he muttered. "It's a dog's life."

The farmer laughed. "Somebody's been putting fool ideas in your head, Joe," he said. "Ma and I wouldn't know what to do without you. Why, we've got almost half a section farm now! Some day it's going to be yours, and you'll have the best place in the country, if I do say so myself. Just forget about that job. You've got something a hundred times better right where you are."

The boy made no reply. The farmer took up the reins and guided his team into the next row of corn. When he looked back, he saw that the other team was close behind him. "Joe can keep up with the work all right," he reflected. "There's nothing in that job he's thinking about. He'll forget about it in a week or so."

On the first of the following week they started with the haying. What with the wild hay to be made from the piece of land purchased the year before, in addition to the meadow-land they already had, the pressure of work became terrific. They were up at daybreak, took care of the chores, milked seven cows, swallowed their breakfast hurriedly, and were in the field before the sun had dried the dew. When they drove home at night, it was always late. Day followed day, and there were haystacks in three fields. The boy worked hard, but he said nothing. The sullen expression on his face never lifted.

When all of the hay had been put up, the oats were ready for cutting. The weather had turned hot, with now and then a violent thunderstorm at night. At noon the humid, heavy air wavered upward, weaving the same unreality over the land as on other summers.

On the third morning of harvest, the man drove his team of three horses down along the edge of the meadow to the field. The boy followed behind, carrying a jug of water in a sack. When they reached the binder at a corner of the uncut oats, the man gave the reins to the boy.

"You hitch them to the machine, Joe," he said, "and I'll tighten the canvases."

The boy was unused to handling three horses, and Vaughn, looking up from his work, saw that one of the horses, a bronco, would not step over the tongue of the binder to its place. Twice the boy drove the animal up, and each time the bronco shied away, frightened.

"I'll show you, you devil!" the boy shouted violently. "You get over there, or I'll kill you!"

"Drive them ahead and then back them into it, Joe," the man advised, "and don't get mad."

Joe tried once more, and again the bronco caused trouble. With a curse the boy threw down the reins, sprang to the bronco's head, seized the bridle with one hand, and with the other clenched, struck the horse repeatedly on the muzzle until the blood streamed. The animal pranced back and forth in fear and pain. The other two horses pulled away, and in a moment all was a tangle of harness. The farmer ran up, seized the reins, and started the horses. The boy moved sullenly out of the way. As they moved ahead, the horses automatically fell into place. Quietly the farmer backed them into position before the machine.

"After this," he said abruptly, his deep eyes blazing, "you'll not hit horses that way. Do you hear!"

"I'll get that devil some time!" the boy cried, his lean face working with fury. "Just you wait!"

Vaughn strode up to his son and struck him on his cheek with open hand, so that the boy staggered. Then, without looking back, he took his seat on the binder and started cutting the grain. After he had completed the round, he saw that the boy was seated beside a shock.

Only mechanically the man watched the operation of the machine. His mind was in a whirl. "I can't help it," he kept saying to himself. "It's no way of doing to hit a horse like that!" On the second round he saw that the boy still sat beside the shock. Then, toward mid-morning, Elias halted the horses and took the lunch from its hiding-place under a shock.

"Time to have a bite, Joe," he called.

The boy did not move. With the lunch in his hand, the farmer walked to his son.

"Come, Joe," he urged quietly. "It was too bad that happened this morning. You were excited, and I got mad. Let's forget about it and have something to eat. We'll feel better."

The boy shook his head obstinately.

"Tell you what, Joe," the farmer said, in a kindly voice, "you've been workin' too steady, I guess. You take the rest of the day off and take it easy."

"No; I ain't tired." The boy looked up. His expression still showed enmity, but it was slightly abashed, too. He reached out for the sandwich that the father held out, and they ate the bread in silence. Then, after they had finished, the man went on with the cutting. When he returned, he saw that the boy was shocking the grain.

After that day, the boy scarcely spoke to his father. The man was silent, too. Often he stared at the thin, set face of his son. He thought about him when he worked. It was just the heat and the work, he decided. Joey hadn't been at farming long enough to get his full strength. When the work let up a little, and the weather turned cooler, he'd feel all right again. Anyway, what were they going to do if the boy left the farm? Lizzie couldn't stand up under it.

After the grain had been cut and shocked, they started with the stacking. They went to the field with the wagon, and both pitched the bundles into the rack. Then they drove back to the farmyard, where the farmer built the stack and the boy pitched from the wagon. Finally the stacking was finished.

"Guess we've earned a day's lay-off," declared the farmer next morning, after breakfast. "What do you folks say to going to Bear River tomorrow? We'll start out early and make a big day of it. The sand plums ought to be ripe by now; it's just the best time for a trip."

Neither the woman nor the boy replied at once, but Vaughn took this as agreement on their parts. All day he talked about the holiday.

They started out next morning before sunrise. The farmer sat on a board placed across the front of the wagon box, while his wife and son sat on the spring seat. It was a drive of almost thirty miles to the northwest, by rough trail.

Some hours of driving brought them to more broken country. "We must be getting near the East Branch," remarked Vaughn. "You'll always find it getting hilly near rivers."

"Is there a bridge?" the woman asked quickly.

"No, just a ford," he replied easily. He saw the fear in her face. "I guess you remember that crossing we made on our way west, Ma," he said, good-humoredly. "But you don't have to be afraid of this one; the crick will be low after all this hot weather."

In half an hour they came to the stream. At the crossing the water flowed swiftly in a broad, shallow sheet over solid gravel.

When the horses splashed into the river, the woman stood up. Grasping the edge of the wagon-box, she stared down in terror at the water.

"Oh, sit down, Ma!" exclaimed the boy. "There ain't nothing to be scared of here."

She looked at her son and smiled weakly. Then she resumed her place beside him.

It was ten o'clock when they reached the bottoms of the Bear River. As they drew to the top of the last hill, they saw, winding in a broad, brown valley, a belt of timber that marked the course of the river.

"Real trees here," remarked Vaughn. "Right out there to the south where the river turns is where I've been getting stove wood for the last five years. You know, I've always sort o' liked the trip. It would be after frost, you know, and the trees would show every color in the rainbow. And then, I always liked to be near running water. Guess you and I don't look at that in the same way, Ma."

In the five hours that they spent at the river, the man was constantly active. He gathered firewood, started a fire, and helped them spread the meal on the grassy bank. After the long ride, facing a steady, cool wind, they were hungry and they ate heartily.

Joe helped gather the dishes when the meal had been finished.

"Come along with me!" the man urged. "Those dishes can wait. I know where there's bound to be plums."

"Guess I'll stay here with Ma," decided the boy listlessly. "I feel kind o' lazy just now."

The man set off alone, carrying a milk pail on the crook of his arm. It would have been easier walking at the outskirts of the timber, but he walked along the river bank, stopping often to look at the riffles in the stream or to stare upward when he came to exceptionally large trees. Finally the heavier timber thinned out into underbrush. Scattered here and there, in dense, thorny thickets, were the wild plum trees, their branches sagging with large, red fruit. Before he commenced filling the pail, he ate a few of the plums. The sharp acid of the juice was a delight to the palate that had known only the monotony of their simple farm diet.

It was not long before the pail was rounding full. With a last, regretful glance at the fruit-laden branches all about him, Vaughn started back.

He found his wife and son sitting on the bank, staring with lack-lustre eyes at the sliding current of the river.

"What! Have you two just been loafing all this time?" cried the man cheerfully. "See what I've been doing!" He exhibited the fruit proudly. "There's bushels of 'em on the trees," he declared. "Wish we had time to get some more." He squinted at the sun. "Past three. Guess we'd better be starting back home."

Their return took them an hour longer than their trip in the morning. The sun dipped farther and farther toward the horizon. A clear green radiance flowed into the western sky. As the sun sank into this field of liquid light, it gathered to itself colors of rose and flame. Then, like a big, patriarchal face, it hung poised on the horizon line for a moment, before sliding down into obscurity. After that, the violet dusk of the afterglow brooded over the land.

The man, driving toward the east, sat on the wagon-box, silent, watching the advance of evening. The horses took their own gait over the uneven trail. In the blue darkness of the east stars came out. Near the zenith hung a wedge of moon. Suddenly, looking down at the woman and the boy, he saw that the latter had fallen asleep. She had moved closer to him, and her arm lay easily about his shoulders.

Lizzie's face was full of quietness. The boy stirred, and she glanced at him with quick concern.

At last the wagon rumbled from the trail to the farmyard.

"Wake up, Joe!" cried the farmer, "and give me a hand with unhitching."

The boy stumbled out sleepily and started to loosen the tugs.

"You just stay right there, Ma, till we get back from the barn," said the man. "We'll be back right away."

They led the horses to the watering-trough. The animals dipped their muzzles deep into the water, blew the spray through their nostrils, and drank in great, sipping swallows.

"I'm just dog-tired!" exclaimed Vaughn, stretching his arms above his head. "It won't take me half a minute to get to sleep tonight."

The horses lifted their heads from the trough. The bridles were taken off, and the animals walked sedately into the barn.

"Well, we ought to feel more like starting with the plowing," remarked the farmer, as he threw the harness on the peg.

"I'm afraid you'll have to find somebody else to help you." The boy's voice came from the darkness with an unnatural boldness. "I'm going to take that job at Junction City. Guess I'll be leaving about Monday morning."

There was a silence in the barn, broken only by the horses as they crunched their hay.

The man moved quietly to the place where he knew that the boy was standing. He placed his hand on Joe's shoulder.

"Better not, Joe," he said, in a kindly tone. "We'll make things nice for you. See, most of the land has been under the plow quite a while, and everything gets smoother each year. And then, I was thinking of painting the house next year. You'll be your own boss out here." The man's voice was low and self-contained.

The boy drew aside slightly. "I can't help it," he said, a dogged desperation in his voice. "I guess I'll have to go anyway; I'm sick of the farm."

"If you go, I'll tell you right now that Ma won't stand up under it. Her mind, you know—" The farmer had started to speak sharply, but his voice trailed away.

"Oh, Ma will be all right," Joe replied quickly. Then he added, the words coming from him violently: "And if her mind *is* kind o' weak, it's your fault, not mine! I guess I know what she's gone through. You had a chance to get your father's farm back East, and you wouldn't take it. So you came out here. This ain't no country for a woman. And then you talk to me that Ma won't stand it!" He ended abruptly.

They walked from the barn to the wagon without another word. Vaughn helped the woman to the ground, and then they walked to the house. The boy went to his room at once.

Vaughn remembered, an hour later, that he had said it would not take him half a minute to get to sleep. At last he got out of bed, quietly drew on his clothes, and walked outside. It was cooler in the open air, and he felt better.

On Monday morning, Joe did not help with the chores. At breakfast time, he came down the stairs dressed in his black suit. The woman looked at him in bewilderment.

"Goin' to town," he explained abruptly.

The man took his place at the table without saying a word. They ate their meal in silence. Then, together, the man and the boy rose from their chairs.

"Afraid you'll have to walk," the man said.

"All right. I sort o' thought o' walking." The boy moved awkwardly to the chair where the mother sat, looking at them with a puzzled expression.

"Good-bye, Ma," the boy said unsteadily.

"You won't be gone long?" she asked.

"No, not so awful long."

"Good-bye, Joey," she said, smiling wistfully.

The boy took up the box which he had carried down from his room before breakfast. He started out of the door, and the man followed him. The two walked in silence down the drive. The man stopped.

The boy also halted. "Well, good-bye," he said casually.

For a moment the man did not speak. Then he said slowly, "I guess you'd better not come back any more."

"I won't," replied the boy.

The man turned and went to the barn, where he spent an hour getting the plow ready for the work of the day.

XXIII

Early in the following spring, the woman drooped into the same malady that had attacked her on other years at this time. For two weeks the man took care of her and, at the same time, tried to get things in readiness for the spring work. Every day, as he looked anxiously down at her thin, gray face, he almost forced himself to believe that she was looking better. At last, however, he realized that her strength was ebbing. One morning, after she had fallen into a light sleep, he saddled a horse and rode to the Schneider farm. As he came to his neighbor's farmyard, he saw Schneider working near the barn.

"I wonder if your wife will come over and stay with Lizzie while I go to town for the doctor?" Elias asked. "She isn't getting better."

Schneider's face showed a heavy concern. "Sure! Sure!" he exclaimed. "You just go for the doctor right now and I'll hitch up the horses and drive my woman over."

Vaughn nodded his thanks, spoke sharply to his horse, and started on his way to Hayes.

Arrived there, he waited in the dingy, unfurnished room above Anderson's store where the doctor had taken up his office a year before. It was more than an hour before the doctor, a young fellow, came bustling in.

"Been waiting long?" he asked.

"Yes, quite a while. My wife's sick, and I'd like to have you come out."

The doctor questioned him at some length. "I'll be out in the morning," he promised.

When Elias arrived at home, he unsaddled the horse and went to the house.

"She seems to be sleeping," Mrs. Schneider said, "but I can't tell so very good. She keeps moving around, but her eyes stay closed." The woman's face, round and healthy, seemed to the man to be drawn almost forcibly into a doleful expression. For just a moment he felt a desperate envy, a wish that Lizzie might have her strength and clear-eyed contentment. He thanked the woman for her help.

"You got to have a woman here," Mrs. Schneider declared. "There's your own work you got to do outdoors. I'm going to send my girl over tomorrow morning, and she'll stay as long as you need her." She looked around critically. "You've been keeping house pretty good, for a man," she announced, "but it ain't like as if a woman's been tending to things."

"No," the farmer said, feeling almost cheerful in the hearty friendliness of this woman, "I guess not." He added, "It's mighty good to help me out this way. Are you sure that your girl will want to stay here?"

"Sure! Greta will be all right, you just see!"

In the morning, when the doctor came into the sickroom, the woman seemed to rouse herself and looked at him with distrust. His examination was short. Then he went into the other room, followed by Vaughn.

The younger man opened his case and took two bottles from the rows that lined the interior. His forehead was wrinkled with the professional frown as he wrote directions on the pasters.

"This ought to tone her system up," he said. "Just let her rest and take things easy."

Vaughn nodded. "What do you think about it, doctor?" he asked hesitatingly. "She'll pull through this all right, won't she?"

The young man did not reply at once. "I've seen other cases like this, out here," he began. "Your wife has just about used up her vitality. Some people are like that: they have just so much strength, and when that's gone—" After an expressive silence, he said again, "Be sure to give the medicine regularly, and let her rest."

After the doctor had gone, the farmer went into the yard, where the girl, Greta, was washing out the milk pails.

"I guess my wife may be sick for quite a while," he said simply. "Do you think that you can stay? I'll be glad to pay you what you think is right."

"Yes, I'll stay." The girl, plump, well-grown, with much of her mother's quiet cheerfulness, straightened up from her work. Her face was red and perspiring. Health shone out of her large brown eyes.

April was wet and cold, and the woman remained in bed, apparently without changing for better or worse.

"She says such queer things sometimes," the girl reported to the farmer one day at dinner. "It seems like she's thinking of a long time ago."

The farmer said nothing but tapped a preoccupied tattoo on the table with his fingers.

Spring came with a rush when it did come. The work of the farm seemed endless to Vaughn, after his late start, and the last of each week saw him a little behind his neighbors. After they had planted the corn, he was just working on the seed-bed. And so it went. Even in June, when days are longest, he rose before sunrise, and at night he ate his supper by lamplight.

"You can't keep it up this way," Schneider remonstrated on a Saturday evening when he had come to get his daughter so that she might spend Sunday at home. "You're just killin' yourself."

Vaughn smiled grimly. "The work's got to be done," he said, "and I'm the only one here to do it."

"Ain't your boy comin' back pretty soon now?"

"No. He won't be back. He had a job at Junction City, but I heard at Hayes that he quit that job. I don't know where he is."

"Too bad, too bad," Schneider replied, taking up the reins. "He'll get enough of it in a little while and then he'll be comin' back home again."

Again the farmer smiled, more grimly than before, but he said nothing. Schneider didn't know how things stood, he reflected. Just within the week Henderson had come over from his farm nine miles to the west, and he had told Vaughn, rather awkwardly, that Joey had taken up with the rowdy element at Junction City. It appeared that Henderson had met the boy and, putting together what he had seen and heard, he had decided to urge Vaughn to go for his son. Junction City was no place for him to be. The farmer had refused, point-blank, to do this, and Henderson had gone away, wearing a rather disturbed expression. Vaughn had a stricken look in his eyes for some time after that, and then his face became grim. Well, it was the end.

On one of those rare days when the farmer made a trip to town for supplies, he saw a disreputable figure walking the road into Hayes. It was just before haying and harvest time.

"Do you want a job?" Vaughn asked abruptly.

"Sure," replied the hobo.

"Jump in and come along," the farmer commanded, making room for him on the spring seat.

On the long trip back to the farm, the men scarcely spoke to each other, and in the days that followed, long, hot days of heavy work, this reticence was not broken. "Jack"—the name the hobo had given himself—worked steadily, ate voraciously, and slept, by preference, in the barn. In two weeks the work had gone along so rapidly that the neighbors were no longer in the lead.

The woman seemed to draw a little strength from the hot summer sunshine. Now and then, when the man sat by her bed, as he did for half an hour after mealtimes and at night, she talked a little, usually to herself, uttering her words in a weak monotone. One evening, she seemed to be more restless than usual, and there was a greater awareness in her eyes.

"Funny that Joey doesn't come," she murmured. "He's been gone so long."

The man reached down and took one of her hands in his, where it seemed lost. His face, covered with new growth of beard, bent over the white face on the pillow. "It's all right, Ma," he said soothingly. "We'll just have to wait awhile. Don't you go to worrying."

The old, far-away expression, filled with weariness, came again into her face. In a short time her breathing became more regular, and she slept.

The summer went through the regular stages of haying, cutting and shocking grain, stacking, and plowing. Long before the first killing frost, the corn stood yellow and ripe in the field, the heavy ears hanging richly down from the stalks. Jack rose before daylight, brought in his two overflowing loads every day, continued to eat an amazing amount of food, and said nothing about leaving.

"When you want your money, let me know," Vaughn told him one day.

"When I get the money, I'll be drifting along," replied Jack laconically.

"Then you'll have to ask for it before you get it," the farmer declared.

On a morning in November, Vaughn had gone to the cornfield south of the house to repair the temporary barbed wire fence which the cattle had trampled down the night before. Jack was in the strip of corn that had not been fenced in, taking out the last few loads.

The farmer worked slowly, but with a deliberate steadiness that had no waste motion. He set in a number of posts at regular intervals, to re-enforce the fence. Even when he straightened up now and then to fasten the wire to the posts with staples, his compact figure, appearing more square and solid in the short jacket he wore, still remained slightly bent. The wrinkles about the eyes had become deeper and ran their furrows into the heavy, weather-beaten cheeks. There was an expression of quiet speculation in the face, an expression that made parallel lines on the forehead. From under the old brown leather hat, the brim of which wavered uncertainly, the iron-gray hair straggled raggedly. Nevertheless, with all these marks which the burden of years had brought to him, still he gave an impression of greater ruggedness than before.

Occasionally, as he worked, the man glanced about him. The sky held a thin scum of gray, through which the sunlight struggled weakly. The morning was quiet. In the southeast, a sluggish bank of cloud hung soddenly.

There was a quick fluttering in the air, and Vaughn looked up to see a large flock of prairie chickens fly past, now beating the air frantically with their short wings, and then sailing stiffly downward until they vanished in a distant corner of the field.

Quick as a flash, the sight of these birds brought back to him the memory of that last autumn he had spent with his father. There had been a great many prairie chickens that year, he remembered. Then his mouth drew into a straight line. He had never heard from his father directly after Lizzie and he had gone away. "Must be getting pretty well along," Vaughn reflected. "Let's see, he'd be past seventy now."

These thoughts had made him work more slowly, but now he quickened his pace. Then he halted again at the sound of a distant call from the farmyard. He looked up quickly and saw the girl, Greta, waving to him, calling out something unintelligible. He jumped into the wagon, struck both horses sharply with the end of the reins, and drove up the short lane edging the slough and meadow to the house.

"You'd better come in!" the girl cried. "She's worse, I guess."

The man strode into the house and entered the room where his wife lay. He saw at once that there had been a change.

"Tell Jack I want to see him just as quick as he can get here," Vaughn commanded the girl. He stood by the bed, staring down at the woman. When he heard the heavy sound of Jack's boots in the house, he opened the door and left the room for a moment.

"Take a horse and ride to Hayes, Jack," he directed in an even, contained voice. "Tell the doctor to come over just as quick as he can."

"She's worse?" asked the hobo, in a curiously subdued tone. Vaughn nodded.

"Better give me my check now," Jack said. "I guess I'll be drifting along. I'll see to it that somebody brings your horse back."

After the hobo had folded the check and placed it in his shirt pocket, he turned again to Vaughn. The men shook hands silently. Then the farmer went back to the sickroom, and Jack left the house.

To the man it seemed that a great weight of silence had come into this room. He sat beside the bed on a low chair from which the back had been broken. He wore the ragged jacket which he had worn in the field. The long, gray hair, rudely parted, fell down shaggily over his temples. Immobile, he sat there, bent forward, hands lying passively on his knees, deep, quiet eyes fixed unwaveringly upon the white, still face of his wife. His breathing was audible in the silence of the room, the deep, rhythmic breathing of one who is asleep.

From the living room came the sound of the clock striking the hour of noon. It drew his attention for that moment. Just so Jack would find the doctor in his office! Maybe he could fix it up all right. His whole being was caught up in a desperate, wordless prayer that she might live.

The woman's face seemed to gather a faint color. She stirred slightly, and then lay still again. In the utter silence came the ticking of the clock in the next room, suddenly invested in the mind of the man with the unreality that may come to most familiar sounds. Timeless intervals of silence were ended each time the clock struck.

When four o'clock came, Vaughn straightened his shoulders. The doctor might come any time now. He'd be sure to come tonight when he got Jack's message. Constantly the man's eyes lifted to the small square of window that looked toward the south.

Outside, with the slow waning of afternoon, the day had turned gray. One by one the distant slopes were blotted out. Stray, lazy flakes of snow drifted aimlessly past the window.

Again there came to her face a change, a certain mobility. Her eyelids remained closed, but her lips moved.

He bent over, so that his face was close to hers. "Something you want, Ma?" he asked in a hushed voice.

Suddenly she spoke audibly, in a steady murmur. "Going on to five …" he heard, "… Joey …" Her voice faded away.

"Yes, Ma," he answered steadily, "Joe'll be here any minute now—most any time, I guess."

Again there was the brooding silence. The light in the room had turned to grayness. A long, whispering sweep of wind passed by the house. "It's coming bad weather," the man thought dumbly. The wind came again, in a stronger gust. The storm door slammed.

"Joey!" the woman cried feebly, her face alive.

The man took her hand. "Yes, Ma," he whispered.

Her hand clung to his. Shortly after that, he saw the weary tenseness in her face become eased and rested, and the light, always dim, flickering during these last years, went out.

She was buried beside the baby out on the prairie knoll where now the cottonwoods were tall. During all these days the man's face was steady and single.

Afterwards, he wrote briefly to her parents that his wife had died.

XXIV

It was a cold evening late in that same winter, and the farmer was about his chores. The stock had stayed in the cornfield, and he set out to drive them in to the barnyard. The cattle were huddled into a ragged mass, facing him, watching his approach with moody eyes. The horses stood off a short distance, pushing through the snow with their muzzles in the hope of finding some nubbins that had escaped the notice of the corn-husker. Vaughn started around them, but they suddenly looked up, heads held high, eyes wide, nostrils distended. As the man approached, they snorted in alarm and rushed off through the crackling cornstalks, their heels throwing up snow and mud behind them. The farmer turned back to the cattle and they filed to the barn. They halted while he lowered the poles that served as a gate, and then walked sedately into the enclosure, the milk cows making for the barn door while the others sought their accustomed place on the sheltered side of the snowcovered strawstacks in the middle of the yard. The milk cows were driven into the barn, where they were fastened to the stanchions. While they were eating the hay; the farmer went to feed the hogs. There was a tremendous screaming and grunting as soon as the metallic sound of the shovel, scooping up the ear corn from the pile near the hogyard, rang out on the sharp air, and the animals fought their way through the small doorway of the low, thatched shed. In a few minutes the tumult had subsided into a contented, grinding noise, as the hogs attacked their food.

After he had returned to the barn and had started with the milking, Vaughn heard the loud, insistent whinnying of the horses at the gate. He finished the milking, poured out a little milk in a tin can for the cat that had waited patiently beside him. After that he let the horses into the barn. They had recovered from their prankish humor and now made eagerly for their stalls. The farmer closed the door, snapped the bridles to the ropes on the mangers, and poured a measure of oats from the bin into each box.

As he went about this routine of chores, a sense of peace and quiet came to him. The interior of the barn was dim, filled with coziness and warmth. The rhythmic sound of the animals crunching their grain was broken now and then by the squawk of some hen disturbed in her rest on the boards nailed between the stalls. The air was sweet with the smell of hay, and touched with freshness, too, as though the animals had brought in the exhilaration of the outdoors.

Before going to the house with the milk, Vaughn went out into the yard once more and threw down bundles of cornstalks for the stock. As he passed the strawstack, snowbirds flew out from their snug hiding places and swirled above him like dead leaves caught in the eddy of a frolicking wind.

The sun was low in the west by the time he had finished feeding the cattle. For a moment he stood in the yard, staring to the west with wide, abstracted gaze. The setting sun hung in the steel-blue dusk of winter evening, throwing a subdued rosy light over the long swells of snowy prairie. Loneliness lay upon the land at this hour; so great a stillness was in the air that it seemed as if all animation had been suspended. The white of the snow dimmed imperceptibly. The red in the west deepened. Black against the glow of sunset, the tall cottonwoods that bounded the yard stood in stark outline. Far away, to the west and slightly to the south, there was the movement of a dark object against the snow. The man's eyes became fixed. The object moved steadily. "Must be someone on the trail," he decided, after a time. "Strange that anybody's walking out there, and at this time of day!"

The sun dipped down below the horizon, and the figure on the prairie was lost to view. The farmer went to the barn, took the pail of milk from the peg, and walked slowly to the house, which formed dimly before him, the windows black and unlighted.

Arrived in the house, Vaughn scratched a match on the stove and lighted the hanging lamp. The room was filled with the shadowy yellow light. The man took off his sheepskin coat, hung it on a nail, and then filled the stove with split wood and opened the drafts. In a moment there was a soft roar as the flame caught the fuel.

After the coffee and the fresh pork had been placed on the stove, Vaughn strained the milk into the pans and set them in the small, dark kitchen which led off from the dining room. After that, he washed himself at the sink and rubbed his face vigorously on the roller towel.

There was a timid knock. The farmer did not answer the summons at once, but stood still, thrumming his fingers on the wooden edge of the sink. Then he stepped quickly to the door and opened it. His son stood there, cap drawn down over his ears, the collar of his overcoat drawn up.

The farmer said nothing. With a touch of bravado in his voice the boy said, "Hello; here we are again." He slipped past his father into the room and walked to the stove, where he rubbed the palms of his hands over its genial heat.

Vaughn closed the door and went on with his work of setting the table.

"Where's Ma?" asked the boy, in a desultory way.

Vaughn had taken the coffee pot from the stove, but now he replaced it again. His shoulders straightened.

"Your ma isn't here any more," he said in a deep, controlled voice. "She's up the hill where the baby is."

The meaning of the man's words did not seem to strike the boy at once. Then he turned.

"What!" he exclaimed in a frightened tone. "Not—dead?"

"Yes." The answer came heavily.

Joe said nothing more. His narrow hands rubbed over one another nervously.

The farmer had placed the food on the table, and now he drew up his chair. The boy stared at him.

"I walked the whole way from Hayes," he said monotonously, "and I'm pretty hungry."

His father motioned to another chair. Joe, after setting a place for himself, sat down.

In other days, Vaughn had always spoken a short blessing before each meal. Now he bowed his head in silent devotion. His son, opposite him, stared at his father with a curious, inert expression. The man raised his face, and they commenced eating. Each took a great slice of bread, impaled it on a wooden-handled fork, and dipped one surface into the bowl of fried-out pork. Then, placing the bread on their plates, they poured sorghum over it. This, with large pieces of meat, washed down with coffee, made their repast.

The man finished his meal first and leaned back in his chair. His eyes remained fixed meditatively on his plate. Joe continued to eat until the bowl of fat pork had been emptied, and then he, too, sat back. He cleared his throat twice, each time as though he were about to speak, but the man's face remained remote, and his son said nothing.

Vaughn looked up decisively. "Well," he asked abruptly, "what do you want here?"

The chair, which the boy had tilted back, came to the floor with a thump. "I got sick of my job," he said complainingly, "and

I got to thinkin' maybe I could hold out just as easy with farm work. It's six o' one and half dozen of the other. So," he concluded, becoming awkward under the man's steady scrutiny, "I come back."

"So you couldn't hold your job?"

"I could hold it all right, but I quit. It's a dog's life. But I c'n get that job back if I wanted it. I wasn't fired."

The father continued to stare at his son. The latter tried to meet his eyes, half defiantly, but each time averted his gaze.

After a long silence, Vaughn said, "Your ma asked about you pretty often." His finger tips were pressed down on the table. Then he continued, his voice growing harsh, "She took real bad last November, the day we were finishing the corn. I sat in the room with her. She didn't know much any more, and she kept asking for you. The wind made the door slam, and she must 'a' thought it was you coming in. I can remember, just like it was happening now, how she called for you, and how mighty glad her face was just then. She couldn't tell the difference, so I took her hand and made out that I was you. You wasn't there, so I lied to her—the last thing she heard me say was a lie." The man's voice rose, heavy, almost menacing. His eyes burned in his head.

Joe's face was filled with blank distress. "Well," he said, "I didn't know." He kept moistening his lips with the tip of his tongue.

As they sat there, motionless, the regular ticking of the clock and the comfortable hissing of the steaming teakettle on the stove became a subdued tumult in the deep silence.

Vaughn got up from his chair and walked into the bedroom. After a short interval, he returned. The boy was standing beside the stove again.

"Here," said the farmer, extending a small leather pouch, "this is all the money I've got in the house. Now you must go."

The boy took it sullenly, without thanks. "Kicked out, heh?" he remarked bitterly.

"You'd better go," the man repeated. "If you want, I'll hitch the horses and take you to town. But you can't stay here tonight."

"You go to hell!" Joe replied. "I'll walk." He took down his coat and cap from the wall, pulled them on jerkily, and faced the man once more. Again his eyes quailed before the contained anger in his father's expression. He turned, opened the door, and slammed it behind him.

After some minutes the man also opened the door and went outside. Coming from the lamplight of the room, his eyes could, at first, distinguish nothing in the darkness. Then, slowly, things about him in the yard took shape. His eyes were directed to the west. Finally he discerned a moving shadow on the snow, growing clearer and clearer as his eyes grew stronger. It was Joey, he knew, walking toward the trail. The black figure paused when it came to the place where the trail met the north and south road. "He's looking back," the farmer thought to himself. Then he saw the figure of his son move forward, to the south.

The moving shadow on the snow became dimmer and dimmer. For a moment he seemed to be lost, and the farmer stepped out into the yard where he again caught sight of the boy, far away now, well along the trail to Hayes. Then the moving object was lost in the hazy whiteness of the winter night.

The sky was radiant with stars. From the north came a scarcely perceptible movement of wind, sharp with cold. The man stood out in the beaten snow of the yard, without coat or cap, his shirt open at the throat. The reflected light from the snow made him seem a graven image. In the square face, crowned with a mat of hair, the deep hollows of the eyes were lost in shadow. Slowly the face lifted to the sky.

There was no sound; a vast silence lay upon the winter prairie, which stretched away from him until it was lost in the night. Slowly the man turned back to the house. For a moment he stood outlined sharply in the lamplight that streamed through the doorway. Then the door closed.

THE END

ABOUT THE AUTHOR

Walter J. Muilenburg was born outside Orange City, Iowa, in 1893. Muilenburg's parents, John W. Muilenburg and Gertrude Van Rooyen, were descended from Dutch settlers who left Pella, Iowa, in the 1870s. Raised on a farm alongside nine siblings, Muilenburg grappled with the challenges of his strict Reform upbringing and the isolation of rural life across his fiction. In 1915 he graduated from the University of Iowa, where he was affiliated with the Athelney literary society. During his career Muilenburg was closely associated with the Iowa City–based little magazine The Midland, founded by his friend and college classmate John T. Frederick. He published six short stories in The Midland along with two other stories in The Forum and Today's Housewife. In 1925 he published his sole novel, Prairie, as the first book by Viking Press. It received generally positive reviews but made little impact on the nation's literary consciousness. From 1923 until 1937 he taught at the University of Iowa and Michigan State College (now University). He later retired to full-time farming and occasional commercial writing at his Glennie, Michigan, farm. After a period of illness, Muilenburg died from a heart attack in Phoenix, Arizona, on November 30, 1958. He is buried near his parents, to whom he dedicated Prairie, in Orange City.